Thin Ice
Silver Lining
A Spark in the Dark
Fire & Ice
Dragons of Las Vegas Boxed Set (The Complete Series)

STANDALONE'S:
Fiery Kiss
Wild Fate

CW01501875

CAPTIVE VOWS

AVA GRAY

ALSO BY AVA GRAY

ONTEMPORARY ROMANCE

His to Claim

THE VALKOV BRATVA Series
Stolen by the Bratva
Kept by the Bratva
Captured by the Bratva
Captivated by the Bratva
Trapped by the Bratva

FESTIVE FLAMES SERIES
Silver Hills' Christmas Miracle
Holly, Jolly, and Oh So Naughty
The Christmas Eve Delivery
Valentine's with the Silver Fox

HAREM HEARTS SERIES
3 SEAL Daddies for Christmas
Small Town Sparks
Her Protector Daddies
Her Alpha Bosses
The Mafia's Surprise Gift

THE BILLIONAIRE MAFIA Series
Knocked Up by the Mafia
Stolen by the Mafia
Claimed by the Mafia
Arranged by the Mafia
Charmed by the Mafia

. . .

ALPHA BILLIONAIRE SERIES
Secret Baby with Brother's Best Friend
Just Pretending
Loving The One I Should Hate
Billionaire and the Barista
Coming Home
Doctor Daddy
Baby Surprise
A Fake Fiancée for Christmas
Hot Mess
Love to Hate You - The Beckett Billionaires
Just Another Chance - The Beckett Billionaires
Valentine's Day Proposal
The Wrong Choice - Difficult Choices
The Right Choice - Difficult Choices
SEALed by a Kiss
The Boss's Unexpected Surprise
Twins for the Playboy
When We Meet Again
The Rules We Break
Secret Baby with my Boss's Brother
Frosty Beginnings
Silver Fox Billionaire
Taken by the Major
Daddy's Unexpected Gift
Off Limits
Boss's Baby Surprise
CEO's Baby Scandal
Scandalous Whispers

PLAYING WITH TROUBLE SERIES:
Chasing What's Mine

PARANORMAL ROMANCE

BLURB

They stole me in the dark—
A daughter traded like blood money.
My father handed me to the Bratva.

Now I belong to **Luka Dubinin.**
Older. Colder. *Sin in a tailored suit.*

He doesn't force my submission.
He *seduces it* with silence and steel.

Builds me a studio. Watches me dance.
Burns me alive with every glance.

I swore I'd never break.
Never beg. Never love a man like him.

But I crave his voice.
His touch. His darkness. *His power.*

He shields me with bullets.

Loves me like war—violent and absolute.

I should escape.
    Instead, *I made a vow behind locked doors.*

Not of love. Not of freedom.
    But of surrender... and survival.

These are our *Captive Vows.*
    And now... **I'm carrying the Pakhan's child.**

But when the truth comes out... will he protect me—
    or destroy me like all the others?

Author's Note: *If you love dangerous men, defiant heroines, forbidden passion, and secret babies... then Captive Vows is for you. Luka and Gabriella's story is dark, sinful, and heartbreakingly addictive. Are you ready to be ruined by the Pakhan?*

1

LUKA

The shredder sucked in the last of the documents. Whirring and grinding, the gears turned, the blades scissored, and the evidence of someone's murder was gone. These remnants and strips of paper would be burned, just in case. After being the boss of the Dubinin Family for decades, I knew better than to *ever* leave anything to chance. I wasn't naïve enough to believe that my staff and men, the entire force who heeded my direction, could be completely trustworthy. I only employed the best. I only retained the loyal. Erasing all proof of life—or death— was my responsibility, and that was what I excelled at. I would always be responsible, and I expected the same attention to detail and diligence from my organization.

Because we sure as hell hadn't obtained this much power and wealth by being sloppy or slacking off.

"Ready to go?" Allen, my personal assistant, asked.

I nodded, not looking away from the removal of those documents. I'd only get up and walk away once I saw that every last sheet of photos was ruined beyond recognition. Technology made things easier. Convenience was the biggest bonus of emails, texts, and other forms of instant communication. It also meant that everything could be more easily traced and hacked. Hence, these old-school glossy photos of a kill that my son, Emil, had overseen.

My son knew how to assassinate without leaving any footprint or clue behind. I trusted him, perhaps more than any other, but it was still necessary to review the proof of a hit done well.

Allen hadn't left. He wouldn't push or nag me to hurry. That wasn't his place. He existed on the top floor of the office building as my executive helper. My comrade in arms, previously. When he was wounded too severely in a turf war some eleven years ago, he'd volunteered to be my administrative right-hand man. It was an arrangement that suited us. While I'd never admit to anyone else being able to finish sentences for me, he intuited when I wanted something. Allen was never one step ahead of me, not truly, but he was often on the same step as me, aware of how this business worked and how I led my life.

"The cleaners are almost through with your car," he added.

I allowed the start of a smile. The mention of that rare antique—the Rolls Royce that everyone called *my* car—reminded me of the triumph I'd experienced when I took it from one of those cocky Italian capos from the Rivera Family. I couldn't stand those fuckers, and that was why it had felt all the more rewarding when I explained that his prized possession was now mine. I'd never forget the glory of striding toward that sleek black car right before my men beheaded him, letting him watch me take his car before we took his life.

It wasn't the best choice for transporting bodies, but I hadn't counted on needing to relocate one earlier. Sometimes, these things just happened. No matter how messy my violent life as a Mafia boss could be, I had plenty of professional and thorough cleaners in my employ to handle it all. The blood, guts, and gore.

Satisfied that the photos were ripped, I stood and buttoned my jacket. Only now did I make eye contact with the bald, gaunt-faced Allen. He seldom smiled, and that suited me just fine. With a life like mine, softer emotions were a waste of time.

"Ivan is downstairs waiting for you," he said, referring to my nephew.

"And Emil?" I asked.

He nodded. "He's ready to go as well."

I arched a brow and snorted a laugh. "I wish this kind of backup wasn't necessary."

"But it is," he said, falling into step with me as I left my office. Outside the ceiling-to-floor windows that made up the entire lengths of two walls, darkness hung over the city. New York City never slept. With glittering lights spread out down below, the sparks of life proved there was plenty of activity.

I could only hope that the meeting I was about to go to would be actionless. I was sick of these headaches, all the whiny rivals, all the back-stabbing enemies, and even all the lying moles and rats. Like any other criminal organization, the Dubinin Syndicate suffered some betrayals from within.

Violence was the currency with which I lived my life, but after so many incidents of having to remind everyone that no one could fuck with us and get away with it, it really did blend into a blur of the same old.

"Backup is always necessary," I replied to Allen. No matter what we did, who we dealt with, or where we went, someone was bound to try to kill us. Even that was getting really fucking old. Tedious.

Boring.

I'd never admit that I realized how dull my life was getting lately, but I couldn't deny the listlessness that was taking hold of me. It was always the same bullshit. Maybe the players were different from time to time, but I was getting tired of having to put up with the same thing over and over again.

"Backup is especially warranted for a meeting with *these* dealers," Allen added as we entered the elevator for the ride down to the garage.

I nodded once, acknowledging and agreeing with him without a word.

Of course, I'd need to be on guard when speaking with the dealers at the warehouse. Going to the docks was risky business for the amount of traffic going on there, particularly at this hour. But it was the fact that I was meeting with the counterparts who had to associate with some members of the Vipers Cartel that pissed me off. The Cartel and the Riveras. Between the two of them, I had no fucking patience and absolutely zero goodwill. I'd never trusted them. Not in business. Not in taking their word as fact, either. Ever since my wife, Maria, was killed near the conjunction of their turf in the city, I'd been committed to blaming them for the death of my wife and unborn daughter.

Blood had been shed.

Fingers had been pointed.

Years had passed.

Still, the anger persisted. Because forgiveness had never and would never be granted on that topic.

Merely recalling those tense, dark times of loss and grief threatened to spike my anger now. Any thought of the woman I'd lost over twenty years ago had the power to sway my mood. Instead of neutral and tense, I could be enraged and raring to fight. Missing her had faded over time, but it was the regret that I'd lost my partner too soon that pissed me off.

Life hadn't been dull or boring when I had a woman to love.

Allen and I reached the garage, and I immediately saw my son and nephew. Emil and Ivan stood waiting near a kitted-out black SUV. Just the sight of them helped to rein in this lurking negative energy that could prime me for killing. They were living proof that the Vipers and Riveras hadn't obliterated all of my family. I still had them and many others.

Emil and Ivan were more familiar with the depth of my fury for those within the other families, though. For that matter, I could rely on them to keep me in check during this meeting.

"You all right?" Emil asked. He tipped his chin at Ivan, leaving him to go into the SUV while he came to join me in *my* car.

"Yes." I furrowed my brow, watching him as he got on the other side of the car. "Why do you ask?" His implication that something was wrong with me didn't bode well. Turning to face him while the driver started the car and exited the garage, I waited for an answer.

"You seem moodier than usual," he answered.

I faced forward and rolled my eyes. "No, I do not." I wasn't in a good mood. But that was generally true for most of the time. I didn't see a reason to expend too much energy on the lighter joys of life.

"You're not acting like yourself."

I turned to look out the window as we sped through the city.

"Not tonight, at least."

Perhaps he had a point there. I wasn't excited or happy to be near some of the players associated with when Maria had been killed.

"Ivan thinks it's old age creeping up on you."

I faced my son, deadpan. "Shut the fuck up." I'd dare him to try to call me *old* in a serious tone. I dared him to repeat that and mean it. His cocky grin hinted that he was joking, but it was a stupid line of humor to go with. One more year was left before I hit fifty, but I was as fit, as toned, and as sharp as men half my age.

"I'm annoyed." Maybe if I tossed him a bone and gave him an answer—not that I owed him one—he'd shut up.

"About what?"

"The same old. There's nothing to look forward to anymore. It's the same fucking old."

Emil studied me silently.

Even the whores were getting to be the same old. Too used up and too eager, like carbon copy blow-up dolls for the amount of genuine interest they were capable of.

"Why—"

I held my hand up, cutting him off. "Leave it." Discussing my mood or any emotional crap wasn't happening.

He replied with a sigh, and for the rest of the ride to this meeting, he didn't poke or prod at me to say anything else.

We arrived with Ivan and the rest of the backup. Pulling up to the warehouse in a line of cars, we showed that we weren't solo, that we weren't weak. All of us were packing, and with practiced confidence, we entered the building as one. Strong, with numbers, and no room for error.

"Boss," one of the men said, bowing slightly as I stepped

into the room where others waited for me. "It is good to see you."

"I can't say the same," I told the middle-level dealer. Maybe he was a supervisor for whoever the fuck he worked for, like an independent broker. As far as I was concerned, though, he was an insignificant piece of shit.

I was expected to attend this meeting, not necessarily to talk much or contribute any new intel. Like a spectator in the background, I brought the weight of my position to this gathering. It was for show. I was here to remind them all who was in charge. Such reminders weren't needed, though, because as the men spoke about deals and the transgressions we had against the Cartel were brought up, I merely watched and listened. I let my men do the jobs they were given. Usually, I didn't play my hand and hover as an overlord. The point was to work smarter, not harder, and I did that by delegating this bullshit to the leaders within my Family.

Every single person in the room eyed me with equal parts respect and fear. As they should.

Only one individual stood out.

Miguel Lopez.

I'd spotted his unwillingness to make direct eye contact with me. Regardless of whether he was talking or someone else was, he couldn't look me in the eye.

What the fuck are you up to?

He was a liaison between the Dubinin Family and the Vipers, but with his intimidated appearance, I couldn't be sure whether he was behaving like he should.

Afterward, when it was concluded that he'd deliver specific pieces of intel to another cell of soldiers near Brooklyn about a big order of drugs that would be dropped there, I wondered if that was a good idea.

While suspecting a man could be a traitor was slightly challenging, this was still the same old, same old. Because it would always end in the exact same way.

No one would fuck with me.

No one would ruin or endanger what was mine.

Afterward, on the ride out of there heading toward the massive building that I considered my fortress in the city, both Ivan and Emil rode with me.

"I don't like this," Emil said.

"I think Lopez is a rat," Ivan told us.

"My thoughts exactly." The weaselly man seemed too skittish, too nervous to be trusted. He had to be hiding something, and I intended to find out what. Secrets would always threaten to ruin us from the inside out. With a heavy sigh, I slumped against the cushions. "Set up a trap. See if you can catch him in the act with this drop near Brooklyn. And make him pay."

Ivan nodded, getting his phone out to do as instructed.

"We'll make it happen," Emil said, drumming his fingers on his knee, likely itching to kill another traitor.

Commanding these ruthless men to play God, to determine the details of life or death, was one more example of how it really was the same damn old. This would be far from the first time I'd had to order a kill or to set a trap. This wouldn't be the last time, either.

The same old shit.

Even this.

Nothing would ever chip away at my need to kill, this bloodlust to protect every part of the Dubinin organization and empire. I would see to the end of every enemy, including the nervous and tense Miguel Lopez.

He'd pay.

Just like everyone else who'd dared to cross me.

2

GABRIELLA

I pressed my shoulder blades to the wall and exhaled a long breath. Sitting back in the corner of the dance studio was the last place I ever wanted to be. This was an ugly twist on being a "bench warmer".

Benches didn't exist in ballet. You were either in the show or not. You were starring or eking out the best you could manage as a secondary dancer who blended more with the props and scenery than the stage.

Back here, idle and allowed to merely watch instead of dance, I tried to ignore the burn of humiliation that I had been selected as one of the outcasts.

The rejects.

The unwanted.

"Maybe next time," Amy, the daughter of the studio owner, said.

I turned my head slightly, just enough to glare at her. I couldn't help it. Timing was everything. Opportunities were fleeting. At twenty-two, I was at the prime age to be excelling as much as I could. To be taking up every chance to dance, audition, and impress.

But not this time. Nope.

I was sitting back here with the few others because I was deemed unworthy.

The dancers still on the floor, practicing and trying to follow the choreography from the guest instructors, were only up there because of who they knew. It wasn't a matter of what we knew. It wasn't a challenge of who had the better skillset. Having the privilege to dance with these instructors came down to who these people knew.

"It's not fair," I whispered to Amy.

She patted my foot. We sat side by side with our legs crossed, but she wasn't in her tights and leotard. A car accident had ruined her chances of ever dancing again. Sitting like this with her knees apart and ankles crossed was a feat for her. Regardless of her inability to dance any longer, she remained a true friend at the studio, a supportive person when I had no one else.

That's the whole problem.

I had no one. I came from nowhere.

"No, it's not fair. But maybe one day, that will change," she said quietly as we watched the lesson carry on for those who were "good" enough.

I didn't have the same kind of faith and hope she enjoyed. When would anything change? I was born in a shitty neighborhood. My mom was killed in a drive-by. My dad was a loser deadbeat.

No money. No prospects. No future.

I winced, watching one of the dancers totally botch a step and leap that I could do in my sleep.

Every one of the dancers up there had wealthy parents to afford all the classes and private instructors they could find. The men and women on the floor were the rich and privileged ones who got to go to fancy camps and courses to further broaden their skills. They knew the right people in the business.

I, on the other hand, knew Amy and her mom, the owner of this small studio. I taught myself a lot from YouTube videos and tutorials, dancing in my tiny bedroom. I got these classes only because I did all the housework for my dad and I bartered with him to pay for these classes. That was all I had going for me.

So, yeah, it was freaking hard to watch others get ahead when all I'd ever dreamed of was to dance. When all I'd ever wished for was to lose myself to the magic of being on the stage and moving my body like a form of art.

"It's just 'cuz they knew these people from that group," Amy whispered, on my side.

She wasn't wrong, though. These classmates of mine were only getting ahead because they were familiar to the guest instructors. As frustrating as it was, I tried to look past the envy and figure out a solution. Being scrappy was how I'd taught myself to live. Without much money and nothing else to lean on as far as a supporting and loving home, I'd had to be resourceful. I'd formed a deep dedication to working my ass off for what I wanted.

Maybe this wouldn't have to be so different.

Paying attention to a pathetically hopeless redhead with the *worst* form ever, I noticed how much the guest instructor smiled at her. How he watched her. How he checked out her ass in that pink leotard. She could barely fill it out, too flat overall.

Dancers tended to have a small percentage of body fat, but I was secretly thrilled I could hang on to my assets while being fit.

Maybe I could be familiar with some of these instructors too...

During the entire class, I let myself dare to dream. To

scheme as well. By the time the "chosen" ones were done with their lesson, I couldn't think of a reason I shouldn't go through with this impulsive brainstorm that had come to me.

I could smile and flirt with that instructor. I could get his attention on me—on my body, at least.

If I couldn't have the means to get to know these elite instructors and be familiar with the staff who could grant me permission to be included in more advanced lessons like this one, then I'd need to use what I had. It was one more way to think outside the box. And that was what I'd do.

"What's that one's name?" I asked Amy with a sly smile lifting my lips.

She furrowed her brow as I pointed out the one I'd watched the most. Tall, thin but muscled, and with a roguish mohawk cut that made him look edgy.

"Why...?" she asked slowly, suspicious of me.

I shrugged. "No reason." Done with taking my ballet shoes off and stowing them in my bag, I slung the small sack over my back. I wrapped my fingers around the thin straps, almost like it was a shield to give me protection.

Hitting on a guy wasn't something I ever wasted my time on. Flirting with an instructor had never crossed my mind before. In all the years I'd succeeded in getting my dad to pony up money for some dance classes, I'd been a diligent, obedient student. I'd listen to their every word, intent on doing my steps right. I'd watch them for how they moved and used their muscles, eager to replicate their gracefulness.

Checking out a dude on the dance floor had never been an option. But hey, I'd do whatever it took.

"Oliver," Amy said at last, still eyeing me like she didn't like what I had in mind.

"And he's in charge of picking who can go for the preliminary auditions in the fall?" I asked, smiling wider. The thought of actually auditioning to go to school for ballet excited me. It was a long shot. It was a pipe dream. But it was *my* dream. Dance was my life and it was all I'd ever wanted to do. That was why instead of accepting a teeny scholarship for a nursing community college outside the Bronx, I got a part-time clerk job at a store so I could perfect my dancing on my own.

Amy winced as she reached out to grab my arm and stop me from going toward Oliver. "Yes, he is. But, Gabby—"

I stepped out of her reach, grinning fully. With a wink for her, I hoped this mischievous feeling could carry me into successfully seducing him.

Whatever it took.

Because instead of dreaming about auditioning and getting into school for ballet, I'd need to start smaller. Just this morning, I argued with my dad about these lessons at Amy's mom's studio. He whined and bitched about not being able to afford them anymore, and that was such a load of bull. I didn't ask for anything. I didn't beg. I didn't covet materialistic crap. I asked for nothing while I did all the housework. On top of that, I gave him some of my money from my part-time job. These dance lessons were the only things I couldn't sacrifice because dancing was just a part of who I was. It was in my blood.

If I can get Oliver to notice me, maybe that'll be my in. And if I have an in, Dad can't just make me stop.

With every step I took to reach Oliver as he left the room, I tried not to look like a stalker. Unfortunately, I felt like one. I felt like a manipulative fool. But that was how stuck I was. That was how far I was from reaching my dreams.

Desperate times sure did call for desperate measures.

Here goes.

I smiled as I bumped my shoulder into his, hurrying to catch up to him and make contact.

"Oh, hey." He smiled kindly, looking me over as he caught me from the collision.

"I'm *so* sorry," I replied. "I'm just so eager to get out of here."

Shit. What? What did I say that for? That's going to make it sound like I don't want to be here when I do.

"I mean, I'm just so sweaty."

Oh, God. That's gross. He's going to think I smell.

"I was on the floor for an hour before that lesson started." I jerked my thumb over my shoulder, as if he wouldn't know what I was talking about.

Lame, Gabby. Really, really lame!

"An hour." He smiled, lowering his gaze to my chest. "Impressive."

Wait. Is he talking about my dancing for an hour or my boobs? I was trying so hard. Keeping this stupid, hopefully sexy smile on my face. Thrusting my tits out. Leaning close. Running my hand down his arm. Giggling. Was I trying *too* hard? Was I too obvious?

God, I'm so bad at this. I was bound to scare him off.

"And I bet this is impressive too." I put my hand on his chest and trailed it down toward his crotch. I'd *never* done something so forward like this. Touching a guy fell into the realm of dancing. When with a partner for the sake of the choreography, I'd be near a guy and brush against him. But this?

Am I doing this right?

It seemed like it. He stepped closer. Then he glanced around as if wanting to make sure no one was watching. As if he wanted to prolong this naughty privacy with me.

"Oh, yeah?" he asked, his voice low and husky.

Uh-oh. I hadn't considered this idea of mine could work too well. I didn't want to sleep with him. I didn't even *know* him. Already, regret was kicking in. This was too complicated. Too risky. Too dumb of a desperate idea.

"Yeah," I replied. I was in this far. I had to keep it going now or I'd look like an imbecile.

He stepped into my space again and put his hand on my hip. Again, that was nothing new. Partners rested their hands there for a segue into a jump. But this wasn't dancing. This was me trying to flirt to get ahead...

And it might be working.

I wanted his attention, and I definitely had it now. He licked his lips, staring at mine.

Fuck. Is he going to kiss me?

That would make this real.

That would push this too far.

"How about we get out of here, then?" he asked, pulling me toward him. "We can get out of here together and get sweaty... together."

Oh, no. No. Let's, um, let's not?

"Uh..." *Now what do I do?* I didn't want to actually have to do anything with him. I didn't want to get involved with anyone at all. If and when I did, it'd have to be someone who'd at least get a spark of interest burning in me. He didn't. I was only trying to use him, and I only now saw how stupid that was.

I bit my lip and hesitated.

He rolled his eyes and retreated. An expression of annoyance crossed over his face. "Knock it off."

"Huh?" He'd seemed so interested and now he was so instantly cold. "What?"

"Stop." He shook his head, like he pitied me. "I'm not interested."

I opened and closed my mouth, torn between relief that he wasn't sincerely pursuing me or expecting anything from me and disappointment that I'd failed. I supposed I hadn't. I wanted to get his attention, and I had. But not in the way I imagined it would go.

"You're way too young for me."

I furrowed my brow. I hadn't actually wanted him, but did he really need to say *that*? He was maybe a few years older than me. How did that count? How dare he make me feel inferior like that.

"I don't know what kind of stupid game you're trying to play, but take this piece of advice." He stepped back again, eyeing me up and down with more disdain. "Don't. Don't play games with people in power who can call the shots."

Fuck.

That sounded like a threat.

I frowned and moved back from him.

The last thing I needed was for him to spread word that I was trying to sleep with instructors to get ahead. Or not. Whatever.

My heart ached as it thumped fast. Panic crept over me, and I wished I could press *rewind* on this whole incident. "No, I—"

He shook his head and left, turning to look at me over his shoulder. "Forget it, kid."

Kid?

Anger replaced the panic. How dare he call me a *kid*? Like I was a joke, an immature idiot who'd never succeed.

Gripping the straps to my drawstring bag, I gritted my teeth and turned to leave. Humiliation warmed my cheeks. Fury quickened my breath and pushed me to flee.

I'm so stupid. Why did I think that would work?

Oliver's words delivered a sharp blow as I hurried home. His mocking rejection was just another reminder of how powerless I was to go for my dreams. How hopeless I was to be a dancer and get into Juilliard.

I narrowed my eyes as I walked the familiar sidewalk, furious and frustrated with the world.

Frustrated with everyone in the world, too.

Especially men.

No man was good. Not my father. Not punk-ass Oliver.

No one.

Just like I had no one but myself to rely on for a decent future of any kind, with or without dance to brighten the dark days.

3

LUKA

I didn't need to go along with the men on this sting to see whether my instincts were correct about Miguel Lopez. Watching him be so nervous was all it took for me to have a good read on the man. I seldom erred with reading others.

However, the next day, I rode along with Ivan and Emil for the trap they'd arranged. While it might have been seen as overkill for me, the boss at the top, to accompany them, I wanted something to do.

I couldn't be sure if Miguel Lopez had captured my attention because he was indirectly connected to the people I suspected as players in my wife's death or if this was merely a way for me to pass the time. Regardless, I was curious about what the sneaky, skittish man was up to.

The trap was simple. We'd arrive in one of the back rooms at the building where the big drop of drugs would happen. An undercover spy would tail Miguel throughout the property to listen in to what he said to the men over-seeing the exchange. If he were to say something incriminat-ing, the Dubinin spy's wires would pick up on it. If that failed, Emil would do what he did best and creep up closer to video the whole thing.

At first, nothing out of the ordinary happened. Miguel showed up to supervise the transaction. Many men labored to move the product. Others idled and watched over, likely expected to make sure no one like the cops showed up to interfere. It was, for all intents and purposes, a normal night.

I'd supervised many of these kinds of exchanges in my career. Before I became the Boss, I had handled these lower-level deals much like Miguel and the other crew leaders here.

The night became extraordinary, though, when the Dubinin spy was close enough to overhear Miguel spilling all kinds of details. He shared the intel with a Viper Cartel spy. Then a half hour later, he identified another drug runner as a mole for the Riveras. He accepted a bribe of cash from him for the same intel he'd given the Viper.

Twice.

Not once, but twice, this rat had turned traitor. The information he sold wasn't the worst-case scenario, but it would compromise our business and we would have to change the future deal up to avoid having the Vipers or Riveras try to fuck with us.

"What a fucking moron," Ivan muttered as he and I approached the rat.

He had no clue what was coming. Standing there watching over the transfer of drugs from the boat to the trucks, he rocked back on his heels. Like he didn't have a care in the world. Like life was just peachy and all things were going as well as expected.

Until he noticed us coming close. Going still, he stared at me like he'd witnessed the devil himself. He was too tanned to go pale, but I could've sworn all the blood drained from his face. Terror crossed over his face with that wide-eyed, *oh-fuck* gaze.

"Mr. Dubinin," he stuttered. "Boss." His Adam's apple bobbed with a difficult swallow. "I didn't expect—"

"This?" I stalked ahead, letting Ivan follow behind me. Without any fanfare, without any further preamble, I raised my arm and reared it for a hard hit. The hook to his face sent him reeling back. The flesh-on-flesh impact was music to my ears. A pained grunt from his mouth preceded his clumsy stagger toward the dirty floor, but he caught himself from falling completely.

"Didn't expect that?" I asked, sneering down at the rat who'd dared to threaten the prosperity of my family, of my organization I would always protect with every ounce of my violent soul.

I swung at him again, landing a jab up at the underside of his chin. Cracks came from the smack of his teeth shutting too tightly together. With the immediate spill of blood from his gasping lips, it seemed like I'd cut his tongue with the hit.

What a dumbass. He didn't even know how to handle taking a hard hit. Maybe he'd bitten his goddamn tongue off. It'd deprive me of the pleasure of cutting it out. But I hadn't gotten far enough ahead to know what to do to him yet.

"Boss, no." He gasped and coughed out blood as he stepped back. There was no hope of escape for him. Emil joined us, standing behind the ugly rat. Ivan and others circled him as well.

Miguel wasn't going anywhere.

"No?" I kicked his knees, dropping him to the floor. "No *what*?"

"Please. No. Don't do this. No. It's a misunderstanding. Whatever you think—"

I laughed, letting him hear the wrath in my dark and sinister chuckle. Nothing about this was humorous. This wasn't some cheap comedy hour. However, it was ironic that he could try to amuse me with such irony. "You have no right to assume what I think."

"No, I mean—" I kicked him again. Aware that I could lose my patience with him too quickly, I glanced at Emil. My son could temper and pace himself while doling out torture. If I tried to vent my frustration at being so bored, I could end up killing this man too soon.

Answers would need to be obtained and analyzed first. Then, like every other rat who dared to try me, he'd pay dearly.

Emil didn't require any further cue from me. He stepped forward as I retreated. It was too bad that beating Miguel this much couldn't appease this restlessness in my soul. If taking out my anger on a liar couldn't boost my mood, I wasn't sure what else might.

Maybe nothing will.

Sticking toward the back, I watched my son interrogate Miguel. Without mercy, he demanded replies to his questions about what he had told those others. Unsurprisingly, Miguel sang like a pathetic canary. Blood dripped from his mouth. One eye was swollen shut. His hand stayed put on his side, as if pressing on the spot where I'd kicked him would make it all better.

"I'm sorry. I'm sorry, Boss." Miguel hung his head, wincing to stay upright on his knees. "Yes, I sold the intel to them."

"Tell me who," Emil demanded. "Who did you sell it to?" He knew. He would've heard the same thing we all had heard on the comms unit. I respected the power my son showed, though, the supremacy I'd taught him. Forcing a target to vocally admit guilt wasn't only to confirm a fact. It was a type of mental warfare for them as well. To speak the truth about a crime done against the Dubinins was to declare your own death sentence.

"The Vipers," Miguel answered, his voice so broken and desperate. "The Vipers and someone from the Riveras."

"Motherfucking two-timing bastard," I muttered as Emil gestured for another Dubinin to beat Miguel all over again.

Once more, I caught my son's attention. With that knowing look shared between us, we were on the same page.

We had the rat.

And we'd dispose of him accordingly.

I approached Emil as he let the soldiers handle the sobbing, crying Miguel.

"Want me to deal with him?" Emil asked, likely meaning that he'd oversee the transportation of Miguel to one of the torture sites to kill him.

I shook my head. "Not so fast."

Ivan joined us.

"Keep him alive for a while yet. Take him captive until I can determine a better price for him to pay instead of only giving us his life."

Ivan raised his brows, surprised.

"I am not showing him mercy," I added with a shrug. "But I am bored. Let's see what else this fucker stands to lose." His life, at this point, seemed like too easy of a price to demand of him.

Emil nodded in acknowledgment, looking back to watch the men drag Miguel away.

"Find out who he has in his life. What he has to live for,"
I told him.

I was getting too used to this dreadful idea that *I* had
nothing to live for anymore. It was only natural to wonder
about what a moron like Miguel had.

"On it," Emil replied, turning away with Ivan.

With nothing left to do here, I returned home. The
second I entered the large building, the "fortress", the loneliness ate at me. The listlessness gnawed at me, making me
feel more aggravated than I desired.

Riding along for that trap we sprung on Miguel hadn't
kept me preoccupied for long. It was a been-there-done-that
scenario. Anticipating an answer from my son about how I
could punish the rat didn't hold my interest for too long.

The only thing I could do was mull over my life. On the
balcony, I looked out over the nightscape of the city. A glass
of vodka hardly changed anything. Not even the whore who
stopped by, Belinda, could entice me.

I wasn't intrigued at all. Nothing captured my interest,
and I feared that this was how the rest of my life would go.
I'd done so much. Years had been spent building the wealth
and power of the Dubinin empire, but now, what did I have
to live for?

Emil didn't need me. My son was grown, and so were my
two nephews. All I had to really keep me company was
anger. Yet, it was wearing on me.

Back when Maria was in my life, when I had a woman to
care for, I was more balanced. But with her, I'd learned the
cruelest lesson of life. To love was to lose. No matter the
circumstances, giving my heart to a woman was the starkest
break of my soul.

Belinda returned to the balcony after I dismissed her the
first time, trying to get me to come inside with her.

I sent her away again. Dismissing her *and* my loneliness at what seemed like the top of the world, I sighed and tried to comfort myself with the reminder that I wasn't the kind of man to appreciate something freely offered.

I relished the challenge. The pursuit. The fight. Because working harder to take something from someone was just that much more rewarding in the end.

Raising my glass to finish my drink, I vowed to do just that.

If no one could keep me company, then my work would have to make do. Focusing on the anticipation of taking something valuable from Miguel would keep me engaged and out of this rut of boredom.

I would take something of his, and the balance of justice in our dark and dismal world of crime would be set right again.

4

GABRIELLA

I hurried home from the dance studio with an urgency to return to my bedroom for privacy to analyze what I'd done. It felt like I was running from my mistake, but I knew that come tomorrow, when I returned for another class, I'd have to face the music. I'd need to overcome the judgment and consequent embarrassment from trying to flirt with Oliver to get ahead.

What the hell was I thinking?

Why?

Why would I do such a dumb thing?

It was almost as if I hadn't been thinking at all. As if all rational thought processes had simply failed to turn on like usual. Desperation had triggered me. But now, I'd have to suffer through the damage.

Focusing on putting one foot in front of the other until I could get home to the tiny apartment I shared with my dad, I relived the humiliation of that damn instructor telling me off. How he rejected me. How he'd mocked me and even reminded me that I was too young for someone in charge like him.

A growl remained trapped in my throat at the injustice of it all. But when I reached the front door and unlocked it, I was bubbling with pent-up rage and irritation. I opened the door, slammed it shut, and rested my brow against it.

Then I let it out. Through clenched teeth, I growled and closed my eyes, wishing I could scream. I could, but then the neighbors would freak out—again—and call that domestic disputes were going on in the building. My dad was not a fan of the cops, and I knew better than to give anyone a reason to come to our place.

Breathing hard from the exertion of that growl and still feeling too wired and riled up, I fisted my hands and wished I could punch something.

"Oh, is the little kitten mad?" a man asked as he came from the direction of the kitchen.

I flinched, jarred from my anger. That wasn't my dad's voice. Startled at the idea that one of his friends or "business" acquaintances could be here, I spun around with my breath caught in my chest.

It wasn't my dad. He didn't seem to be home. But somehow, Tony, one of his supposed friends, had let himself into the apartment when no one else was here. Holding a half-empty bottle of liquor in one hand while he rubbed his crotch with the other, he approached me.

"What the hell?" I snarled.

He didn't waste a second to pin me to the closed door. This close, I smelled his body odor faintly masked with too much cologne. The mix of scents nauseated me, as did the booze on his breath and the stink of weed he had to have smoked in here.

I dodged him, shoving my hands at his chest.

But he was quicker, slamming his hand to the door and trapping me from stepping sideways.

Panic rose. The urgency I'd hurried home with sharpened into fear. "Leave me alone, Tony."

My dad's friends were all assholes, jerks who would openly check me out even if my dad was nearby. They were all misogynistic creeps who didn't respect women. Deadbeats without jobs who wanted handouts. Losers who drank too much and had nothing to give back to society.

Tony fit every one of those criteria.

"No, I ain't leaving you alone, little kitten." He picked up some of my long brown waves resting on my shoulder, curling them around his finger as he grinned down at me. "Now that you *are* alone."

Oh, fuck.

This was just what I didn't need. Not now. Not ever. One of Dad's friends trying to get close when he wasn't here fell under the category of my worst nightmares realized.

I never questioned what my dad got up to. He probably sold drugs and stupid things like that. He was too much of a conman to ever want a normal job with a steady paycheck. Yet he was too cocky to be able to stay in an unconventional position of earning income.

His friends and buddies weren't any better. They all probably did stupid, illegal shit to pass the time. For the most part, they didn't make a habit out of directly bothering me. I was never here to be near them. I would lock myself in my room and dance, then barely acknowledge them when they were visiting.

"What the hell are you talking about?" I replied hotly, shoving him back again.

I could be proud that I wasn't a flat, skinny dancer. I had some curves. I had some meat on my bones. I could even call myself athletic.

But Tony had about one hundred pounds on me and

was at least two feet taller. Stinking and looming large, he leaned over me as if to remind me that he was bigger and stronger. As he groped at me, I resisted and damned how helpless I was.

Again.

Hopeless.

Helpless.

And he was right.

I *was* alone. My dad wasn't here.

"Get off me," I shouted when he didn't answer me. He kept pawing at me, crushing his hips to mine to wedge me against the door. Between holding my breath to avoid inhaling his godawful stink and slapping him away, I didn't accomplish anything. My protests and slaps seemed only to encourage him to try harder. Spit from his lips smeared on my neck as he tried to kiss me.

"You're all alone now," he taunted, unzipping his pants while he used his other hand to shove me up against the closed door again. "Miguel ain't coming home tonight, little kitten."

I grunted, kicking out at him as hard as I could. He'd blocked me from smashing my knees into his dick, though, his pale, skinny cock that he got out from his sagging jeans.

Oh, fuck. No. No. Fucking no!

This couldn't be happening.

This couldn't be my reality.

I didn't have time to wonder about what he was saying. I didn't want to slow down and think about why my dad wasn't coming home. He was probably shit-faced or high, too out of it to make it back to the apartment. And knowing that I'd be alone and unprotected, Tony thought he could help himself to being here and raping me.

"Get off me!" I shouted it louder.

He didn't. Laughing harder, he slapped me. I gasped, lifting my hand to my cheek to ride out the pain, but that was the lapse in fighting back that he must have been counting on. With my arm up, he could ram it above my head. Faster and faster, he shoved at my shorts and panties. Every scrape of his grimy fingers on my skin sickened me. Each taunting laugh and needy growl of lust threatened to make me pass out from sheer horror and fear of the unthinkable happening.

I couldn't catch up to understand why and how this was happening. How my dad could be such a lowlife as to let his friend have a key to get in here. How my only parent could be such an uncaring idiot not to be concerned about my safety. Nor my happiness. Expecting him to wonder if I was happy was a ridiculous joke. But how much worse of a human could he be to not even give a damn about my safety? About preventing a sicko like Tony from raping me?

Over and over, he yanked at my clothes. It took every bit of my strength to squeeze my legs together. Staying upright was critical. I couldn't let him get me down. He'd cover me and never let me back up—not until he got what he wanted. Keeping that nasty dick away from me was all I could focus on. I refused to lose my virginity like this. He wouldn't reconsider, too frenzied like a wild, feral predator with this need to rut.

"Stop!" I screamed it that time, wishing the neighbors would hear and call for help.

No rescue would be coming, though. No one knocked on the door to inquire about the sounds of a struggle. I didn't want to let myself cave to the alarming idea of my dad being dead and never coming back. If I let that fear overpower me, I'd be frozen and useless, too scared to fight back.

Because my life was this unfair and because I had no

one to guard me or help me, this was it. It was a fight to the death as far as I was concerned. I would *not* be defiled, not like this.

To the best of my ability, I fought Tony off and tried to get enough distance between us so I could wrench the door open and escape. It felt like an eternity of hell, resisting his touches and squirming to break away. A smearing blur of anxiety and dread gave me the energy to fight, and at last, I managed to pull on the door knob.

I yanked on it as hard as I could, letting the edge of the door smack into Tony's face as he lunged after me. Spinning quickly, I dropped low to dodge his outstretched arm.

Then I was gone.

Running right back down the hallway with half of the lights out or blinking, I escaped the one place I was supposed to be able to count on.

My home was no longer safe.

Nowhere felt safe.

No one would make me feel safe ever again. My dad never had done well in that department, but after this incident, I knew I couldn't live with him for much longer. Not when he'd let creeps into the apartment. Not when he'd associate with rapists.

Sprinting down the sidewalk, I scanned my surroundings. Panic fueled me. The adrenaline rush of fighting Tony back and then fleeing had me primed and aware. All my senses were heightened. With every movement I spotted and each sound of the city nightlife that I picked up on, I wheezed and strained to steady my breath.

He's gone.

He's not coming after you.

I jerked around to check that Tony wasn't chasing me out on the street.

You got away.

You're alone.

I couldn't dupe myself into thinking everything would be all right. Nothing would be okay ever again.

I'd had a lesson in how others with privileges would always get ahead at the studio.

I'd experienced a harrowing near-rape incident in the supposed security of my home.

Out on the street, afraid to go to my room and lock myself in, I feel utterly spent and scared.

With nowhere else to go, I grabbed my phone and called Amy. She was a friend who'd want to help me out, but it wasn't like she could be my hero. Her apartment was too small. Her sister—who'd just had a baby—was sleeping on her couch. There was no room for me to come over.

I didn't have a long list of friends to rely on. With all my waking hours spent cleaning for my dad and working at the store, I only had the free time to dance, not socialize and have friends.

"Hello?" Amy answered.

"Hey, um." I cleared my throat, hating how croaky my voice was from the fear and running I'd done. "Long story short, I, uh, need a place to stay tonight."

"What?" She peppered me with questions about what was wrong. I wanted to avoid admitting I'd almost gotten raped in my home. And I didn't wish to rehash any details for her at the moment now. The less I allowed myself to think about what just happened—or didn't happen—the better my odds were of not freaking out.

"It's a long story," I said, hedging an actual answer again, "but could you open the studio?"

It was the only other location where I could feel safe. I'd be safer there than at home.

"The dance studio?" she asked incredulously.

"Yeah. You don't have room for me at your place. I don't have enough money for a hotel room. And I can't go back home."

"Why? What happened?"

I shook my head as I walked, knowing she couldn't see my gesture. "Please, Amy. Can you unlock it? Just for the night." I didn't know what I'd change before tomorrow night would come, but I could buy myself time for tonight. I had to figure something out. This couldn't be my future, dammit.

"All right. You know where the spare key is for it." She sighed. "I'll text you the one-time guest security code when I get it. But you owe me answers later. You hear me?"

"Yeah, Sure."

Yeah, right.

I didn't feel like telling the only semi-friend I had that I'd almost been raped. I was used to being the poor girl. The outcast. The loser no one wanted to be near because I was supposed to be inferior. But to admit that I'd almost been raped? That was more humiliating than how I'd struck out flirting with Oliver.

Amy was true to her word. She texted me the code to get into the dance studio.

The second I was in the place that I considered my second home, I sighed and scanned the empty space. I didn't dwell on how I'd failed to hit on Oliver. I didn't let myself relive the flashback of Tony trying to rape me, either.

Here, I was safe. I was free.

All night long, I compartmentalized my trauma of the night in the only way I knew how to pull through this. I danced.

And danced.

And danced some more.

Losing myself to the beat of the music and seeking the comfort of the steps and choreography that I knew by heart, I stayed at the studio all night.

The bench near the restrooms would serve as a cot. The locks and security system wouldn't fail me.

But come tomorrow, I'd need to prepare myself for another day of disappointments, namely, my dad.

What's new with that, though?

He always let me down, and I bet that he would try to neglect me for the rest of his life.

Because no man is good.

None of them.

I closed my eyes and snuggled into the warmth of my hoodie, taking that morose thought to heart as I slowly drifted to sleep on the tiny bench.

5

LUKA

Emil came through with information about Miguel Lopez. He didn't keep me waiting for long. No matter the target and regardless of the reason someone had to be investigated, my son could get his hands on whatever intel he required to get the job done.

"A daughter?"

I glanced up from the documents he'd handed me. I was back in my office at the end of a long day of reviewing the documents and reports that encompassed several businesses within the organization.

Allen was just exiting the room with Emil's arrival.

Emil nodded and yawned, clearly staying up late, as was his style. He kept odd hours and was often on the go, all over the world.

According to the file Emil had gotten his hands on, Miguel Lopez had a daughter. Family members were always an option for collateral damage or leverage. I would know. My wife had been killed as an attack on me.

"No wife?" I tossed the file to my desk, uninterested in perusing the material inside it just yet.

"No. Or he did." Emil shrugged. "It seems like she was killed many years ago in a drive-by."

"Hmm." It stood to reason that Miguel would be all his daughter had, and vice versa. Their bond would be strong, I bet. And that would work in my favor. "Any other assets of note?"

"None that I could find. He's a deadbeat who seems one OD away from death."

"Then I imagine these hours he's been held are hell on him." Withdrawal was one of the easiest means of torture and one we didn't need to do anything to accomplish.

"From the reports of the men at the holding cells, he's been alternating between sobbing, begging, and praying."

"For mercy?" I guessed.

He shrugged again. "Who fucking knows?"

"Then let's find out what he thinks about losing his daughter instead of his life." I stood and headed out with my son. Emil was all I had. Just father and son for us, like Miguel and his daughter. If anything were to happen to my son, I'd be devastated. I'd move mountains to ensure his well-being, but with time, and especially with Emil's propensity for and excellence at killing targets, I'd come to learn to trust him to be in control of his own safety. Letting go as a parent was never a simple feat, but I knew without a doubt that if I were ever captured and my son's life were dangled on the line, I would tell them to take me. To kill me.

What the fuck? Maybe this is as good as it'll get. Such dark and morbid thoughts weren't the norm for me. I surprised myself with these thoughts, that maybe I'd done all I could in this lifetime. I was only about to turn fifty, yet my mind was veering toward a nonchalant attitude more suited for a ninety-year-old nearing the end of his life. With this idle-

ness and lack of interest that accumulated every day, I had
to wonder what I had to look forward to again.

I'd raised my son and my nephews.

I'd strengthened the family.

I'd proved our might to our enemies.

What else—

"We're here," Emil told me. He might have assumed I'd
lost track of where we were going with how I'd looked out
the window of the car the whole ride.

Jolted from my thoughts, I nodded. "After you."

We entered the building and went directly to the basement where the worst of the worst were keeping our hostages
and captives in line. Miguel had his own cell at the end of a
dark corridor. His cries and begging pleas were audible before
we walked down the narrow length. At the sound of his
misery, a kernel of excitement lit up in my chest. The prospect
of delivering justice would give me some degree of pleasure.

But will it last?

*When will I be committed to something other than working
like this?*

Once more, I consciously shoved those thoughts aside.

"Please, Mr. Dubinin," Miguel cried out pathetically
once Emil and I entered the room.

He was a mess, and he'd made a mess of himself. No
matter how cocky, strong, or numb a person could be, after a
few hours of torture under my skilled, hardened men,
they'd be pissing or shitting themselves in fear. Ammonia
from urine offended my nose. The reeking hint of dried
fecal matter didn't help. But it was the metallic tang of blood
in the cell that stood out the most.

Miguel was more a sack of bruised and bleeding skin
over broken bones than a man. He lay on his side. Tears

streaked over his cheeks, but the blood coating his skin had already dried over so thickly that the moisture from his eyes couldn't rinse it away.

Between moans and wheezing inhales, he could barely lift his head. Yet, I forced him to get up anyway. I'd be damned if I bent to accommodate him.

Emil and another guard dragged the broken man to the only thing in the room. A chair that he'd likely been tied to could barely keep him upright. So I gave him a hand. It was the least I could do. Gripping his hair, I twisted tightly until he screamed. With that hold, I wrenched his head up so he'd face me.

If he could.

Both eyes were swollen. One wouldn't open at all.

Yet, he was paying attention to me. Begging.

"Please, Boss. It won't happen again. I swear it won't."

The stupid fool was under the impression I'd ever let him near any official Dubinin business again. It went without saying that he was fired. Fired and awaiting punishment. "Oh?"

"No. I swear. I'll never lie again. I'll never sell any intel ever again. Just please, let me live."

How the supposedly mighty fall. I rolled my eyes. "No, I'm not here to kill you."

"You're... not?" He sniffled, disgusting me and annoying me more.

"No. I expect a much more personal currency."

He stiffened, moving his thighs closer together. I couldn't blame him for worrying he'd be raped or otherwise abused like that. It would be a fear for anyone, but that wasn't our style.

"More personal like this." I dropped the file Emil had

given me. He'd grabbed it when we left my office, and I used it as a prop now.

"Like what?" Miguel asked, trying to lower his head. I still held on to his hair. Releasing him with a shove, I stepped back and waited for him to reach for the papers on his lap. They'd scattered. A couple of photos fell to the bloody floor. But with a weak slowness as if his arm were broken, he moved his fingers to pick up a page. Then, straining to move again, he brought the photo closer to his face to peer at it as though his vision were compromised.

"Gabriella?" he whispered.

"Your daughter," I confirmed. Clasping my hands behind my back, I paced from side to side.

"You... want Gabriella?" he asked, confusion clear in his shaky, tired tone.

"No. I don't *want* her," I replied. He was a moron to assume I'd lust for his child. As I paced past a fallen photograph of a young woman at a dance studio, her back to the camera, I huffed a weak laugh. Like some teenager would entice *me*. "I expect you to give her to me."

He didn't reply for a long moment. "You want me to give you my daughter? In exchange for my freedom?"

"You will deliver her to me," I stated plainly, not replying to the matter of whether he'd be free after he saw through this act of giving me his child. I could still very well decide to end his life, but it would not happen without a payment of something of his. That was how it worked. This was how I restored the balance of justice in a world where I was the king to dictate the rules.

"My daughter?" he repeated, at a loss and starting to look more like the nervous man I recognized him as. No, he wasn't a man. Just a rat. A liar. The worst kind of traitor.

He lowered his gaze, deepening the lines of wrinkles on

his brow that were already red from a beating. Dried blood cracked on his face, the only indication that I could reliably follow to guess that he was frowning.

"*You* want *my* daughter?" he asked.

It wasn't a matter of his being confused about what I was demanding.

With the emphasis of that last repeated question, he seemed unable to comprehend why I, the Boss, would be so taken with his daughter. I laughed loudly, truly amused that he'd be so bold as to assume that his daughter was anything special. That she was something rare that even *I* would covet.

"Don't overthink it," I teased, tapping his head hard as I paced past him.

"Oh—" He cleared his throat. "Okay." A feeble nod accompanied his reply. "If that's what you want..."

Again, I didn't *want* her. It wasn't a matter of needing to possess his daughter over any other woman. It was the basic transaction of stealing something of value of his. To right his wrong, or at least to start that concept.

"I will bring her to you," he said. Nervous and skeptical, he spoke slowly, as if testing out the words to see if they were the right ones to tell me.

"You'll sacrifice your daughter?" I asked again. The more that I witnessed him caving and complying, the more I despised him. I'd take Gabriella whether he wanted me to have her or not. In fact, kidnapping her and holding her captive would've been an alternative to informing him of his payment and punishment. One on hand, this could've been psychological torture in itself. To give him the idea to get used to it. To torment him with the premonition of pending loss.

The speed with which he agreed irked me.

He hadn't hesitated for long. No. He had only seemed reluctant to react because he wanted to make sure he'd heard me correctly.

It wasn't that he didn't want to lose her.

No love would be lost between them.

And that lowered her value. His acquiescence reduced the severity and cruelty of this punishment. If he didn't seem to care about giving her up, was it even a punishment?

That was why I struck out, smacking him with so much force that he flung from the chair. Crying out in both surprise and pain, he dropped to the filthy floor. Rolling once, he moaned like a dying man.

Disappointment filled me that he wouldn't argue with my terms.

Irritation followed. How could he not want to protect his own flesh and blood?

Why wouldn't he fight to save her?

How come he acted like he didn't give a shit about giving me his daughter?

She couldn't mean much to him. Or perhaps it was a matter of his choosing his life over hers, deeming his life more valuable than hers.

Fuck it.

She wasn't going to mean much to me, either. This woman was just a pawn. A payment.

I could always sell her later. I could hold her until I could somehow get more value out of her.

I scowled down at Miguel after I beat him. Breathing hard, seething, I once again damned this spineless idiot for trying to betray the Dubinin organization.

6

GABRIELLA

Sleeping on the bench at the dance studio wasn't comfortable. I tossed and turned. At every little noise I heard, I panicked and couldn't return to any semblance of drowsiness. Sometime throughout the night, I gave up trying to stay on the narrow bench. Using some yoga mats from a closet and a few clean towels from storage that people used for sweat rags, I made the best bed that I could.

And I slept in it.

That was the story of my life. I made my bed and slept in it. I tried to make the best choices that I could, and I stood by them. I owned everything like that, including the crap I'd had to put up with yesterday.

It was only my fault that I got the hare-brained idea to hit on Oliver. And it was only my fault that I might face backlash from that. He could spread the word about me in a terrible way, and that would backfire epically. But there wasn't anything I could do about it now. It was done.

I also partly blamed myself for thinking I could be safe in my own home. It had been my choice to stick with my dad after I became a legal adult. Four years had passed after the milestone of my eighteenth birthday, the date when I was no longer a minor. I didn't *have* to stay with him. I could run away and start over somewhere new, on my own. Yet, I chose not to leave. If I ran and tried to control a new life of my own elsewhere, I'd be further from Juilliard and my dreams to dance on stage. Taking off to live in a different area wouldn't increase my odds of succeeding in ballet.

I owned my mistakes. I always would.

As I woke up, stiff and sore from trying to sleep on that bench and the floor, I was determined to own my next mistakes, too. Because I'd always make them. That was simply part of being human.

After I stowed the yoga mats and towels back where I found them, I left the dance studio before Amy or her mom could show up to open for the first class of the day. My stomach grumbled, reminding me that I hadn't eaten since lunch yesterday. My skin was grimy, another unwelcome reminder, one that I needed to shower, and badly.

Heading home, I tried to keep my head held high and concentrate on what I'd do if my dad wasn't there. I had to be smart about the possibility that Tony, or any other friend of my dad's, could be loitering there. Depending on how bad my dad's hangover was, he should've shown up by now. Like something the cat would drag in, he'd be there, grumpy and dehydrated, but likely not rethinking his choices like I always tried to do.

If Tony was still there, I'd have to wait him out. Calling my dad was useless. It had gone straight to voicemail. I tried his number as soon as I got to the studio last night.

There was no way in hell I'd go into the apartment with that creep in there. The closer I came to the building, the hotter my anger ran at the idea of his being in my home.

The audacity to let himself in just so he could try to force me into having sex with him. The nerve of barging in and preventing me from reaching my room, the one lockable safe haven I thought I could count on.

When I reached the building, I moved cautiously. Tony had been in the apartment, not out in the open and stalking me. Yet, as I walked up the stairs and continued down the hallways to reach my unit, I couldn't help but fear someone could be watching. A sixth sense to be alert was triggered. I couldn't shut off this need to be on guard. Anxiety would stick with me until I knew that no one was in my home, until I could lock a door between me and the rest of the world. This need to be *on* and never relax dragged me down, but there was no other option for how to survive.

No one approached me in the hallway. Not a single jump scare reached me or had me flinching.

Still, I paused at the door. I knocked. I *knocked* on my own damn door, as if I were a guest, not a member of the "family" there, not a person who contributed to the rent.

"Hello?" I called out after my knocks.

Nothing came. I didn't expect Tony to answer, anyway. He'd enjoyed catching me off guard last night. He wouldn't get away with that again. My hope was that if he were still here, I could know and retreat before going inside.

I knocked again. "Hello?"

Nothing. I tried the doorknob, finding it locked. Narrowing my eyes, I used my key to unlock it all while hanging on to a hammer I'd found in the closet at the dance studio. I'd bring it back. It wasn't like I wanted to steal it. I doubted Amy or her mom would need to even use a hammer today, or any time soon. They wouldn't even know that I'd borrowed it for the sake of self-defense.

I pushed the door open and waited.

No one lunged at me.

I blew out a deep breath and waited anyway. This anxiousness was going to drain all my energy on top of the shitty sleep I'd gotten last night.

I took one step in, hammer in hand. Once I was all the way in and no one showed, I exhaled another careful breath. I didn't release the hammer until I checked the entire apartment.

Tony was gone.

My dad hadn't returned.

I was alone, blissfully by myself. At last.

Without a second thought, I hurried to get in the shower. The hammer came into the narrow, stained stall with me. Just in case.

I stood under the hot water for as long as I could. It didn't erase every ache and pain, but the steam sort of soothed me. The longer I could calm down and try to relax in my own space, the more clearheaded I felt. Instead of being on guard and in a defensive mode, I could allow myself the chance to think back to all that happened.

Never minding my error in attempting to seduce Oliver, I dwelled on the fact that my dad hadn't come home. Tony hadn't counted on his coming home either, but somehow, I doubted my parent was dead.

He'd be alive if for no other reason than to trap me in this life.

But am I trapped?

I can leave. I can get dressed, walk out of here, and never come back.

I could just go and figure out how to get money and start a new life.

Doing so would end my chance of being near the resources to dance, though. It wasn't much, but each time my dad paid for a lesson, it was one step closer to the dream I never wanted to quit on. If I ran, I'd have no backup to pay for any lesson at all. I doubted I'd meet another friend like Amy, either, and I wouldn't be able to show up at a dance studio like I could now.

"Why does life have to be so hard?" I mumbled to myself as I got dressed in loungewear to make myself a late breakfast. Lunch. Whatever. I was so hungry that I'd lost track. Preparing food would only be feasible if anything was in the kitchen, and with Tony helping himself to this place last night, I doubted I'd find much.

"Thanks a lot, Dad," I muttered as I walked into the kitchen. It was his fault he'd befriended an asshole like Tony who'd try to rape me. I wanted to blame him for my mother's death too. Because he hung out with the wrong people, she'd been near the violence of a drive-by. Out of the goodness of her heart, she'd tried to help someone who was wounded.

And what did she get for it? Death.

I'd never forgiven my father for exposing her to a violent life. And I wouldn't be quick to forgive him for not showing up last night when his presence might have prevented Tony from trying to get me.

As I scrounged in the kitchen for the bare basics to slap together a sandwich, I sighed and wished I could be more like my mother. To hang on to beauty and sweetness like she had and not let the anger and frustration eat me up. My mom would've wanted me to be sweet and not so jaded, but in my opinion, she might have been too sweet. Too naïve. Too caring at the expense of her own safety and life.

Being raised like this, depending on no one but myself, I'd learned to always fight. To be abrasive and determined.

To be cutthroat and scrappy. That was the only way to survive.

That was why when my dad showed up, I was ready to fight like hell.

The door opened right when I realized we had no bread. Not a single slice remained, and it sucked to put together a sandwich with two slices of cheese and pickles. The deli meat I'd bought was gone too. Hungry and angry, I spun at the *click* of the door's hardware slotting into place.

I faced him with a serious scowl, but I struggled to keep a straight face like this.

He walked in slowly, limping like he could barely move his body. His face was littered with the evidence of pain. Bruises. Red, swollen blotches. Open cuts that looked like they'd bled a lot. One eye was shut, but he slitted the other one open enough to peer at me.

"What in the hell?" I demanded. Propping one hand to my hip, I looked him up and down. It even smelled like he'd peed his pants. "Dammit, Dad." I shook my head. Just seeing him renewed my fury. Seeing him like *this*, a pathetic and hungover mess, enraged me. He was good for nothing, too stuck on associating with deadbeats and getting high without a regard for anyone else.

"Where the fuck have you been?" I shouted.

He winced. Or maybe he didn't. It was hard to tell with how his face looked.

He must have gotten so high and messed up that he'd fallen somewhere. I didn't care. I was running out of patience, let alone compassion. He never gave any to me, and I was too burned to want to be "sweet" to him.

"You've got to be fucking kidding me, Dad. You were out all night—"

"Gabby, that's not true." His voice was slurred, as if something was wrong with his tongue.

"That's not true?" I parroted with every bit of seething anger I could muster. "That's not true? The hell it isn't. You weren't here last night when I got home. But Tony was. He knew you were out all night doing whatever the hell you wanted while he let himself into our home."

"What?" He stopped walking into the room, staring at me seriously. "Tony was here?"

"Yes! And he tried to rape me. Your buddy tried to take advantage of me the second I got home." I crossed my arms, too livid to stand straight without hugging myself. "He tried to *rape* me." Saying it out loud made it all the more real. It wasn't just a thought or a figment of a possibility. Speaking about it cemented it as a fact. As something that had happened. It was every woman's faraway fear, but it had almost *happened.* I struggled to accept it, wishing I could just be mad and yelling at him like this to avoid thinking about what if Tony had succeeded.

"He—" Dad took another step but had to put his hand on the table to support himself.

I furrowed my brow at the bruises and cuts there. It looked like he'd tried to fight with a clawed animal or something.

"Did he touch you?" he asked.

Like you care. "He tried to."

"But did he?" He lowered his head before staring me down. "Gabby, did he do anything to you?"

Not for one second did I think he was asking because he cared. Because he was worried. It seemed more like he needed a factual retelling, nothing more.

"No. I got away. He came on to me and was ready to take advantage. But I fought him off and ran away."

"Good." He exhaled a wheezy breath. I couldn't convince myself he was relieved *for* me, though. "You're still..." He cleared his throat, as if it was hoarse from screaming. "You're still a virgin, aren't you?"

I narrowed my eyes, ready to add to the bruises on his face. How dare he ask me that? How dare he prioritize my "purity" like that? Anger spiked in me all over again, and I wondered if it was possible for a person to combust from being so mad.

"Fuck off," I told him, sick of this. Sick of him. And sick of this life. This was his reaction? Just to make sure I remained a virgin?

"You can be as mad as you want, Gabby," he said, almost mockingly, "but it won't change anything."

I didn't need him to tell me that I was stuck in this life with no hope. I didn't understand what he was trying to say, though. I could be mad, but too bad, so sad?

"What?" I watched him lower his head again. As he stood there without a reply for me, I realized he hadn't closed the door behind him.

In the void of the doorway, another man appeared behind him. Dressed in a suit and wearing a somber, serious expression that warned the world not to mess with him, he strode right into the apartment.

"Dad?" I lifted my hand to point at the intruder. He moved too fast, though, and the urgency of him entering my home triggered that fight-or-flight response in me.

I backed up, smacking my hip on the counter. I couldn't fight this guy. He was too big. Too sinister. Just one look at him had me worried he was with the Mob.

"No. Get back! Dad?" I shot him a panicked look.

He didn't stop the man as he rushed toward me. He didn't blink. Didn't flinch.

"Dad?" I backed up into a corner where the counter met the fridge. "No. No!"

I had nowhere to run. My heart raced as the man pulled out a syringe from his pocket. Darting toward me and capturing my wrist, he moved too efficiently, jabbing the point of the needle into my upper arm.

"Dad!"

He didn't react. He didn't move.

Staring at me as the man struggled to hold me still, he witnessed my being captured right before his bloodshot eyes.

"No!" I screamed it as loud as I could, praying someone might hear and give a damn enough to intervene.

My own father wouldn't.

Deep down, I knew that no one would be coming to save me.

The only person who'd ever tried to accomplish that was myself.

7

LUKA

To no surprise, I woke up expecting this day to be exactly like every other one. The same fucking old. Nothing changing. After a workout, I headed into the office to oversee what was going on. Just like I had yesterday. Just like I would tomorrow. Always constant.

What's the fucking point of this anymore?

I couldn't pinpoint when my mood had soured so drastically. All I knew was that it dragged me down so far and so deep that I barely noticed Allen entering my office in the middle of the day.

He was good at blending in. His chameleon effect worked well for us. Without bothering me or becoming a distraction, he could seamlessly come in and out of my space to better assist me with whatever I might have needed. What I needed right now was something to jolt me back into the living.

He cleared his throat, a wordless cue that he had something to share.

I turned my head to stare at him, wondering what it was now.

"Alexsei has just arrived," he stated.

My other nephew was more of a protective services guru. Unlike Ivan, who excelled at negotiations and making deals, Alexsei was the product of what happened when a skilled combat expert tweaked his focus more toward security.

That didn't mean anyone had to herald his arrival at the office building like this. My son and two nephews went wherever they wanted or needed to without any approval or check-ins with me. They were the men I depended on most.

"All right," I replied, wondering why my personal assistant was taking time to share this news with me.

Allen cleared his throat again, looking as somber and monotone as ever. "He accompanied Emil on the delivery, or rather, the collection of Gabriella Lopez this morning."

I set my pen down. Perking up a bit at that fact, I tilted my head to the side. "Oh?"

He nodded.

"I wasn't aware that Emil would've asked for backup." Going to get Miguel's daughter should've been a routine exercise.

"It should've been," Alexsei said as he entered the office. His face showed the grim lines of a severe scowl. The red mark high on his cheek was what captured my attention the most.

"Did Miguel resist?" It came as no surprise that the sniveling bastard would try to renege on the punishment I'd told him to expect. His daughter as payment for his sins. His debt for turning traitor. There was no gray area contingent on that transaction, but clearly, he'd protested and struck out at my nephew.

"No." Alexsei rubbed his jaw. "*He* did not." He winced as he opened and closed his mouth. "How bad does it look?"

I sighed, hating that he'd be this worried about coming

home with a bruise. We lived a hard life. Bruises and cuts were expected. Not a single member of the Dubinin Family went by unscathed. Yet, I understood why Alexsei was bothered about this at all. His son, five-year-old Misha, had unfortunately wandered enough to find some men in a holding cell. Tortured enemies weren't something a child *that* young should have to witness. I didn't want to shelter the boy, nor did Alexsei, but Misha seeing those beaten men was too much at his age.

Alexsei's wife had been killed, and it was up to him to raise and shepherd the boy in this life. It was unfortunate that the boy was more nervous than usual about anyone in our family looking wounded now.

"Not that bad," Allen replied, cool and calm as ever. "I'll order an ice pack to be sent up."

"Thanks," Alexsei replied before exhaling a long breath. "Your payment is now at your place," he told me, smirking.

"Did Miguel have someone there for protection?" Someone had to have hit him.

"No. He dragged his raggedy ass home to find Gabriella alone."

I raised my brows. "Someone intervened in the building when you took her away?" I guessed.

"No." Alexsei rolled his eyes. "She didn't go easily. She wrestled to get away."

"Hmm." That was to be expected. No woman wanted to be taken. It would only be a matter of time before she'd learn her new reality, the one that dictated she was my possession now, all thanks to her spineless, lying father. "Was Miguel bothered by any of it?" I imagined a teary, pathetic goodbye. Maybe an apology that he'd dragged her into this mess.

"No," Alexsei said. "No, he wasn't. It happened quickly, but as far as I could tell, Miguel didn't react at all."

"You let him live?" Allen asked.

I tipped my chin at the door, indicating we could all leave now. With news that Gabriella was in a holding room at my fortress, the large mansion I owned as a residence and subsidiary office, I wanted to see what the fuss was about.

They both walked with me, exiting the office. Nothing was keeping me there anyway, at least, nothing I couldn't resume handling later.

"Yes. That was the order. We didn't kill Miguel," Alexsei said. "Emil didn't exactly leave him in any state to live for long, though."

I didn't mind if Emil left a farewell of a beating on the rat. He deserved it.

"Is there a chance Lopez can sell any other information?" Allen asked.

"No," I replied. "And if he tries to cause me any more trouble, it *will* be his life that he'll owe me." It wasn't my nature to leave threads loose like this, but Miguel had been tortured and questioned so extensively that it didn't seem like he had anything else to sell to the Cartel or Italians.

"At any rate," Alexsei quipped dryly, "you'll need some good luck on your side if you plan to sell Gabriella."

"Why?" The only assumption I could reach was that she was hideous. Unattractive. Such a lost cause that she wouldn't be desirable to anyone. "She's not a virgin?" I didn't often concentrate on selling women as a business, but it was common knowledge that virgins would always fetch a higher price. I hadn't looked at any of the photos of her up close. She could be a freak no one would want. Or she could be too used, damaged goods already.

"Oh, no. It sounds like she's a virgin," my nephew said. "It's just that she's a handful."

I gestured for him to get into my car as we reached it in the parking garage. Allen handed over the ice pack someone had brought for him, and with a wave, he excused himself.

"A handful?" I huffed a laugh. Alexsei knew how to manage a handful of anything. Danger. Angry men. A stubborn young son. And uncooperative women. "Just because she fought to get free?" That wasn't uncommon. Some people actually had a survival instinct.

"She fought to get free," he replied as we were driven toward my home. He pressed the ice on his face, proving that he was still the tough man I needed him to be but also soft in not wanting to look too rough for his son. "She also faked being drugged. With how difficult she was to grab, I couldn't be sure I got the needle in her arm properly. When she went lax, I carried her down to the car while Emil gave Miguel his personal goodbye. Emil carried her out of the car, and that's when we realized she was only faking it. She wasn't drugged or unconscious. She lashed out and got him really good. A few of us had to grab her before she escaped." He stared at me, likely wondering if I'd order anything further in regard to Gabriella's treatment.

I had nothing to say—yet. But I was intrigued. This *was* different. Most women deferred to tears and begged to get away. Questions would be wailed as they wondered why this was happening to them. Sobs would go along with their pleas for mercy. Most gave up. Once they realized they were outnumbered by strong men, their survival instincts would peter out.

Submission was imminent.

Defeat was implied.

But Gabriella was a fighter. And just like that, I was very curious to see what kind of a woman she was.

Alexsei answered a call about something else as we rode. He lifted a finger to indicate for me to wait a second. I acknowledged him with a wave, dismissing him and leaving him to his responsibilities. Instead of talking about this woman any further, I looked out the window and wished we could hurry this drive. Nothing had given me this urgency lately. Nothing had excited me, but I cautioned myself against admitting that this was exciting. That this was going to be something different to embrace.

We arrived, and I strode straight to the security room where all the footage from the basement rooms was monitored. This was my personal home, but security like this was still a must. These few rooms where hostages could be held were all equipped with cameras. Guests seldom stayed here, but Gabriella was an exception for now.

In the biggest room that was more furnished than the others, Gabriella lay slumped on a bed. She was out now, clearly drugged despite the hassle of her faking it the first time. As she began to stir and sit up, she gave me the first view of her face. It was a shame it was through this camera.

She was young, but not so much so that I wouldn't be turned off. Gabriella was a woman, elegant with high cheekbones, sharp eyes, and a heart-shaped face. Even though the image was grainy, there was no mistaking her beauty. Her athleticism. Her curves. In the scowl she gave the room, sitting there and surveying the place, she showed her defiance.

With her looking around, as if scoping for a threat, she demonstrated that she had a fighting spirit.

For how long? Hmm? How long will you stay tough and delude yourself into this idea of control and power?

I hadn't counted on her being gorgeous, not like this. Not in a way that robbed me of breath. Not so strongly that I was mesmerized, watching her as she stood and investigated how she could get out of the room.

She couldn't. But when Ivan appeared to bring her water —likely to check on the captive's vitals, too—she reacted in a snap. Instead of curious and nervous, prying at the windows and doors for a chance to run, she positioned herself to attack.

"What the fuck is going on?" she demanded of him, trying to beat him back.

He, like Alexsei, was too trained and experienced to let her get the best of him. In a matter of seconds, he turned her around and had her dropping to the ground. Without using too much force to wound her, as was expected from me so far, he showed her that she wasn't going to escape.

"Stop—"

She didn't. Chest heaving, she shot back up and tried to charge at him. She was deft on her feet. Spinning and ducking to dodge him, she showed how athletic she truly was. Nimble and fast.

But no match for a Mafia man.

I rubbed my chin, watching as she fought Ivan and shouted at him to release her. With this much sass, this much fight, she was no common, ordinary woman. *Why would Miguel act as though she has no value? Why would he dismiss her so easily?*

Why give her up?

Ivan told her to settle down.

"Settle down?" she shot back, getting up as she gritted her teeth and seemed ready to lunge at him again.

He held up a gun, clearly peeved with her antics. She backed up then, not stupid enough to argue with a gun.

"Yes. Settle the fuck down," he ordered. "Someone will be in with food soon." He exited the room, and she didn't neglect to flip off the closed door and curse him out once he was gone. Resuming her search in the room, she hunted for a means of escape. Or perhaps she was looking for a weapon.

I couldn't stop watching her.

When a guard brought her a tray of food, she again tried to fight her way to freedom. Ivan must have ordered them to go in threes. If not for the two extra guards accompanying the one bringing the food, she might have succeeded.

Still, she cursed them out and eyed them warily, like they were rabid animals encroaching on her space. Witnessing her fire tempted me to go down there and put her in her place. To explain that no matter how much she resisted and fought it, she was my property now.

There would be no chance for her to leave until I said so.

Yet, I couldn't leave the security room. I was drawn to watch her. She would be a challenge to handle, and as of yet, I wasn't sure how I'd want to go about that.

Ivan entered the security room. Emil walked in behind him.

"The fuck..." Emil muttered.

I stifled a laugh at the black eye she'd given him.

"I see you're home," he said. Gesturing at the screens on the wall, he sneered. "So is your latest toy."

"Toy?" I wasn't ready to convince myself that this spitfire would be my toy. "I have no idea what to do with her yet."

Emil shook his head, walking out. "Well, good luck with whatever the hell your plans are."

Ivan studied me, stepping further into the security room to join me and close the door behind him. "At least this will snap you out of being pulled into that depressive mood you've been stuck in." He sat, undeterred by my sharp look.

"What?"

"Alexsei said you've been in here watching her for hours now."

It's been that long? "So what?"

"So... it seems that you're intrigued." He smiled at me, too cocky for my liking.

I laughed, shaking my head that he thought he had me figured out like that. But I sobered quickly because I could remember all too well when Ivan was depressed, truly, legitimately in a dark mood after he suffered through a bad breakup. I would never forget how depressed he'd been during those days when he walked away from his love.

Which was ridiculous.

No love would be happening here. Not between me and this sassy, defiant woman.

Gabriella was a payment. A pawn. Nothing else, no matter how much she captured my interest at this moment.

"Intrigued," I admitted to my nephew.

But not stupid.

8

GABRIELLA

Waking up groggy and disoriented was the first indication that something was wrong. Feeling the after-effects of whatever drug that thug had shot me up with was another.

My dad never gave me an indication that he was a good guy. I knew he was associated with some sketchy people.

But until now, when I woke up in a locked bedroom after being dragged out of my home, I hadn't realized he knew people in the freaking Mob.

As in the Mafia.

Like all these suited guards and militant men who entered my room to provide me with cold glares and food. If I were the kind of person to wallow in being a victim, I'd convince myself that I deserved these glowers and expressions of loathing. I hadn't made it easy for them, fighting each person to come in here for the sake of getting the hell out of this place.

But I didn't. I *was* a victim. I hadn't asked to be taken. I hadn't put myself in any position to warrant being kidnapped like this and held captive.

I refused to wallow and accept it, though.

They had me *now*. They were keeping me here against my will for the time being.

I'd be damned if I took that as my fate, though.

Every time the locks clicked open, I tensed and braced myself to fight back and figure out an escape. Any chance I could get to bolt, I'd take it. They were quick to realize I was capable of protesting, fighting back, and squirming to get free.

At first, they came one at a time. That one bastard thought that aiming a gun at me would kowtow me into a defeatist attitude.

It hadn't. I wasn't stupid. If they'd wanted me dead, they would've killed me already.

They hadn't.

If they wanted me harmed, they wouldn't have hesitated to beat me and mark me up.

They didn't attempt to wound me.

Putting a gun in my face was just a scare tactic, and I wasn't falling for it. Yet, seeing how all these men were packing was no joke. These men were members of a criminal organization. The Mafia. I heard the Dubinin name mentioned, and that alone was plenty to convince me to watch it.

My captors weren't amateurs. They weren't imposters. Each and every one of these guards who entered was capable of killing.

So, when on the fourth day of being held here, I tried to fight my way free, I saw how far I was pushing my luck. Luck seemed like a cruel tease. I wasn't lucky to have been kidnapped without a damn explanation. I wasn't lucky to have been shoved in here with no weapons, no means of escape, not a single way to contact anyone. And I sure as hell wasn't lucky to be taken from my life, to be held away from Amy's studio and the freedom to go to my few dance lessons that were the sole purpose of my life.

They came in threes now, one man to bring water, food, or clothes and then two more as backup. Always packing. Always with their hands on their guns, ready to defend themselves or to remind me that I had no power here.

"Let me go," I ordered. It was the starting line of a greeting I gave them. No matter which rugged and stone-faced brute it was, I told them all the same thing. Submission wasn't happening. Not from me. So long as I could breathe and stand, I would fight to get out of here.

This captive bullshit wasn't the life I was supposed to live. I was supposed to be on stage or learning how to get there. I was powerless and outnumbered. I still didn't know anyone to save me. But dammit, I couldn't give up.

"No." That one-word reply was all the guard said as he set down a pile of brand-new clothing. A short stack of it was accumulating on the narrow side table where the other garments sat untouched.

I'd drunk the water so I'd stay hydrated. I ate some of the food so I could keep my strength up. But I'd be damned if I acquiesced to wearing the clothes they brought in. To do so would be a step toward admitting defeat. It would give them another clue to assume I was accepting the fact that I'd been taken and would be held.

Too many questions pinged in my mind. All day and night, trapped in here with nothing to do but worry and panic, I failed to answer any of them. Why I was taken. What the Dubinin Mafia would want with me. Why my father hadn't tried to help me. So many questions plagued me during the torment of waiting for answers from these men.

But I knew better than to ask them for an explanation. They were all the low-level grunt men, the soldiers and guards. I needed to speak with someone in charge, and once I did, I'd demand my release.

"Then let me talk to your boss." I crossed my arms and tipped my chin up defiantly. These assholes wouldn't see me weak. Yet, as I stood straight, I felt tired and nervous deep inside. Tomorrow would be five days, and I wasn't sure I could manage to remain this tough.

The man who offered me the clothing started to smile. Dark and sinister in a suit, he showed me a cocky smile I didn't care for.

"You want to see the Boss?" he mocked.

"I want to talk to your boss," I repeated.

"Just talk?" With a slow, leering look that he roved up and down me, he suggested that if he were to have his way with me, he'd have other things in mind than merely talking. So far, none of them had tried to touch me. But that didn't mean they wouldn't surprise me yet.

I tightened my arms over my chest and pressed my lips tighter together.

"The Boss will deal with you as he sees fit," the man replied in that damn teasing tone again.

Hearing him mock me was too much. I got it. I got the big picture. I was stuck here with no defense, no options. And I was sick of feeling helpless and without power.

"Then tell him that I demand a discussion about why I am stuck here."

"Oh. *You* demand?" he taunted, leaning closer to sneer at me. "You're nothing. You're no one. And it might do you well to accept it."

If he'd said anything else, I might've been able to rein in my temper. But he'd chosen to demean me and remind me of this supposed inferiority that I was supposed to be okay with.

I wouldn't.

And I showed it by punching him. I'd struck out at them before. I'd kneed men in the nuts, like Tony when he tried to rape me. Self-defense was something I'd taught myself, just like I had learned to dance by watching dance tutorials and videos. I bet my form was all wrong, but I'd done it right. My fist popped him in the face. A sickening crunch came with my hit. From how he groaned and staggered back, his hand over his face, I'd gotten him good.

The other two raised their guns, and this time, as the other man reeled back and growled in pain, I worried they really would shoot me.

I wouldn't take it back, but I feared the repercussions I could face for fighting this hard.

"What the fucking— You bitch!" The man I punched lowered his hand and scowled at the blood in his palm. Deep red and flowing fast, it leaked from his nose.

"Let's go." The thug to his right grabbed his arm and propelled him to retreat. The third, the man on the punched one's left, kept his gun trained on me as they backed up toward the door. It closed after them with a slam. Despite watching them go and knowing the door would shut with a bang, I flinched.

Then as I stared at the door for another long moment, partly afraid and partly curious whether they'd realize I wouldn't ever stop trying to get out of here, I wished this wasn't happening to me. That I'd been born to someone else. That I'd lived elsewhere, somewhere on this planet where I had an ally and a friend. Anyone.

But it's just me.

I would always only have myself.

With that depressing thought, I let out a deep exhale and hung my head. It wasn't a simple matter of being alone again and having the luxury of lowering my guard. I couldn't. I wouldn't dare to relax just because I was the only one in the room now. Cameras were no doubt posted on the walls. Eyes were on me. Ears, too. I knew better than to assume I wasn't being watched, and with how I'd just punched and broken that man's nose, I wondered how long it would take for someone to come and react to it.

Shaking out my hand that stung with the punch I'd thrown, I spun away from the door.

Giving it my back felt like a stupid mistake, though. As soon as I pivoted, the locks clicked once more. Someone was already coming in here.

Tense and shaking with how tightly my muscles bunched, I waited for the men to enter again.

Only one did.

A taller man with graying hair strode into the room like he was in charge. His eyes were just as cold and serious as the others'. But this hulking individual wasn't one of them.

I knew from just one look.

I felt the change in the air.

He exuded power. Dominance. Authority.

Refusing to show an ounce of fear, I narrowed my eyes as I faced him squarely. With every second of him stalking toward me like a predator hiding in the disguise of a finely tailored suit that clung to him perfectly, showing he was as fit and toned as his soldiers and men, I wanted to quiver. The instinct to cower and tremble hit me, but I resisted it. I was too determined to stand tall and strong. Letting this brutish but distinguished older man see a hint of intimidation would only be the start of my downfall.

Extending his arms, he lowered his hands to straighten

the cuffs of his jacket. Even those movements were fluid and graceful. He moved like a panther, like a powerful being at ease with his identity and unafraid to control everything that could impact him.

Watching me stare at him, he arched one brow. It wasn't a sign of amusement. It wasn't an expression of anything but what I could interpret as mild intrigue.

"What?" I demanded, pissed at how shaky that single little word was as it came from my lips.

"You asked to see me?" he replied.

Cool yet raspy. Deep yet smooth. His voice was the whiskey-laced kind of smoky growl that had me snapping to attention.

I cleared my throat. "You? I asked to see *you*?"

What the fuck?

What the hell am I saying?

I didn't know where this ridiculous bravado was coming from. It wasn't like the naïve and risky attitude I used when I tried to hit on Oliver at the studio. This false courage and tough exterior weren't *me*.

He didn't stop until he stood right in front of me. I was within reach. If he so pleased, he could snap his arm out and grab me by the throat. He'd squeeze, too, able to end my life. Like all the others, his minions and soldiers, this guy was a killer. The dark aura that emanated from him was unmissable, but somehow, I clung to this stupid idea that I could still be tough around him.

Stopping still to loom over me, he breathed in and out once. His chest rose and fell as his lean face remained unreadable and unwelcoming. No smile. Not a smirk, either.

"Yes." His reply was clipped and brokered no nonsense.

"I asked for *you*?" I huffed, rolling my eyes.

I was signing a death sentence, trying to mock him, but I

couldn't stop. I had to do *something*, and fighting like this was all I could think of.

Ever so slightly, he edged in closer. One placement of his foot toward me. That was all he did while glaring down at me. Nothing else. A single step closer and I wanted to buckle down and cower.

Instead, I forced my throat to swallow and refused to back down.

"You asked to speak to the boss." He tilted his head toward the side as he peered at me.

"You're the boss around here?"

"I am the boss." He wasn't confirming what I'd said. He told me that statement like it was a law I should know. No questions asked.

"Fine." Dammit, that came out shakily too. "Then release me."

Nothing. He stared me down. I wished I could claim to be stronger, but I wasn't. Pinned under his hard stare, I weakened. I snapped. I just couldn't take his scrutiny this directly.

"I didn't ask for this. For any of this."

He shook his head without breaking his glare. "You didn't."

Now we were getting somewhere. He agreed.

"Then release me. I don't belong here."

Again, he shook his head. "You do."

"What?" I dropped my arms and gaped at him. "No. No, I do not. I don't fucking belong here. You had no right to have your goons kidnap me. I've got nothing to do—" I shook my head, but it wasn't the slight movement he did. I jerked it from side to side, as if denying what he said with vehemence would make things go my way. "I refuse to be kidnapped like this."

"Too late."

You asshole.

"I will not accept this."

He raised both brows in a silent challenge.

"I won't!" I clamped my lips shut and fought back the urge to punch him.

"Just as I will not accept your attitude or your eagerness to break my guard's nose."

I opened and closed my mouth, settling on grinding my teeth. "He deserved it. I *don't* deserve this. Please. Get a hold of my dad. He'll set this straight. I don't know anything about what he does or doesn't do. I don't know anything about any of you. I'm innocent. So just figure out your issues with him."

"Innocent?"

I narrowed my eyes once more. The way he asked that chilled me. *Innocent as in untouched? Is that why Dad was asking if I was still a virgin?*

The possibility that this wasn't some random mistake quickened my pulse so suddenly that I feared I'd pass out.

Please. No. God, no. He couldn't have...

I forced another hard swallow down my dry throat. I'd never been so scared before in my life. "Miguel Lopez."

He nodded once. "I'm familiar with your father."

"Then set this straight with him. I shouldn't be here. Deal with him. Not me."

"I have dealt with him." He drew in a deep breath, making his chest rise high again. "And this—you—are the deal."

"What?" I scowled, terrified but masking it to stay strong. "What the fuck are you talking about?"

"Miguel gave you to me."

"I'm not a *thing* to be given!"

"No." He dragged his gaze lower. "You most certainly are not. Not when you insist on fighting the truth."

"The truth?" I gritted my teeth, fighting back the urge to hit him and to cry. "The truth is that you've kidnapped me!"

"Your father gave you to me." Looking down his nose at me, he paused with his cruel honesty.

"He *sold* me to you?" I refused to believe it. I couldn't. Yet, he had been so deliberate with asking if I was still a virgin.

"He gave you to me. As a payment for a debt."

Oh, God. Oh, God. Oh, God. Bile rose up my throat at this news. That my own parent would give me to this Mafia monster and think it was perfectly fine. That...

Oh, fuck.

No.

Oh, fuck no.

I shook my head again, furiously. "No. Fuck that shit. No. You hear me, *Boss*? You're not—" I staggered back a step. "You're not getting *anything* from me."

He laughed lightly at first. Then as he shook his head again, a wicked smile transformed his face. He was mocking me. *Laughing* at me and pissing me off like no one had ever done before.

"You hear me?" I shouted. Only the fear of knowing he was in charge kept me from hitting him as he turned to stride out of the room.

"Hey! Do you understand? You're not getting anything from me!"

Not my virginity. Not my submission. Nothing. I vowed to never stop fighting.

Stopping at the door, he turned to give me one last hard look. "But you do belong here, as a payment for your father's debt. Like it or not, you *are* mine." With those last words, he exited and shut the door quietly before the telltale click of the locks fell into place.

Alone and bewildered from the experience of speaking with the Boss, I fisted my hands and growled out the scream that was trapped in my chest. I was trapped. I was well and truly fucked, captured and stuck here where no one would save me.

My dad gave me to this Mafia boss.

All this anger at him would never fade. But it was the hopelessness of being confined and kept from my dreams that threatened to break me more.

9

LUKA

If she hadn't struck out and broken that guard's nose, I probably would've let her stew and stay in that room for another week. Just to break her in. To wait out her initial reluctance to realize she was no longer free.

I wasn't afraid of her hitting any more of my men. After Simon's nose was reset, I bet none of them would take her for granted again. And yes, he had deserved her wrath. He didn't need to be so cocky toward her, so smug. He'd poked the beast and gotten what he deserved.

Instead of being livid that she'd wounded one of my men, I had to admit I was impressed.

She wasn't acting. She wasn't putting on a show or pretending to be tough. Like a caged animal, she was reacting under that survivalist instinct. After so long of the same old, of the typical captives crying and begging like pathetic defeatists, Gabriella intrigued me.

She wasn't going to stop fighting this new reality she had to adjust to.

She wouldn't quit.

That bold determination *was* admirable. However,

watching her from afar was wearing on me. Every time I settled in to view the footage from her room, I struggled against the itch to experience being in her presence again. To feel the burn of her scathing scowls and stares. To let her dole out her anger and wrath, waiting for her to push her luck.

I wasn't a glutton for punishment, but—

Fuck.

I huffed a single laugh.

Ivan was right.

Gabriella *was* pulling me out of that shitty depressive streak.

I sat back on the executive office chair that the men had brought to my home office. The security team had rigged it so I could view the direct feed to Gabriella's room. Nightly—hell, even daily—I watched her in captivity.

She hadn't cowered. She still glared at the men who brought her food and water, then the clothing too. She'd changed out of the loungewear but didn't peruse the variety of the garments brought to her.

But she didn't bottle up her anger and frustration. No. She let it out. She vented in the form of dancing.

And that was the obsession I couldn't shake.

Watching her like a stalker, I glued my gaze to the screen of my computers and witnessed her grace. Her athleticism. Her natural beauty as she moved to music in her head.

Every night, beginning in the late afternoon or evening after her dinner was delivered, she'd dance. Too soon, I felt cheated to be reduced to only this indirect view of her, but I wasn't ready to face her again.

I didn't know how to play this game with her. I wasn't sure how I wanted to handle this.

In the meantime, I could enjoy all I wanted.

Emil entered the office and strode up to me. Hands in his pockets, brows raised with curiosity, he smirked. "Again?"

I shrugged, looking back at the ballerina I'd captured.

"You're watching her again." He leaned his hip against my desk. It should've been a question but he'd said it like a statement.

I couldn't help but want to watch her.

"What, you want a private dance?" he teased.

I lifted my head to shoot him a look. "She's not that kind of a dancer." Nothing about the way Gabriella moved suggested that. She wasn't an exotic performer. She wasn't grinding and hinting at anything. "She's an artist." Her passion was obvious.

I made a mental note to have music sent to her, perhaps on a new phone that I could track. She hadn't left her room yet. The more I watched her and wanted to experience her stubbornness and passion, the more I readied myself to release her to the rest of my home.

"She's a debt paid from a rat," Emil reminded me dryly.

I hadn't asked for a reality check but he'd given me one anyway.

"She could be a debt payment of my own," I muttered. Gabriella was gorgeous, and that alone would fetch a nice price for her. This show of her passion and skill for dancing just made her more expensive.

"You'd sell her?" he asked, watching her dance in the room.

I shrugged. "I have no plans yet." Other than appreciating more of her defiance, I wasn't prepared to claim my intention with her. "But I could." I could definitely sell her or give her away. I took things. I was always the one in control, but I could just imagine the interest other men might send her way. She could be a critical tool of leverage. A delicious carrot to dangle and entice even my worst enemies.

Rubbing my jaw slowly, I sighed and dismissed any hurry to make up my mind about what to do with her yet.

All I could make a move on right now was this intrigue. This curiosity.

This desire to watch her more up close.

The next evening, I went to her room and opened the door. After I stepped in, I leaned against the doorframe, teasing her by leaving it open. She wouldn't get past me.

The second I ended her privacy, she stopped. Breathing hard from the exercise of dancing, she glowered at me.

Her huge breasts heaved. Her slim waist remained flat. Her legs, so slender, ceased moving. But it was her eyes that captured me. Those dark, rebellious eyes. Her lips stayed parted, but the longer I stared her down, they turned into a scowl.

"What?" she snapped.

I crossed my arms. "Nothing."

"What do you want?"

"What makes you think I want anything?"

She rolled her eyes. "This question-for-an-answer shit won't bother me." She shrugged, but it seemed more like she was rolling her shoulders in a stretch.

I didn't leave. Merely staring at each other, we entered a tense test of who'd break first. I knew she would.

"What do you want?"

I considered the repetition of her question. What did I want? Where she was concerned, I wasn't sure.

"Dance." That was my reply, though.

She barked a wry laugh. "For you?" She stepped toward

her bed where a hand towel waited for her. As she wiped the sweat from her brow, she smirked. "No."

"You don't want to dance for me?"

"As if I haven't been already." She gestured vaguely at the room. "As if you don't have surveillance on my room. You've seen me dance enough."

"So, you'll stop? You'll quit?"

She slitted her eyes. "Never. But I won't dance for *you.*" With that, she turned and hid in the bathroom.

Stubborn brat.

The next night was the same. In my office, seated in front of my computer, I'd watch her dance until I couldn't take it anymore. Then the second I opened her door, she'd stop, huff or growl in frustration, and leave to go to the bathroom.

After two weeks of captivity here, it never changed. With me, she was sullen. For me, she was tough and sassy, not backing down at all. Each time she was rude to me, she antagonized me and pushed me that much more to make her break. Whether I came to watch her dance—not that she would for me—or to bring her a meal, she was tough.

And when I realized we'd entered a routine, I grew irritated with this sameness. The lack of change. The challenge she presented was still there, but this waiting game, this distance, was stagnant.

That night, I entered her room before dinner.

She blinked, sitting upright from a nap. "What— Why..." She cleared her throat. "What's going on?"

"Dinner." I extended my hand toward her.

She frowned.

"Get up."

She slowly swung her legs over the bed but didn't fully put her feet on the floor. "I'm not hungry."

"Too bad." I thrust my hand out more.

"I don't want dinner."

"Do you think you're privileged enough to get what you want here?"

She stood, getting in my space and glowering. "You're an asshole."

"I'm your owner. I'm the Boss." I snatched her hand and tugged her out of the room with me. With every step I took, I seriously wondered if she'd attack me. And if she did, how far I'd take it to remind her who was in charge. "If I say you're accompanying me to dinner, you are."

"Why?"

I pushed her against the wall near the door to her room. Once those dark eyes locked on me, I leaned in closer. "Because you are mine to do with as I please."

She licked her lips and glared at me. Only because she was so young, I doubted that she realized what a fucking tease she was, wetting those plump lips like that. "And dragging me to sit through dinner pleases you?"

"Maybe."

When she rolled her eyes and shifted to get free, I put my hand back on her hip and yanked her in front of me. "From now on, I expect you to be near me."

"Why?"

"Don't question me," I warned. I took her hand again and led her out of the room. Merely feeling her soft, warm skin against mine was a thrill. Handling her at all was a challenge to beat. I had no doubt she'd slip away the first second she could.

"Why?" She persisted, asking again in the hallway as she tugged to wrench her hand free.

"Just because."

She growled, and I almost smiled.

"That's not a reason."

"I don't owe you a reason." I glanced at her, wondering why a defiant pout was suddenly so sexy from her. "But if you want one, consider this. You will accompany me to every meal—"

"*Every* meal!"

"—for no other reason than to remind you that I own you."

10

GABRIELLA

I set my water glass down and exhaled through my nose. Three days now, I'd been dragged out of my room for meals. For three mornings, afternoons, and evenings, I'd been "released" from my room to sit through a meal with Luka.

Luka Dubinin.

I only learned his name when a bald man who looked like a butler called for him.

Luka.

It was a bold name for a bold man.

But I filed it away. Calling him an asshole suited me just fine.

When the first thug joined us for dinner tonight, it seemed that introductions were in order. I didn't want to know anyone here. I couldn't let go of this need to be out of here. The man who helped capture me referred to Luka as Father, and at first, I wondered if that was a Mafia title thing. It wasn't. The more I studied them, the more their family resemblance was clearer to see. The father and son spoke in riddles, just like Luka did every other time anyone else came near during these stupid meals in his stupid mansion.

I didn't give a damn about their Mafia business.

I didn't care to learn any secrets.

I wasn't here to spy or anything like that.

Yet, they never divulged details about anything.

Belatedly facing me near the end of the meal, Luka gestured at the man I'd attacked when I faked being drugged. "Gabriella, this is my son, Emil."

Emil gave me a cocky grin. "Oh, we've met."

I didn't reply with anything other than a glower.

"Nothing?" Luka asked me.

I stared at him. *I hate you.*

"Allen."

The butler-like man came to stand next to him. "Yes?"

"Every time that Gabriella doesn't reply to me, tally it."

Allen nodded.

I pressed my lips tighter together.

"What's the tally going to be for?" Emil asked. I almost could've thanked him. I wanted to know that too, but I was too stubborn to stop this silent treatment.

Luka didn't take his dark, smoldering gaze off me. "That's to be determined."

An empty threat? *Ha.* I set my fork down and didn't break eye contact.

I wouldn't dance for him.

I wouldn't speak to him.

Sooner or later, he'd realize I wouldn't ever break.

It just made no sense. I couldn't understand why he wanted me out of that room. To come eat with him? To walk around the huge mansion with him? To sit in that weird conservatory-like sunroom with the pool and hot tubs no one ever used?

I had no idea what kind of game he was playing with me. If he'd taken me from my dad to exploit me, he sure had a kink for waiting.

No matter how much time I was forced to spend near him, I couldn't determine what I was. He hadn't made it a secret that he owned me. That I was a possession. But for what? Why? To have me be a human trophy? A piece of décor to place in his home?

Finished with eating, Emil stood and nodded at me. "I'd say it was nice seeing you again, but, well..." He shrugged. "Your first impression lingers."

I flipped him off.

He chuckled, and I could've sworn Luka almost smiled.

Seated at the table as the plates were taken away, Luka and I stayed put.

"You do remember that I own you," he said, breaking the silence.

I sighed, resting my chin in my hand, my elbow on the table.

Like I could forget.

"I could sell you at any second."

Uh-huh.

"I could give you to someone else and let them put up with you."

I blinked. *You think that hasn't crossed my mind?*

Moving so quickly that I couldn't be prepared, he startled me by gripping the corner of my chair and shifting it suddenly. The feet scraped on the floor. My hair whipped into my face. I'd been seated to his right, my chair perpendicular to his. Now, with his jerky movement, I was leaning forward, nearly nose-to-nose with him.

I held my breath. I locked down, too tense to dare to exhale as I focused on his heated stare.

"Nothing to say to that?" he asked in a low, gruff growl.

I licked my lips, hating how I stared at his.

He wouldn't beat me at this game. He wouldn't make me break. I would get out of here, and I would do so without defeat.

Another long stare-down tormented me. He didn't push, he didn't demand. Only watching me like this, so close and in a bubble of our own, he tested me.

What?

What is it?

What do you see? What do you want to see in me? You say you own me but you don't. You never will. Why can't you just give up and let me go?

Getting sucked into his orbit would be the stupidest thing I could do. That was why I resisted, why I fought. It was why I stubbornly protested how my body reacted. In my mind, I could be strong and stand up to him. I could carry on without talking to him. But under his dark, hungry gaze, I reacted.

My nipples stiffened.

An ache blossomed and spread from between my legs.

And this illogical and nonsensical need to close the distance between us just so I could feel him was shredding my patience.

"Or..." He leaned in to grab the armrests of my chair to drag me closer yet. "Are you getting used to how *I* put up with you?"

Lifting my head, I met his gaze and scowled.

No.

You won't win.

You won't break me.

No matter wh—

"Come." He stood, almost chilling me with the absence

of his body so close to me. He hadn't touched me, not really, but just being this near him, I felt all the warmth emanating from his big body.

On his feet, he straightened his jacket and extended his hand toward me.

I'm not a dog.

I'm not a thing to order to heel, goddammit!

Yet, I stood. All I could do was let him feel my ire in the intensity of my stare.

"I've explained to Allen that you have permission to be in my personal wing." Leading me up the stairs from the vast dining room and open floor plan of the first floor, he carried on. "I've already asked the staff to relocate your things."

What?

Wait.

What?

Personal wing? Like, your bedroom? You expect me to sleep with you now? Keeping all these questions unspoken burned me. I was itching to blurt them out. More clarification was necessary, but I refused to ask. He could design any damn game he wanted with me, but I wouldn't play along.

"You will reside in the room next to mine."

Oh, thank God. I exhaled in relief, letting my shoulders sag. He must have noticed from the hand he held. Glancing back at me, he raised his brows.

Even though he was changing things up by having me be closer to him, he didn't make any other move to suggest he wanted to own me in any other way. He was still gone for hours. Sometimes, I wouldn't see him at all during the day. Only late at night.

And still, I refused to speak to him.

I'd dance in my room, then wait for a sign that I could be free of this.

When he wasn't near, I'd overhear the staff. Emil was often around. He hadn't warmed up to me. Nor had Ivan, the man who'd first pulled a gun on me here. He was Luka's nephew. Another nephew, Alexsei, seemed familiar, and I realized he'd also been in on my capture.

Guards and soldiers always talked in code or riddles. But one night when I was dancing in my room, a guard burst in.

I jumped back, nearly tripping over my own feet as the bloodied man staggered inside. He grunted, holding his head like he was lost and confused. With the clarity of a memory to guide me, I knew instantly that he was high. Drugged. Not with it.

As he latched his gaze on me, he squinted and lifted his bloody arm to aim a gun at me.

"No!" I backed up, hiding behind a chair as he sluggishly advanced toward me. Holding my hands up, as if that would magically ward him back, I retreated until I was cornered by the windows. All locked. Everything was locked. There was no escape for me—ever. Even now, as this dazed and drugged man pursued me, talking in Russian gibberish.

"Get back!" I ordered, terrified that he would be so out of it as to shoot me.

"Get down!"

Luka's voice roared. He was there, rushing in after the man. More shouts spewed from him, then another, but I couldn't tell who was in my room now. I dropped to the floor as instructed. Crouching low and ducking to cover my head, I tried to make myself as small as I could, into as tight of a ball as I could.

The sounds of a struggle reached me, nonetheless. Grunts. Thuds of flesh against flesh. Moans. And growls. I couldn't tell who was where and what was going on. All I knew for a fact was that like this, here, I was powerless. I *was* hopeless, and it was with that sobering fact that I hugged myself and prayed this wasn't the end.

"It can't be the end," I muttered to myself just as strong arms wrapped around me.

I squeaked, shaking my head and keeping my eyes closed as I was lifted off the floor. Carried up and walked backward, I refused to open my eyes and see that I would be taken. Or killed. Or hurt.

"Can't be the end," I muttered again, shaking my head. "Not done. My dream... Not the end yet..."

Fingers bit into my upper arms, then I was shaken. "Stop."

Luka.

I blinked, gazing at him as he walked me further into my room. Behind him, the sounds of a struggle continued, but it wasn't any episode of danger toward me. Emil and another guard dragged the drugged man away. They were handling the situation. They were taking the intruder away.

"Gabriella."

Luka's smoky voice barely reached me. He sat on my bed, keeping me on his lap as he watched me. "Gabriella." Again, he shook me.

But I wasn't jarred.

I was too coiled up. Too tense. Too overwhelmed with the stress of being kidnapped, captured. Then the endurance to maintain this silent treatment and never show weakness.

When that man burst in, it was the most direct example of violence I'd faced yet.

Just like when Tony tried to rape me.

Just like when I was snatched out of the apartment.

It was just too much.

Locked in this trauma response, I could only stare back at Luka.

He framed my face, forcing me to address him. "Gabriella."

I swallowed, dizzy from the panic attack of someone in here and the dreadful worry that I'd be dead.

"Not done yet," I whispered, almost drunkenly.

"It *is* done. He's gone. He slipped away and is still too... It *is* done," he commanded. "You're not in danger."

I nodded feebly, wishing I could believe him. I wasn't in danger from whoever that bloodied, wounded, drugged man was. But I was very much in danger from *him*.

Like this, Luka stared at me with concern. Not expectations.

Alone in here with me, Luka watched me out of worry. Not irritation.

"I meant..." I cleared my throat. My voice was scratchy from the lack of use.

"What?" He didn't release me, and the more I acclimated to the hardness of his body serving as an anchor for me, I didn't want him to. "What did you mean?"

"I meant that my life can't be over yet." I licked my lips and lowered my gaze.

He lifted my face again until I was stuck in his dark stare. "No. It's not. Not on my watch."

I huffed. Then I laughed once more. "You've got to be fucking kidding me."

He furrowed his brow.

"You can't win like that."

The lines on his brow deepened. "What?"

"That's... That's cheating. You got me to talk."

He sighed, lightening up. "For fuck's sake." As I tried to

stand, preferring fighting with him to letting him see me weak and vulnerable, he tightened his hold on me again. "Stop. Enough with the silence."

I rolled my eyes.

"I will not let anyone harm or kill you here."

I frowned. "What about this tally system? When I don't reply?"

He smirked. "Don't think you can get away with changing the subject right now. You were scared."

"You won't hear me admit that."

"Fine. I respect that. In fact, *don't* admit it. Always guard your words."

I laughed once, wryly. "Why do you think I haven't been giving you *any* of my words?"

He gave me a hard glare. "No more silence."

"Fine." I doubted he'd kidnapped me to hear me talk, anyway.

"What were you saying?" he asked, undeterred. "About not being done."

I shrugged, sheepish that I'd said anything in my moment of fear. "Just that I'm not ready to die. I'm only twenty-two. I used to think that I had my whole life ahead of me." I narrowed my eyes. "Which is clearly false. That's why it's ironic that you'd tell me that my life isn't over on your watch."

"Are you doubting that I will keep what is mine safe?"

Does he even realize how he objectifies me and makes me a thing and not a person?

"No. But it's bullshit to call *this*"—I gestured at the room —"a life. I'm a captive... whatever. Hell, I don't know what I am. A thing. A possession. A... hostage?"

"I'm not negotiating with anyone to release you," he stated plainly.

"Okay, then I'm back to square one of having no clue why you're keeping me here." Now I stood. Then I took a step away. He was too tempting to lean on and the fact remained that I could only count on myself.

How the hell can I lean on you when you're the reason I'm here at all?

"I am keeping you because your father owed me."

"Great." I flung my arms up. "Great. I'm a transaction." I backpedaled toward the bathroom, hoping a long, hot shower could reset my head straight again after that scare and Luka's comfort. "I'm a thing that was traded in a business transaction. Got it. Thanks for clearing that up."

"What do you want to be?" he demanded, getting to his feet and following me as I beat a hasty retreat.

"What?" I stopped, pissed that he'd tease me. "Don't be this cruel. You won't release me. You just said it yourself. What point is there to sharing my dreams with you when they won't happen?" Before he could reach me, I slammed the door shut and locked it.

He could break in. I knew he could. He owned this big-ass mansion.

But he didn't. I stood there staring at the door for a moment until I heard him leave.

After starting the shower and getting in, I shook my head and dismissed the possibility that he could actually *care*.

11

LUKA

"Is she okay?"

I turned toward Alexsei as he approached me outside the dining room.

"I heard about Petyr coming back shot up and drugged. He was looking for you to give you a head's up about the activity uptown, but he found her in her room."

I nodded. "She was startled."

"But unharmed?"

I nodded again.

"Good." Then he furrowed his brow and glanced at me. "That *is* good, isn't it?"

I sighed, peeved to be questioned like this.

"Sorry, Uncle. It's just that none of us can tell what your plan is with her."

Count me in on that. I was just as confused. "Neither do I."

"She's not..." He frowned again. "You're not going to have her be a whore?"

Fuck no. I couldn't even imagine letting anyone see her, let alone touch her.

"Then are you going to sell her?"

I winced, not a fan of that option either. The more time I spent near her, the more reluctant I was to give her up.

"I don't know what my plan will be for her." I gave him a stern look. "Leave it at that." A man could be undecided from time to time.

At the sound of her coming down the steps, wearing one of those skeptical frowns, I had a fleeting desire to see her smile.

It occurred to me only then, while my nephew walked away, that she hadn't given me one yet.

Gabriella hadn't given me anything.

And I couldn't shake this nagging interest in her.

I didn't want her to give me *something*.

I wanted her to submit and give me *everything*.

Stop. Listen to yourself. What is this bullshit? Just stop.

As she approached, I walked toward her and snapped my fingers. "Change of plans."

She raised her brows, stopping on the last step of the staircase, putting her slightly higher than usual.

"Let's enjoy this on the balcony."

She shrugged and gestured for me to lead the way.

"I thought you agreed to no more silence."

"I thought you dictated that it wasn't allowed."

There. That's better. I relished her spunk and fire. Taking her hand, I nodded at the staff to move our dinner placement to the private balcony on my floor. The sounds of the city would reach us, but that never bothered me. It was still private and sheltered, too high up for anyone to see us in that particular space.

"For the record," she added dryly as we headed to the elevator, "I'll never 'agree' to anything you want."

"You think so?" I let her enter the elevator first.

"I know so." She gave me a haughty look.

"Hmm. What about if I offered you a chance to reach your dreams?"

She scowled. "You don't know what my dreams are."

"Then tell me."

"No."

"Why not?"

"Because you can't care enough to make them come true."

I watched her lean against the elevator wall, curious. No, that wasn't true. She fascinated me, fighting me at every turn. It was the ultimate taunt, pulling me under her spell.

"What if I could?"

She lowered her gaze. "Let's say you could. You have no vested interest in making my dreams come true. You *kidnapped* me, remember? I'm a *thing* to you."

"Then what's the harm in telling me your dreams?"

"Because it's something secret that you can't have."

"But I do. I have you. You're mine to own."

She crossed her arms and gave me the start of a coy smile.

And fuck if that wasn't the last straw. Taking two steps toward her, I caged her against the wall and stared down into her brown eyes. Her breasts pushed against my chest as her breath quickened. Her lips parted in surprise.

"You almost smiled."

She rolled her eyes. "Are you trying to goad me into being happy about being here?"

I traced the line of her jaw, excited when she seemed to shiver from my touch. There was no missing the heat in her gaze.

"Would you be happy if I made your dreams come true?"

My stomach continued to react to the rise of the elevator,

but this giddiness was all due to her. This thrill. This intrigue. Hell, she really was getting to me.

"Why would you care if I'm happy?"

"Weren't you the one who critiqued the concept of answering a question with a question?"

She opened and closed her mouth, stumped. We reached the floor, and the doors opened. I took her hand and led her out. "What are your dreams? To dance?" I pulled a chair out for her at the table while the servers brought dishes out from the other end of the balcony, coming up on their service elevator.

"Yes," she replied glumly.

"To be on the stage?" I guessed as I sat across from her.

"Yes." She said it with a glum reluctance. "I've always wanted to get into Juilliard. Then be on stage."

"A performer at heart."

She narrowed her eyes. "Don't mock me."

"Don't try to tell me what to do."

"So, I have to sit here and let you mock me about my dreams? Yet, also convince myself that you want me—your thing—to be happy? Sure. Why not embrace this oxymoron?" She made a face before reaching for her water glass.

"I'm not mocking you." I meant that. But her hurt expression lingered. "How did you get into dancing?"

She lifted her face. "I'm still not dancing for you."

"I didn't ask."

She opened and closed her mouth.

"How did you start dancing?" I asked again.

After letting out a heavy sigh, she explained her interest and how she was mostly self-taught. It was a drastic departure from her previous silent treatment. While asking her to talk about ballet and her passion for dance opened her up, she was still holding back. I could tell. She was factual about her experiences, or lack of them. But she wasn't enthused about the matter.

The next day, at lunch, I asked her about it again. She didn't disappoint, sharing more about how she taught herself from videos.

The following day, she told me about the studio where she was supposed to be taking classes.

She talked. But she wasn't lowering her guard.

Keeping her near me at home messed with my head. Even if she was trying not to allow any connection between us, it was inevitable. My reluctance to give her up or sell her worsened. I didn't need Ivan or Emil to comment on my interest in her. It was implied. With great difficulty, I had to be honest with myself and admit I was getting *too* interested in her.

Don't. Just don't even think about it.

The last time I allowed myself to be interested in a woman—to truly desire their company, and not just for sex —I'd lost her. I'd lost the last woman who'd genuinely captured my interest. My wife had given me this same drive to learn about her. And I'd lost her.

Missing Maria faded long ago. What I suffered the most from now was the loss of companionship.

Admiring a portrait I'd ordered to be painted of my late wife back when Emil was just a toddler, I sighed and tried to remember what she sounded like when she spoke. When she laughed. I focused on the artist's image of her and strained to recall what she felt like. How small her hand was in mine.

Gabriella would never replace her.

She would never compare to the docile sweetness Maria gave me in her short life.

Stop.

I couldn't let my thoughts go down this path.

Hanging my head, I shook it and sighed.

Gabriella was too caustic. Too spirited. She was just a challenge to entertain me until I'd get rid of her.

Right?

If that was the truth, I wouldn't be energized to be near her. If she was nothing more than a thing to preoccupy me for a while, I wouldn't be so hesitant to see her unhappy.

And if she was supposed to be a pastime, a temporary presence in my home, I really wouldn't be rushing to find her.

Pausing outside her room, I lurked in the shadows and spied on her. Stalking her like this was becoming second nature. I couldn't help it. I couldn't stay away. I'd learned too quickly that if I nudged her door open an inch, she'd be too lost to the music playing from her ear buds to notice she had an audience.

So I'd watch.

I'd admire.

And I would inch that much closer to caving completely.

Would it be so bad to spoil her for just a bit before I'd get rid of her? Would it be so terrible to give her a taste of something good before I sent her to someone else? She wasn't an ideal partner for me. Not in the long run. She was too young. She was too full of hopes and dreams. She wasn't hard enough to withstand the violence of this life, as evident by her fear when Petyr crashed into her room.

She'd suffer away from me. I could treat her so well here. But she wasn't destined to stay as mine forever.

That was all life was—suffering. Suffering with slight rewards along the way.

Oblivious to how I watched her, she carried on like the

artist she was. Spinning, twisting, jumping, and bending. Her body was the paintbrush of motion through the canvas of the air. Despite her admittance of no proper training, she was a treat to watch. A gift to treasure.

I turned away and got my phone out. It was time to reward myself. And if ordering a private dance studio to be made for her was the reward of my choice, then that was how it would be.

Contacting Allen first, I requested him to find me the contractors to make this impulsive idea a reality. All the while, as I considered the project, I wondered if this was what it would take to truly make Gabriella break. I had to imagine how she would react.

And I dreamed that *this* would finally net me a smile from her.

A real one.

Regardless of how foolish it seemed to care.

12

GABRIELLA

Luka and I finished breakfast on a bad note.

"It's semantics," he growled.

"It's semantics that matter," I protested, fed up and unsure whether I was being problematic for the hell of it. It seemed like I was getting too comfortable and losing my edge to fight back and keep an escape plan in the back of my mind.

I could *not* be softening toward him.

I could *not* be okay with being placed here against my will.

No matter how grateful I was for the food and place to rest, for being spared creeps like Tony, I wasn't going to be deluded into thinking it was acceptable to be kidnapped.

"Calling me a guest is a joke."

"You *are* a guest in my home," he argued back as he tossed his napkin to the table.

"I'm not. You kidnapped me. And you're keeping me here against my will. There is no other way to paint that picture." I threw my napkin down to the table as I stood. Before he could get another word in, I turned and left.

I hadn't walked away from him yet.

I hadn't had the last word.

Only now did I have the courage to leave the dining room before he'd excused me or escorted me out. Taking back that little bit of control felt good, but as I marched out of there to go back to my room, I hated how bratty I sounded. How defiant I was to push back.

He didn't speak to me all day, sending me a text on the phone he gave me that he'd be gone for lunch and dinner.

"Shit. He *is* mad." I shook my head and focused on dancing. Worrying about whether my captor was mad had to be the joke of the century.

He was the enemy. He was the bad guy. Or, at least, he was supposed to be. Something was getting awfully twisted in this narrative if I was starting to see him in a good light.

As the hours passed by, I dreaded the possibility that he could seriously be upset and irritated with me. He was still a Mafia boss. He was the leader of the Dubinins. The man ordered people killed. He'd killed people, probably with his bare hands.

And here I was, the moron to think I could push him and stand up for myself about terminology.

When he showed up in my room later that evening, his thunderous expression alarmed me.

"Hey!" I jumped back, jarred from the concentration I'd locked into to perfect my steps.

"Come on."

"What? No. It's not dinnertime anymore. Or—" Anything else I could've tried to say was lost. He grabbed my wrist and urged me to go with him. "Wait! What's going on?"

"You'll see," he bit out impatiently.

"But—" I growled, digging in my feet.

"No." He shook his head, doubling back to hold on to

me. "Do you want to walk?" Dipping lower, he aimed to pick me up. "Or do I have to carry you?"

"What?" I squeaked, alarmed when he crouched low to hoist me over his shoulder. "Hey!" I slapped at his shoulder as he nearly picked me up. "What are you doing?"

I couldn't tell if he was mad or what. All I could do was try my hardest not to let him see me smile. Like this, he was almost playful. Maybe that was just in my head, though, because every time he touched me felt like a new adventure in which I had to decide whether I wanted to enjoy the feel of his fingers or hands on me or not.

"I am trying to show you something." Realizing I was too quick to escape him from picking me up, he pivoted us until he'd spun me. With my back pressed to his chest, he could band his arm around my stomach and walk me forward.

I was trapped, moving with him, and I'd be a liar if I said I didn't feel *all* of him. His muscled thighs behind my legs. His rock-hard wall of abs bracing me. His thick arm heavy over my stomach. His hand over my chest. His...

Oh, God. No. Don't think about that.

With every step we took, the bulge of his dick was there too, pressing against my backside. He wasn't hard, but I could still feel him. The implication of him.

"You weren't kidding when you said you'd never agree with me," he growled as he walked me toward another room.

Now, because my back was to him, I gave in to a small smile. "Nope. I wasn't."

He moved his hand over my collarbone, resting it more over my heart—and my breasts—than my neck. "Your heart is racing."

I wasn't surprised. Desire quickly built up in me and

made me delirious for him. A spark of innate need took hold of me.

"Are you excited?" He tightened his arms around me.

"Um." I furrowed my brow. "Until you showed up, I was sort of convinced you wanted to order me killed for arguing with you at breakfast."

He grunted a single laugh. "Over that trivial nonsense?" His fingers spread out over my skin. In a tank top like this, I could easily envision him dipping his hand beneath the fabric and really copping a feel.

Don't delude yourself.

Not him.

Not like this.

I couldn't deny this attraction taking root, but I wasn't blind. I wasn't that naïve. Luka was a rough, violent, and hard man.

Like Oliver had warned me almost a month ago at the studio, I had to be careful if I tried to play games with older men in charge, the ones who called the shots. I wasn't trying to play any games, but this stupid part of my mind that was directed by lust and hormones had me wishing Luka would play with me. At all. In any possible way he wanted.

And he surely couldn't want someone like me.

Not when he went to such lengths to remind me that I was his thing. His possession to own.

Nothing more.

"I'm not going to kill you," he stated plainly, almost bored.

"Then wh—"

"Shh. What do you think of this instead of an assumption that you'll have a death sentence?" He pushed open one of a pair of double doors. The movement of using his foot to nudge it open pressed his leg alongside mine. Every torturous second of that friction teased me, but I didn't have long to dwell on the naughty thrill of imagining my bare leg rubbing against his.

Because we were in a studio. A dance studio, to be exact. He'd dragged me out of my guest room to show me a brand-new dance studio. I smelled the new wood. Even the hint of stain clung to the air. The mirrors stretched across the entire wall to the east. On the other side of the spacious room, floor-to-ceiling windows showed the nightscape of the city. Other odds and ends that made this an area to dance in were installed or set aside. But it was the quietly playing music from one of my favorite ballets that really got to me.

I was stunned.

Speechless and in awe, I roved my gaze around the room and tried to convince myself that this wasn't a dream. That I wasn't hallucinating.

This was a dance studio. But was it all for me?

"I believe that's twenty-eight now," he whispered in my ear.

I blinked, so surprised and in a trance at the beautiful studio space that I hadn't realized he still held me. Leaning my back against him as he kept his arms around me, he secured me in a possessive hug.

"What?" I furrowed my brow.

"Twenty-eight on your tally marks of the silent treatment. You didn't answer me."

"I—" I turned, facing him and not entirely eager to push him away. Being within the embrace of his arms felt... good. "I don't know how to answer you."

"Say something."

"I..." I blinked again, putting my hands on his chest to

steady myself as I looked around the room again. "What is this?"

"A dance studio."

"You just happened to have one in your home all this time and are only now telling me?"

"I had it built for you."

I gaped at him.

"What do you think?"

I couldn't speak. I could only stare at him and try not to cry.

He leaned in, teasing me with the possibility that he might kiss me. He didn't. Closing in until he could whisper in my ear, his big hands braced on my back to keep me snug against him, he whispered, "Twenty-nine."

I laughed. The burst of amusement jarred me, and I reared back. "What are those tallies for, anyway?"

"To be determined," he answered cryptically. "Tell me. What do you think, Gabriella?"

"I think..." I stepped away from him, too overwhelmed to endure his touches any longer. "I think this is wonderful. It's beautiful. It's perfect. It's for *me*?"

He shoved his hands into his pockets as he watched me. "I got to thinking that maybe you refuse to dance for me because you don't have a studio to dance in."

I rolled my eyes. "Like you don't spy through a crack in the door," I teased back.

He shrugged.

"This is amazing." It was kind of him. It was even sweet of him. And it made absolutely no sense at all. He'd told me over and over how I was his possession, nothing more, yet he'd go to the extremes of gifting me something like *this*?

"Amazing enough that you'll dance for me?"

I lowered my gaze, smiling wide. "Turn up the music." If he wanted me to dance for him...

I would.

It no longer felt like a war, to withhold from him. To hide myself from him. I'd been here for a month now. While I was no closer to understanding what he wanted from me, I was tempted to believe I was living a better life—in some ways—like this than I had before.

He walked toward the panel on the wall that controlled the music. As the volume rose, I tamped down this excitement that he'd done this for me. That this rich and powerful man had a dance studio created all for little, old *me*. The nobody. The outcast. The poor girl from the bad neighborhood.

The woman who was given to a Mafia boss as a payment.

Shutting out all my thoughts, I let the music reach me. Like always, it flowed through me and I moved. I followed the beat. I practiced my steps. Like this, I *was* free and would be forever.

While I danced, I felt his stare burning on my skin. All those heated looks he gave me were tangible touches I craved. But like this, while I danced for him in this gorgeous state-of-the-art studio, I wondered if this pleased him. If his giving me something as grand as this meant he had a heart after all.

Maybe he did, but I couldn't lower my guard any more than I had so far.

I couldn't.

Not for any man. Not even him. It had been drilled into my head and my heart for too long that the only person I could truly trust was myself.

The song finished. Then he clapped. Slowly and steadily, he clapped as he pushed off the wall he'd been leaning on as he watched me. As he stared at me like I'd given him the greatest reward of all—my submission.

Over my dead body.

"Thank you, Luka." I did a little curtsy.

"I feel like I should be thanking you." He approached, shoving his hands back in his pockets as he eyed me from head to toe.

13

LUKA

Gabriella was happy.

She wouldn't admit it. That would be too much of an allowance for me.

But I saw it.

Since I showed her the studio that I'd ordered to be built for her, she was there all the time. When she wasn't near me to eat with me and be civil, accompanying me to meals, she was dancing. If she wasn't sleeping, she was dancing.

Giving her that studio was the ultimate reward for me, too. Because while a big question mark loomed about what I'd do with her, it felt too damn good to know I'd given her this.

Her passion only grew. And when I sought private instructors to come and give her lessons, she seemed more content than ever before. Vetting the instructors had been Allen's task, and once I witnessed the professionalism they exercised, I trusted the situation.

Watching Gabriella open up as a dancer was a beautiful thing to experience. She was still guarded with me. Even with Emil, Ivan, and Alexsei when they joined us for meals.

But it was so clear that dance was how she truly expressed herself.

Every night, I was beholden to watch her and see with my own eyes how her skills improved, how she executed her moves more precisely under the private lessons. After a month of these private lessons, even I could witness and track her progress and improvement. She wasn't frilly or girly. Strictly a studious athlete under these instructors, she excelled.

It was an expression of art, which could've been surprising with how hard her life had been so far.

More and more, she talked with me. I had to ask. I had to initiate the conversations, but she was sharing now. About how her mother passed away. How Miguel was never there for her. How she fell in love with dancing.

One night, after she said she'd had enough in the studio, she walked with me toward my private wing of the house. While I enjoyed her softening toward me as much as she had been, I still wondered how to get that smile from her.

"What would you say if I arranged a private audition for you?"

She stopped short and grabbed my arm. I looked down at her fingers on my sleeve, then slowly dragged my gaze up to her face. She had no clue what it did to me when she initiated a touch like that.

"What?"

I nodded. "I could do that."

She tilted her head to the side. "As in you could pay off someone to give me an audition?" She shook her head quickly. "No. Nope. I don't want to be— No. You can bribe someone to pretend to let me audition. Then bribe someone to just give me a part. I want to earn a spot on the stage— any stage."

"Then earn it." I smiled at her stubbornness, her earnest desire to work for what she wanted. "I can arrange the audition, but you have to go through with it."

She gawked at me and almost smiled. "You'd do that?"

I nodded.

"You have connections like that?"

"I have all kinds of connections." Or I'd make them. Money did grease the wheels that made the world go round.

Still, she was hesitant. I urged her to walk again, ready to call an end to this long day of being in the office, checking on some things in the field, and then dealing with more headaches that came with running multiple businesses. Those parts were the same old. But coming here to see Gabriella dancing was my secret vice.

"You'd do that for *me*?" She asked.

Fuck. She was still too nervous to trust me. I sighed heavily as I opened the doors to my private wing.

"I'm hesitant to believe it. To trust that you'd want to do this for me out of, I don't know, the goodness of your heart. If you have one."

I shot her a look. One she returned in kind.

"I'm serious. I never know how to read you or interpret what you do. I'm warning you..."

I snatched her by the waist, pushing her against the wall to cage her in as I laughed. "You're warning me?" Pulling her close, I stared her down and wondered how she'd react if I just decided the hell with it and kissed her. If she'd ever been kissed before. If she—

Stop.

I was getting too carried away with these damn thoughts and moments of desire.

"Yes." She tipped her head up and gave me an indignant,

smug expression that made me laugh more. "I'm warning you not to play games with me."

"Oh, really?" I stepped into her space, wedging my leg between hers.

I didn't miss how her breath hitched. I sure as fuck didn't miss how she put her hands on my chest. The sparkle of lust in her eyes was obvious too.

But so was her inexperience. She frowned, almost as if she were confused about how to follow through.

"Do I need to remind you that I can do whatever I want with you?"

She stared at my lips and furrowed her brow. "I think you've made that point perfectly clear."

"Hmm-mmm." I pushed my hips against hers, fighting back a growl at how she jumped and curled her fingers into the fabric of my shirt.

"Does that mean..." She drew in a deep breath and lifted her gaze to mine. "Does that...?"

I waited, watching her closely and wondering how I could be this much of a saint to endure not taking what I wanted. "Go on."

"Does this mean that you *do* want to play games with me?" she asked.

"I don't *play*, Gabriella." I leaned in to whisper into her ear, "I just take. I take what I want."

And right now, I want you.

Pressing a light kiss to the skin near her ear, I waited for her reaction.

She sagged, arching both into me and against the wall. She sighed, letting out such a swoony sound of need. And she didn't protest.

Instead, she turned her head as if to seek my lips for a real kiss.

Perhaps her first.

She's too young. She won't know how to do anything. On the tails of those thoughts that should've been enough to scare me away, I got hooked on the idea of being the one to show her. To teach her.

"Bullshit," she whispered, still defiant despite how rattled and shaken she was. I saw the desire in her eyes. I heard the need in her short breaths. She was just as attracted to me as I was to her. And she had to be wondering —confused and reluctantly disappointed—why I wasn't making more of a move on her. "You don't only *take*. You gave me that dance studio."

I laughed once, stepping away from her and grabbing her hand to escort her the rest of the way back to her room. The space between us was jarring, but it almost worked to clear my mind. If I wanted to take this path with her, I had to be sure I could give her up after I'd had her.

"I'm shocked that you haven't reminded me that I also took you."

She smirked. "And I'm shocked that you haven't reminded me that I'm yours to own."

She said that as a parting shot. Letting go of my hand, she turned toward her room, but not without one last look over her shoulder. A look that suggested she was wondering why I might not act on making her mine in every way that counted, like the most intimate closeness two people could share.

A closeness where we'd be one as we fucked—with me deep inside her and claiming her not as my captive, not as a thing to possess and lock up, but as my woman, as my lover.

14

GABRIELLA

Losing track of time happened too often. Although I was trapped in his house and never given the right to leave or choose anything about my existence here, I fell into the routine of enjoying what I could while I was here.

The studio.

The food.

The lack of wondering whether someone would bother me while I walked home.

At first, it was a simple feat of tracking days and hours by realizing how many classes I'd missed at the studio. How many open-studio hours I was skipping to practice. Once I was given the ultimate gift of my own dance studio and a rotation of tough but excellent instructors to tutor me, I had all that I could have ever wished for.

Under Luka's provisions, I could catch up to all those privileged dancers who never had to stress about money.

With nothing else to burden me here—no responsibilities other than to be with Luka when he came home to join him for meals—I was free to dance and study and learn.

After a month of dancing here, I felt fit and toned, more precise with my movements. No simple, silly mistakes happened to frustrate me.

And all the while, I accepted that low-burning tension and apprehension of waiting for Luka to watch. He was busy, commenting about long hours at an office or being out "in the field" on other days. I didn't ask. I didn't want to know any details. The less I was aware of, the better, because I wasn't fit for this Mafia life of violence.

Allen and Emil explained weeks ago that the bloodied soldier who'd come into my room drugged like that was a mistake. That he had been helped appropriately after a fight. The experience had traumatized me, but the other, smaller incidents that followed didn't send me into a lockdown status of shock.

Now and then, I spotted wounded men coming through. From Ivan and Alek, I was given vague details about how Luka's fortress of a home was under lockdown. That was a joke for me. I was already locked in, but they always gave me a heads up when danger was higher than usual. Violence was a part of these men's lives, but so long as I stuck to the studio and stayed out of sight, I could do my best to keep it apart from my existence here.

No matter what, Luka always came home. He never defined his expectations of me. For as much as he wanted to emphasize that he'd gotten me from my father and I was now his possession, he left the obvious follow-up question open-ended.

He owned me... for what?

I didn't know. But the more he came to watch me dance and stare at me with that ravenous, sinister gaze, I let my mind wander.

I dared to fantasize about the chance that he might be keeping me here to truly *own* me—body, mind, and soul.

Submitting to him wasn't happening, not with my heart or head. I wouldn't be able to fully lower my guard and trust him when I spent my whole life only relying on myself. But with my body? Surrendering to this older, stronger man didn't seem like such a horrible concept. Not anymore.

Desire gripped me when he was near. Longing fueled me to think about him when he wasn't. It didn't matter what I was doing and where we were. These slowly igniting embers of need wouldn't be extinguished.

Each time I felt him watching me, mostly without a single word, I enjoyed the thrill of him stalking me. Of him planning to prey on me. Or I hoped he might. I wasn't sure if I could withstand this nonverbal tease of him watching me without following through on what had to be desire.

When he'd kissed my cheek, that felt like barely controlled desire.

When he'd caged me against the wall, it seemed like he was about to cave and devour me.

What is wrong with me?

I paused in the middle of a sequence of steps, distracted by these thoughts about the older, sexy man I had no business wanting at all. Hanging my head as I tried to collect myself, I resisted this needling obsession.

I had to stop wondering what it would feel like if he really kissed me. If I'd pass out from the thrill of him really touching me. This teasing game we were keeping up, a mutual suspension of desire, couldn't last for long. Maybe it could. I wouldn't know. I had no experience with this.

Just like when I hatched the hare-brained and impulsive idea to flirt with Oliver, that dance instructor at the studio, to get ahead, I felt so out of my comfort zone. Going after men wasn't something I knew how to do. Pursuing someone and expressing my lust for them weren't something I felt confident about.

And that scared me. It rattled me to consider telling Luka that I wanted him. Those times I asked him what he wanted from me were supposed to be my attempts of getting clarification. But they failed. He still wouldn't just tell me what I was here for. Then when I reminded him that I was here against my will, his *thing* to own, he wouldn't elaborate on why.

It's not like I can just tell him that I'm interested in him.

He'd never believe me.

I can't come on to him.

That was definitely not happening. After my failed attempt to seduce Oliver, I knew better than to overestimate myself and my ability to wow a man. Luka watched me. I saw how he looked at me, like a starved man wishing for a feast. But he wouldn't make a move. He wouldn't initiate anything like that.

Shaking my head, I tried to hold on to logic. It was stupid to even think about lusting after this Mafia boss. I was supposed to get the hell out of here. To be free. Yet, if I did that, I'd miss out on his hungry gazes. I'd cut off this dangerous thrill of his interest. And I'd lose this gorgeous studio and the instructors he'd provided for me.

But why?

If I was here to be a kept woman, why wasn't he going for me?

If I was given to him to be his sex toy, his mistress, then would he take me like he said he could?

"*I don't play, Gabriella. I just take. I take what I want.*"

He'd whispered those naughty words to me, but he had yet to act on that power.

Thinking of how it would feel to be under his touch, in his grasp, and kissing his lips, I couldn't shake off this sensation of being small. Helpless. Inexperienced. It almost reminded me of the fear when Tony almost raped me, but more than that, I was addicted to exploring whatever Luka Dubinin would show me.

He'd be a hard lover. There was no question about that. But I was getting ahead of myself. Until he could make a move and let me know that he truly wanted me...

"I thought this room was for dancing."

I jolted at his deep voice. He came up behind me, stalking so quietly like the powerful, predatory man he was. I hated how I flinched, but as I turned to face him, I damned this stupid blush that warmed my cheeks. "I was thinking."

"Ah." He raised his brows, coming to stand right in front of me. His hands were in his pockets. His stance was relaxed. It wasn't fair how he could look so cool and chill when merely trying to make eye contact heated me up like this. "And what kind of thoughts are keeping you so preoccupied?"

I licked my lips. That teasing, sexy tone affected me, making me hotter and more on edge.

God, I just want to...

I fought the urge to just kiss him. To give in and cave to this seductive man. To admit I wasn't strong enough to be smart and know that I shouldn't want him.

What's wrong with me?

He kidnapped me.

He captured me.

He tilted his head to the side. "Thirty."

I cringed. "I—"

Stepping closer, he pulled me into a loose hug. Having his hands on me at all was nearly my undoing with how drawn I was. His presence was a magnetic force, tethering me to him.

"Hmm?"

"I was thinking about you," I admitted.

He pulled me closer, tightening his arms around me.

I couldn't breathe. I couldn't think. I was stuck under this desire that made my pussy wet and my nipples hard.

"Go on," he urged.

"That's it." I cleared my throat. "I was thinking about you."

"Ah. Well, you can think about this instead." Leaning in, he tormented me with the suggestion that he'd kiss me. Instead, he smiled and watched me as he stroked his finger along my jawline. "I've set up an audition for you."

I gasped, staring at him in awe. Just when I wanted to reconfirm how he was the bad guy, he had to go and do something extraordinary like this.

"With the people you mentioned. The ones who'd select their dancers for the show next year. It's preliminary yet, but I've secured a private audition for you."

"I..." I couldn't speak. I was so blown away, unable to comprehend him and why he'd do this. No one had *ever* done something like this for me. No one had ever expressed this much support of my dreams.

"I..."

He tipped my chin up, keeping his two fingertips there as I met his gaze.

"Say something, Gabriella."

I blinked, so moved and touched. Yet, still so twisted and confused by how badly I wanted him. Deep down, I fought the worry that this had to be a trick. That his kind gesture would come with a catch. "Why?"

"Because I want to see you smile." Caressing my cheek, he made a slow move of cupping my face and leaning in.

"A smile?" I huffed a weak laugh, feeling delirious in his embrace like this. "You didn't have to go to such a grand gesture to get a smile from me."

"I didn't?"

I stared deep into his eyes. "No. I mean... just kiss me already. That'd probably do it."

He didn't wait. Crushing his mouth over mine, he kissed me. He brushed his warm, wet lips over mine, so smooth and demanding. Under his touch, I was taken out of this world. I was floating, suspended in this fantasy I'd kept to myself for so long. I was sinking, drowning with the urgency to experience more and more.

He pulled back, staring at me as he breathed hard. "You're not smiling."

I furrowed my brow and reached up to tug him back down for another kiss.

And another.

Another.

His growls turned me on more. When I whimpered with need, he slid his tongue into my mouth and stole a taste. Groping him to hold him close, I explored this raging heat to kiss and be kissed. To devour and be claimed.

That tension snapped at last. This delicious race to surrender to him scared me, but as he made out with me and clutched me close, I couldn't imagine ever stopping.

Leading me toward the wall, he proved how quickly his control could unravel. He pressed me against the hard surface as he gripped my hips. His touch was rough and demanding, but I wasn't scared. I was only that much more feral for him, that much more impatient and desperate for his kisses. For his needy gropes and pushes of his hips against me.

When he broke for air, I gasped and clung to him. With that one wicked look he focused on me, as if he were searing me from the inside out, I sagged and wished he could just show me how good it would be. I waited for him to take me —just like he said he could.

"Luka..."

He trailed hot kisses down from the tender spot beneath my ear. His hands squeezed at my hips, but it was the drugging, hot suction of his lips on my neck that made me squirm with more need. "Oh, Luka..."

He pulled back. Keeping his head low, he didn't give me the privilege of eye contact. But it was when he stepped back fully that I wanted to cry out in protest.

"Have a good night, Gabriella."

What?

No.

Seriously?

No!

What the hell?

I leaned against the wall as he turned away. Relying on the surface at my back to keep me upright, I panted and tried to unscramble my mind long enough to know what the hell had gone wrong.

In a millisecond, he was just over it. He was done. He was walking away from me without another word. Without any explanation.

He declared that when he wanted something, he'd just take it. He didn't play games. He merely got what he wanted because of who he was.

As I watched him go, I lifted my trembling fingers to my lips and pressed them to the warmth he'd left there. Kiss-stung and swollen, I felt shaken to my core from just that tease.

Was he teasing me?

Was he messing with me on purpose?

What is going on?

All I knew was what he'd told me. That he took what he wanted.

And if he could walk away after kissing me like that, I had to accept the disappointing and wretched truth that he didn't want *me*, the thing he'd taken because he could.

I shook my head slowly, hating myself for ever desiring him when I was clearly so unworthy of his touches and kisses.

15

LUKA

I almost lost control. If I hadn't reached for the last reservoir of patience, I wouldn't have been able to hold myself back. With her mewling in need for me, her lips so eager and hungry against mine, I was lost to doing what I did best.

Taking what I wanted.

I never asked.

I didn't beg.

Playing games was a waste of time, too.

But with Gabriella, I was suckered into a spiral of need so intense that I nearly lost sight of why I wanted to resist her. She felt too good. She tasted so fucking fine.

From one kiss, she'd reduced me to a needy, desperate man.

And that transfer of power wasn't something I could handle. Not with her. Not when I still felt too torn and undecided about how she could actually stay in my life or fit as my woman.

Even though she kissed me back, I noticed her inexperience. While she was eager to push against me and mutually seek out that friction of rubbing her body with mine, she lacked the finesse and confidence of how to go about it like a real woman.

Because she's a virgin.

I had to remind myself of that single fact. When she uttered my name, so needy and breathlessly, it tore me out of the sensual haze of kissing her and holding her. That broke the spell, and with that clarity, I had to remember her value.

She was a virgin.

If I took her, I wouldn't get as much for her if I sold her to another. That was the only thing that forced me to walk away and not take her for myself.

Yet, today, as I headed out to lunch with a few men, she was on my mind. I couldn't stop dwelling and obsessing about whether I would be able to give her up now.

After a fucking kiss, I was stuck on her.

How the hell could I sell her or dispose of her now with only that sample to sate my curiosity?

"Uncle?" Ivan glanced at me from across the table.

"Yeah." I shook my head, wishing that would clear my distracting thoughts of Gabriella from my mind as well. I didn't need to glance around at my two nephews and son to see that they'd noticed how distant I seemed. I had to get my head in the game and stop thinking about her.

"We got a call from the house," Ivan said, arching one brow. "Someone tried to corner Gabriella near the kitchen."

I swore, pissed that these new recruits were all a risk like that. New blood was necessary. Men died. Soldiers and guards were lost. But for fuck's sake, wasn't any new man on the staff loyal anymore? We rooted out the moles and threats. I personally double-checked the men in the house. But some slipped through.

"Allen said the situation is handled." He cleared his throat. "She, uh, punched one."

Emil chuckled darkly. Alexsei rolled his eyes.

"But he had to shoot another."

I furrowed my brow, hating that time was running out until this meeting would begin. Behind them, the people we were here to speak with entered the restaurant. "Is she all right?"

"Shaken," Ivan said, "but seeming to handle it. She's in her studio."

I nodded, expecting her to retreat to her "domain". That studio was her place, her sanctuary, and I was glad I could provide it to her while she acclimated to the Mafia life in my home. For now.

Fuck. Why can't I make up my mind about her?

All through the meeting, my thoughts wandered. I stayed on task and appeared to be fully engaged with the discussion. But I was distracted. Veering back to thinking about her and wondering if she was okay from this latest scare, I debated how I could go forward.

Sell her.

Or keep her.

Resist her.

Or fuck her.

When the meeting concluded, I was in a hurry to get back to my home and check that she was all right. Seeing her would be the final proof to know that she wasn't traumatized again.

Emil rode with me, perhaps sensing that I wasn't being myself. Then when we were stuck in traffic, he came right out and asked.

"You fuck her yet?"

I cringed, giving him a hard look. "Do you always keep my fucking sex life in mind?"

He laughed, shaking his head. "No. Hell no. Trust me, it's the least of my concerns."

"Then why the hell are you asking me something like that?"

"Because you're distracted. We covered for you at that meeting."

Dammit.

"And if you're distracted, it's got to be her."

I rubbed my face, sighing heavily. "I almost lost my control with her."

He watched me, studying me and likely trying to interpret the meaning of my words. That line could refer to me losing my control to take her or kill her, I supposed. "I almost..." I shook my head. Emil and I were close. I raised him myself. Well, I raised him as a single father and the rest of the Dubinin Family as my backup. Some people liked to say it took a village to raise a child. That was true for a Mafia "village" as well. While we were close as father and son, there were boundaries to some topics, like this one. Yet, I wasn't uncomfortable to confide in him this much. That was how much I trusted him and valued his opinions—usually.

"So?" He shrugged.

"I can't tell if it would be a mistake."

"Only one way to find out."

I shot him a dull smirk.

"Or you could just sell her now and then you won't be tempted. If you don't want to be tempted."

"No." It left my lips as a single word of a refusal, one I couldn't take back. I hadn't been comfortable with the concept of letting another man have her. Not after I'd kissed her, not once I saw how strongly she lusted for *me*. "I'm no longer in the mood to sell her." Fuck, I hated the idea of losing her at all. But in wanting her, I was endangering her.

"It's not like it'd be a terrible thing to have a woman to pursue," he said with another indifferent shrug, watching the scenery slowly pass by out the window. We were back in "my" car, the Rolls Royce I couldn't let go of. Tinted windows precluded the rest of the world from seeing us in here, and I enjoyed the freedom of this privacy to talk about this with my son.

"Because she's an innocent," he reminded me. "It's not a matter of your having to worry about her being a trap or a spy."

I nodded. That, unfortunately, happened far too many times to count. Whores and other women would use themselves to get intel for our enemies. Gabriella didn't fall in that category. She knew nothing about what Miguel Lopez was up to. She seemed naïve that he was a drug runner at all.

"She won't trick you into anything," Emil added.

I nodded again, easily agreeing with him. Gabriella wasn't a threat like that. She was only a temptation. A siren. Nothing more.

"But she is not fit for this world." That seemed like the most direct argument I could count on. Distancing her from me made the most sense when I pointed out how ill-suited she was to be with me for anything more than the short term. She couldn't belong with me for good.

"That's true," he replied. "She's too innocent."

Gabriella was innocent in every sense of the word. Untouched as a virgin. Clean without any crimes or wrong-doing, no blood on her hands.

"She doesn't necessarily scare easily, though." Raising his brows, he almost seemed amused. "When I went to pick her up, fuck, she fought like hell. Not only protesting and fighting to get free to run, but she was also calculating. She was strategic in faking that she was unconscious from the drug to try to get away again."

I had to smile at that. Gabriella's fight and spirit were admirable. I enjoyed how defiant she could be. It was almost something to be proud of, that she wasn't a fool and could operate like that under pressure.

"But she's too soft. Too good." I sighed. "Too…"

"Delicate?"

I narrowed my eyes. She wasn't delicate, though. That invoked the impression of a dainty weakling.

"Too precious."

"Fuck." He laughed softly, shaking his head. "You're getting smitten with her already?"

I scoffed. "Smitten?" I shot him a stern look. Now he was just being ridiculous.

"Listen to yourself. You think she's *precious*?"

Ah, fuck. I regretted my choice of words.

"Yeah, I can't see you selling her now."

"I still could." Reinstating distance was critical now. I appreciated how she was a break in the monotony of my life, but the idea of her being a permanent source of pleasure wasn't wise. "She's a temptation." One I hadn't counted on being so intrigued about. "But nothing more." I shrugged, feigning a disinterest I wished I could fully embrace. "Nothing more, Emil."

It sounded less like a denial and more like a realization of the truth.

Downplaying the impact she had on me would help me in the long run. I didn't have to feel bad for desiring her. I didn't have to worry about wanting her and being weak for being under her spell.

After I fucked her and got her out of my system, like I could have done with any other woman on this planet, I wouldn't be so caught up in wondering what it would be like to take her. To have her—for now.

Because it was all too clear that she wouldn't be staying in my life forever.

16

GABRIELLA

Days passed and I practiced as much as I could. As the hours crept closer to the private audition that Luka arranged for me, I suffered through the turmoil of so many mixed feelings.

At the top of the list was nervousness—about being a kept *thing* here but unworthy of being wanted and desired by Luka, the strong Alpha male who stated that he took what he wanted. Those nerves collided and twisted with the worry that I wouldn't be ready for this preliminary test.

The only way I could combat the anxiety that kept me so tense was to dance. To practice. And to dance and practice some more.

I had a break from being in the studio to grab a light dinner one night. Maintaining a proper diet was essential for dancing this much. I'd come a long way from merely eating what was offered to keep up my strength for escaping to speaking with the cooks on staff for the ideal balanced meals I'd need for endurance to perform on stage.

Luka wasn't there. As if I needed another reminder of

how little he wanted me, he had to keep his distance from me and be too "busy" to eat with me.

Emil and Alexsei were there, though.

"Ready for the competition?" Emil asked.

He and I weren't exactly on friendly terms. We had gotten to a point of not glaring at each other on sight, and that was probably as good as it would get.

"It's not a competition." I rolled my eyes.

"It's an audition," Alexsei confirmed. He wasn't getting off my shit list just yet, either. He'd been there to capture me as well. While he almost seemed milder than the other violent thugs here, I wasn't lowering my guard to think he was a good guy, either.

"How come it matters so much?" Emil asked, taking a seat at the table. Alexsei sat across from him, diagonal from me.

"The audition?" I raised my brows. "How could it not matter? If I want to get closer to being considered for Juilliard or any other decent school, I need to be judged and vetted."

Alexsei shrugged. "I think he means why bother with ballet at all?"

I narrowed my eyes. "Because it's what I'm passionate about." I huffed, paying attention to my food instead of facing them. "Trust me, I'm not counting on you to understand."

"To understand being passionate about something?" Emil taunted. "Ask the whore I took to bed last night how hot my 'passion' runs."

I shook my head. "Of course you'd be vulgar like that."

"Prude," he shot back.

Hearing the son of the man I lusted after call me a

prude, of all things, seemed like too cruel of an insult to accept. "I'm not a prude."

"You're a ballerina," he corrected. "A wannabe ballerina. With passion."

"What's so wrong about being passionate about something?" I folded my hands on the table and peered at him. I couldn't help but get defensive about this.

"Hey, passion and drive matter," Alexsei said. "We're passionate about our jobs."

"About killing and kidnapping people, you mean."

"About whatever is required of us as loyal Dubinin men," he replied gruffly.

"Having a purpose is important," Emil said. "But how the fuck is ballet supposed to give you a sense of mattering at all? It's dancing on a stage. Big deal."

I furrowed my brow, hating how they could mock me like this and challenge me. "It *is* a big deal. Or it should be. Ballet is art. Art matters." I didn't want to interpret their harsh words as a critique that I wasn't good at the medium of ballet or dancing. Besides, I wouldn't take *their* word for it. What did they know?

As I ate, vowing to ignore them until I was done, I knew that they'd never understand my life or my world just as much as I would never adjust to theirs. I couldn't relate to this world of crime, of killing and seeking power. Even though I had always suspected my dad wasn't exactly a law-abiding citizen, I never broke rules or the law. I was a good person.

After I left them in the dining room, I struggled with holding my head high. Their words cut deep. I wasn't feeling so confident now. In light of all that these dangerous men did, my passion and love of dancing had to seem so trivial and frivolous. So petty.

I hated to feel so stupid as to have what they'd consider an insignificant dream. That low mood carried into my steps, into the usually fluid motions I'd practice. Hours passed well into the night, but nothing could jar me out of this funk.

Worrying about being a joke wasn't something I needed to deal with before an audition. But that wasn't something I could fix by merely dismissing what they'd said.

When Luka showed up, lingering near the door like he typically did, I was still stuck in this lowness, this bitter sadness and dejected attitude.

"What's wrong?"

I shrugged, not bothering to face him as I tried to get through a sequence of complicated steps again.

He ambled closer, chill as ever. Cool and calm, hands in his pockets, a blank face so I couldn't read his expression.

"Gabriella."

Clumsy steps and poorly executed spins were my reply.

"Gabriella."

I continued to ignore him, trying to move faster so he'd get the hint that I didn't want to talk.

It seemed that his sternly calling my name weren't all he was ready to do to get my attention. Rounding back toward the door, I was stopped short. He reached out, grabbing my waist and forcing me to change my spin and topple against him. Catching me securely, he held me in a hug.

The abrupt stop of my momentum caught me off guard. So did the heated intensity of his dark stare as he lowered his gaze toward me. Breathing hard and fast from the exertion of the exercise, I licked my lips and willed my heart to slow down. It had to be racing from dancing. From rehearsing. Not because of this slow rise of warmth that spread through me at being in his arms again.

"Tell me what's wrong."

I shook my head.

He tightened his hold on me, narrowing his eyes.

"It's nothing," I replied, then cleared my throat. Damn him for being so commanding and sexy. Screw him for toying with me and finding me unworthy. If he didn't want me, why'd he kiss me at all? If he wouldn't take me and give me more of himself, then why care if I was in a bad mood or a good one?

He made no sense, twisting me upside down with emotions I couldn't control anymore. That was how off-kilter I felt around him. It was even worse with his arms wrapped around me like this.

"Tell me and I will decide if it's nothing."

Oh, like you decided to just snatch me out of my home and keep me here?

"It's nothing for you to worry about."

"I'm not *worried* about anything. What I am is impatient."

"Why do you care if something is wrong?"

He tipped his head lower, intensifying his glare. "Answer me."

"I was talking with your son and nephew earlier." I hated to cave. But dammit, he was too much to resist. Too commanding and larger than life to ignore for long. "They were asking me about why I bother to be interested in ballet and care about this audition. And since we spoke, it's made me feel like my... my passion is wasted and insignificant."

He huffed a wry laugh. "Your passion is worthy."

I rolled my eyes and began to turn my head to look at the wall. He stopped me, gripping my chin and forcing me to face him.

"It is inspiring."

I couldn't help but laugh bitterly as I yanked out of his grip, removing his hand from my face. "Oh, stop. It's a waste of your time and mine for you to humor me."

He gripped my chin again, with a little more force. "Are you accusing me of humoring you?"

I arched one brow. *Yeah, I guess I am.*

"You don't believe me?" he challenged.

I had no reply ready. I wasn't sure what the hell to believe anymore. If he wanted me or not. If I was wrong to wish he'd want me. If I was smart to try to resist him. If he thought I was a joke or something valuable. Nothing was clear anymore.

"You inspire *me*, Gabriella." He pressed his lips to my cheek as he lowered his hand. The slow, gentle drag of the back of his fingers teased my flesh. In the wake of where he stroked his fingers down my neck, then my arm, and then even lower until he could take my hand in his, he kissed me like he wanted to suckle and savor every inch of my skin.

Holding my hand, he maneuvered, pushing it between us.

Further and lower, he guided my hand until my fingertips brushed against the thick, hard bulge of his erection.

I gasped, stunned by how strongly he could show me his interest like this. This was an answer to stop me from wondering. He was giving me a vivid clue of how he wanted me.

"Don't ever doubt how you can..." He urged me to cup his long erection trapped beneath his pants. "Fuck. Gabriella..."

I stroked up and down gently, rewarded by his growl. "Don't ever doubt how you inspire me."

I didn't think I could after this. Feeling his rigid hardness in my hand, I knew he wasn't as indifferent to me as I imagined when he walked away from making out with me a few days ago.

This wasn't the time for any doubts.

Staring into his eyes, I reached up on my toes to press my lips against his, relishing the instant spike of heat and lust that charged through me as we kissed.

17

LUKA

Gabriella didn't release me. Not with her lips. Not with her hand on my cock. She kissed me like she'd wither away if we stopped. She caressed me like she wanted to explore. Between both of her moves, she was cautious but eager. Nervous but willing.

And I couldn't get enough.

Ripping my mouth away to suck in air, I stared down at her. It was too easy to get lost in the depths of her gorgeous eyes, shining so brightly with uninhibited lust. I wasn't in the mood to be mesmerized like that.

"Do you doubt me?" I pushed into her, letting her feel the erection tenting my pants.

"I..." She shook her head, all that I would allow from her before I grabbed the back of her neck and hauled her closer for another kiss.

She couldn't fucking dare to deny that I wanted her. With my dick stiff under her careful, uncertain caresses, she felt how badly I wanted her. As I robbed her breath and sealed my lips over hers, she could taste how much she inspired me.

This young woman had power over me whether I wanted her to or not.

Only her.

Gabriella Lopez, the daughter of a rat.

A survivor making her way through this world on her own.

She had no goddamn clue how much power she held over me like this, but it was about time I gave her a lesson on what happened when an innocent like her could taunt the beast.

"Do you doubt how much I want you?" I demanded.

Watching her hooded gaze as we broke again for air, I pivoted until she reached the short stage I'd had installed along one wall. It wasn't large, nothing like what she'd need to prepare for at her audition. But it was a higher height of the flooring. And it was an ideal level to set her on. I lifted her, squeezing my fingers into the delicious juiciness of her round ass. Then I hoisted her up to sit on the stage, bringing her mouth more level to mine.

"Do you doubt how crazy you make me feel?" I growled, tugging her loose exercise shirt off.

She shook her head, watching me with a hunger I wanted to erase. Leaning back as I slanted in, she kissed me back and framed my face. Even that touch was light and tender. Too sweet. Or maybe it was just her confusion and nerves.

"Do you doubt yourself?" I asked as I kissed down along her slender neck, seeking the heaving swells of her breasts. The bralette she'd worn under her loose shirt was too tight and confining for me to experience the touch of her skin, the peaks of her tight nipples that beaded and showed through the fabric.

"On... on stage?" she asked, so clueless that it only turned me on more.

Her inexperience showed. I was stunning her, twisting her off the axis of her world. Instead of bothering me or annoying me, I relished the privilege to be the one to show her how this could be. I looked forward to the exquisite pleasure of introducing her to sensual bliss.

I looked up at her as I slipped my hands under the short skirt she'd worn to practice in. "You *are* on a stage," I reminded her.

As I pushed my fingers further up her silky thigh, she furrowed her brow. That resistance wasn't gone. Her fiery need to refuse me was still there. I'd never forget how hotly and fiercely she'd told me that she'd never get anything from me. It was a sweet memory to recall now as I prepared to give her the start of something she'd never had before.

Perhaps she wasn't fully submitting to me yet. Her body betrayed her. I felt the evidence of how turned on and aroused she was. Warm slickness greeted my fingers as I reached for her panties to tug them down. Her nipples begged for my lips, hard and pushing against her bralette. I lowered my mouth to suck on them through the thin fabric, and she arched into me with the sexiest, neediest sound.

In her eyes, though, she wanted to tell me no. In her mind, she had to be protesting and wishing she could tell me to stop.

But she didn't.

"Do you doubt that you can make me want you like this?" I asked, pleased when she lifted her thighs to accommodate my removing her panties.

"I... I... I don't—"

I pulled her in for a hard kiss to quiet her nervousness. As I sucked and nipped at her lips, excited about how she proved to be a quick learner and responded in kind, I rubbed my fingers around in her juices. All that arousal slickened my fingers. I smeared it around her slit, massaging her pussy. I wasn't too gentle, impatient to show her how good it could be to submit. I wasn't too rough, demonstrating that I was in charge. I followed her reactions, marking every hitch of her breath, each clutch of her fingers on my arm as she held me close. She adjusted to my touch, one she'd never had before.

Mine.

Right then and right there, she was *mine* and no one else's. The exquisite right to her was a heady sensation to overcome, but I didn't lose myself to the ride of this experience. I wouldn't get too selfish and greedy and end it too soon.

"Luka." She moaned as I dipped one finger in, stretching her tight sheath. "Oh, fuck. Luka…"

Goddamn. Her breathless groans were music to my ears. Sweet, sinful admissions. I knew what she wanted. I tracked how much she needed me.

I wasn't going to trick myself into thinking I was giving her anything. I was taking. Like this, I'd take away some of her innocence, all to show her how worthy she was. How breathtaking she could be when she took a risk. On the stage, or with me.

"I've never… I've never done this," she confessed as I dipped over her, urging her to fall back further.

"Never what, Gabriella?" I taunted her, too high on the exhilarating rush to touch her and caress her. Adding another finger to her pussy, I resumed sucking on her nipples as she lowered to the stage. Reclined with her hands behind her, her arms locked, she had the ideal vantage point to watch me trail kisses lower and lower. Flipping her skirt up bared her to me, and I grinned at the naughty gasp she let out. Perhaps seeing my fingers in her cunt shocked her. Or maybe it was the view of her legs spread wide to make room for me.

"Never been... touched," she whispered as I went down and down.

"Like this?" I dropped my face to her sweet pussy. The musk of her arousal was too tempting to deny myself this taste. At the first touch of my lips on her cunt, she arched her back and cried out. Then as I swiped my tongue around her entrance, lapping up her cream and all that juiciness she dripped for me, she let her legs fall apart even wider.

"Oh. Oh, my. Fuck. Luka. Are you sure— Oh, *fuck*."

Hearing her lose her mind to my tasting her sweetness was another memory I'd take to the grave. I'd never forget how she trembled and shook. How she watched with awe and shock. Licking and sucking, I left no inch of her untouched flesh neglected. But it was when I moved on to her clit, flicking it with the tip of my tongue before sucking on it over and over, that she came for me.

Her first orgasm was mine.

The gush of her arousal was mine.

All those cries and strained growls of reaching that blissful release were mine.

Gabriella was fucking mine. To take. To keep. To fuck.

Yet, as I watched her quiver and close her eyes tight at the intensity of her orgasm, I knew I couldn't rush any more of this.

I couldn't let the hunt and chase be over already. She was the salvation, the break to my same-old depression, and I refused to take too much, too soon. I had to endure the challenge, to wait and pace myself before she, too, would be spent and used, no longer a new thing to intrigue me.

Stepping back from her was the hardest thing I'd done in years. Her legs remained parted as her thighs trembled. That pink, glistening pussy was bared for me to see. Leaning back, her head hanging down so her hair tumbled like a curtain behind her, she was lax and open. Exposed and all for me to take as I pleased.

I didn't.

Retreating one step, then another, I licked my lips and damned how delicious she was when she finally surrendered. I wanted her. I lusted for her with every fiber of my being, every cell of my body. Still trapped under my pants, my dick strained and ached to be freed and slammed deep inside her.

I wouldn't. Not like this. I had to prolong this challenge and intrigue for as long as I could.

Without comforting her, without offering her any solace or guidance for how to recover from an orgasm like that, I backed out of the studio and closed the door behind me.

"Fuck," I whispered as I leaned back on the closed door. Shutting my eyes, I tried to grasp and cling to the threads of how sweet and sexy she was, opening up for me to take what I wanted. To give her what she sought.

Leaving her alone felt wrong.

Yet, at the same time, it was the only right thing to do.

If I stayed to hold her and comfort her...

No. Just go.

Worried that I could be too soft, that I could care too much, I walked away and left her to handle the aftermath of what happened when she doubted how deeply she could inspire me. She could make her own opinions about what it was like when she tried to dismiss how much I appreciated her and all she'd done to change my life this far.

18

GABRIELLA

I hadn't caught my breath from coming so hard before the sound of the door clicking shut reached my ears.

Luka left.

Before I had a chance to come down from the high of my orgasm.

Without a word.

Not a second thought at all.

He came in here to distract me with his wicked touches and sinful kisses. Then he was gone. He'd left me here just the way I was as I came so intensely from his mouth and fingers on me. My legs remained draped over the edge of the stage. My feet dangled, my panties caught at one ankle. At the shake of my arms from reclining on them for so long, I cringed and tried to sit up to relieve the pressure on them. All of my muscles were raw, my limbs too loose from how he'd shaken me. But it was the cool air on the exposed skin between my legs that registered the most.

He'd left me here like *this*, spent and open. Bared. Used. Teased.

Willing my heart to slow down from the rush of coming,

I sat there and continued to catch my breath. That confusing, damning Mafia boss gave me pleasure orally, then took off.

I bet he hadn't even looked back.

Giving up on the stupid thought that he might've merely left to get something to clean me up, I scooted off the ledge to stand. My legs were still shaky, but holding on to the stage helped.

I couldn't risk falling. No injuries would be welcome now.

My audition was in two days, and I surely had no business exercising like this. The first couple of steps I took sharply reminded me of precisely how Luka had touched me. How he'd proven to be a master of me in a way no other man had.

No one had ever touched me like that. Hell, besides a couple of little kisses, no man had ever kissed me like that, either.

Now, I knew what he meant when he said he'd take what he wanted. Clearly, he'd wanted me. Just not enough to linger and get something in return.

Why?

Why would he leave me like this?

Does he think I can't handle him? That I can't repay the favor?

I'd never done anything with a man before, so perhaps he was right to guess how ignorant I was. That didn't mean I wouldn't teach myself. That I wouldn't figure it out and pay attention to his cues.

Feeling cheated and rejected, I shook my head and grabbed my panties. Bunching them in my hand, I turned off the lights to the studio and left. There was no point in hanging out here. My concentration was shot. Those former worries about whether my commitment to ballet was trivial were forgotten. As I walked to my room, the only thing on my mind was that I'd crossed a boundary with my captor. The fine lines of resistance were blurring where Luka was involved, and I couldn't be sure if I was forfeiting or adapting to my new reality.

I slowed down as I passed his room. Both doors were closed, as they always were. I had yet to even peek inside his personal quarters, but I wondered now what he was doing in there. His erection had to be tended to. That furious need in his eyes had to be dealt with.

Is he in there... doing that?

I sighed, shaking my head at how forbidden it seemed to even think about him pleasuring himself. Or why he'd choose that route instead of being with me in the studio.

Come on. Stop. Think about what you're suggesting. Losing your virginity? To him?

This was nonsense. Or it was supposed to be. He wasn't supposed to be the one to make that spark of interest flare this hotly inside me. He wasn't supposed to be the man to make me feel so alive and needy.

I showered and went to bed, restless with the flashbacks of how he'd pleasured me. When I woke up the next day, he was the first thing on my mind.

Throughout the day, I waited for him to approach me. To offer me guidance of how it would be now. Of what to expect next.

He didn't. Not once did he come to me. To talk to me, to check on me. To even look at me. That distance was between us again. A couple of texts gave me the hint that he wouldn't be available, busy with work. Allen, the ever-present butler-like assistant, told me not to expect him home any time soon.

I hated it, but I got the message.

Luka had taken what he wanted—my submission in that orgasm.

And that was all he'd wanted.

Instead of dwelling on his reaction to being intimate with me at all, to showing me how I "inspired" him, I put all my energy into preparing for the audition. Luka could do this hot-and-cold, close-and-far routine all he wanted. I wished I could know why he'd go to such extremes to kidnap me and keep me locked up here and within his convenient reach when he'd just avoid me again.

Every time I tried to analyze and wonder why he'd play with me like this, I doubled down on practicing and prepping for my audition.

Still, he was there, lurking in the back of my mind. Shame grew as I realized he'd spurned this newfound lust and interest that I couldn't turn off. The more he stayed away, the more I wanted to experience that sensual danger of letting him kiss and touch me again.

Focus on what matters.

I wanted to. Trapped here, I was given so many things I couldn't take for granted. He'd built me a studio. He provided instructors. He'd secured a *private* audition. I had no clue how many strings he'd had to have pulled to make that happen. Those were all gifts I'd never receive otherwise, so when I put it in perspective like that, I struggled not to feel selfish to want *him* when he'd already given me other things to bring my dreams closer to coming true.

On the night of the audition, I felt like a wreck. Mentally, I was a mess. Physically, I was ready and primed to impress. Any time my mind wandered and I was more prone to thinking about him, I rehearsed my steps in my mind. I walked through the music and moves I'd need to complete.

"Ah," I quipped as Emil escorted me to a car. This was the first time I'd been outside in almost two months, reduced to viewing the outside world only through windows. "Free at last."

He rolled his eyes as he held the door to a car open for me. "You're not going anywhere yet."

That *yet* should've intimidated me. With how nervous I was about the audition, I couldn't multitask and worry about my future with these Dubinin men.

"You know, I understand what you were saying the other day." I tipped my chin up, studying this killer. That was how they all referred to him—the assassin. "When you mocked me for wanting to be a dancer and go through this audition at all."

"I wasn't mocking you," he replied, proving that he would always want to argue with me. "I just don't see the point."

"And now I understand it. What *is* the point? Why should your father fuel my dreams, give me that studio and those lessons? Why would he go so far as to arrange this audition when I'm just a possession to keep behind locked doors and armed guards? What *is* the point?"

He furrowed his brow at me.

"It's not like he'd allow me to go to school. It's not like he'd grant me the freedom to travel on tours to perform for others. Right?" I shrugged. "In that regard, it is stupid of me to even try."

He had no reply.

"I get it now," I said again, hating this defeatist attitude before performing. There was no clarification about what my future could be like. The only constant was that Luka owned me.

"Don't overthink it," he advised wryly.

I sighed, glancing around at the evening sky, relishing the fresh air while it lasted.

"And don't break a leg."

I raised my brows. "That's not how it goes. You're supposed to tell me *to* break a leg."

"You want your legs broken?"

"No." I clamped my lips shut. I couldn't expect a Mafia assassin like him to comprehend it. He broke bones for a living, probably torturing people before killing them.

"No. It's a saying," I explained. "For showbusiness in general. Telling someone to break a leg means wishing them good luck."

"Oh. Fine. Good luck, then."

I shook my head. "I don't need luck." So long as I kept his father out of my thoughts, I could—and should—rely on my skill. "Only hard work and determination."

"Then..." He shrugged, gesturing for me to get in the car. "Have fun with that."

I slid into the car, noticing the flutters of nerves in my stomach. This would be a chance to run, to escape, but I had no desire to do so. Why would I rush off when I was being driven to a private audition? I never could've counted on Luka Dubinin to get me closer to my dreams, but there it was.

Before the door was closed and the car sped off, he slid in after me. I hadn't counted on him to show up like this. Much less get in the car with me.

"What are you doing?" I blinked, surprised that he'd be near me after the distance of his avoidance. Those flutters in my stomach intensified with that now-familiar excitement he made me feel. "Why— What's going on?"

"I'm coming with you." He arched one brow, not lightening up on his serious expression as he set his phone in a pocket inside his suit jacket.

"*You're* coming with me?"

He nodded once, peering at me like I had lost the plot. "Yes. Why wouldn't I?"

I narrowed my eyes. Talk about mixed messages. Wasn't he the same guy who avoided me after eating me out? "Why *would* you?"

He rolled his eyes, gesturing at the driver to drive.

I sank against the cushion, watching this confounding man.

"What, do you not trust me to be out of your house? You're thinking I'll run away while I can?" That was my best guess for him to personally escort me to this audition.

He didn't reply, simply staring me down.

"You don't trust me outside the walls of your 'fortress'?"

"I do." He straightened his cuffs. "Or rather, I trust my men to supervise you outside my home."

It was my turn to roll my eyes.

"Besides, if you run, I will find you and bring you back."

I grimaced, so sick of this confusion he doled out on me. "Why?" Before he could reply, I kept going, letting out this frustration he instigated in me. "If I'm a possession, just a thing for you to own, why treat me like this? Why would you tease me and lead me?" I swallowed hard, finally relieved to speak my mind after days of not seeing him. "Why would you... pleasure me like that?"

He shook his head, furrowing his brow like he was disappointed or annoyed with me. "Stop. Stop this. Focus on your audition. Not me."

"But—"

He held his hand up. "This is time to concentrate. Don't think about me or what is going on between us."

I wanted to scream.

It wasn't as though I wanted to be attracted to him.

It wasn't a matter of choosing to think about him.

I just did.

He was always there, in my mind and my memories.

I was desperate to know if there even was anything going on between us.

"Don't, Gabriella. Shut it down and *focus*."

Blinking at him slowly, I let his harsh words sink in. He wasn't dismissing me or trying to downplay his actions. He was lecturing, he was commanding. And he was right. This wasn't the time to be stuck in my head. This was go-time. This was the moment to ride the determination to succeed.

And I would. I resolved to heed his advice. As I sobered up and nodded at him, I turned to gaze out the window instead of pushing this issue with him. Maybe he'd never answer me. Perhaps he intended to keep me confused and on the edge of this dance of desire for him.

Deep down, as the sleek black car brought me closer to the building where I'd perform in a private audition, I appreciated that Luka could be so tough like that. To be so strict and harsh and steer me back to where I needed to be.

I was grateful to have him tell me to focus on what I cared about.

My dad never did.

No one had ever supported me or given me a pep talk like that. It seemed cruelly ironic that the man who'd taken me would be the one to encourage me.

All these weeks I'd been stuck in his house, I wanted the freedom to dream and prioritize about what I wanted out of life. Secretly, though, I had to admit that I wanted *him*. More than I had any right to.

19

LUKA

Keeping away from Gabriella was supposed to have served two purposes.

First and foremost, I needed that step back to cool it. After making her come in the studio, going down on her like she was the feast I'd been waiting my whole life for, I knew that more distance was smart. She tempted me. She taunted me. Walking out of that studio with her taste lingering on my tongue wasn't easy. But this would be better in the long run.

I couldn't let her become too familiar. I couldn't permit *myself* to be that familiar with her yet. Once that happened and it was the same old, the allure of having her in my home would fade. I wasn't ready to return to that nothingness of boredom and only having work to preoccupy me.

Secondly, I had to give her a chance to focus on what she wanted. Oh, there was no doubt at all that she wanted me. I bet she'd sat there stumped and miffed, put off by how I'd walked out of that studio room without a word or another glance.

Maybe she felt rejected. Used and discarded. That

couldn't be further from the truth, but so long as she assumed such, she would be free to concentrate on her rehearsal and practice. With this all-important audition coming up, she didn't need to be distracted by me, by wanting me.

Her dream was to dance. To be on stage. To perform in the art of ballet.

I wasn't her dream.

I couldn't be when I wasn't sure if she'd even stay in my life for long.

Crossing my arms, I shifted my weight on my feet as I stuck to the back of the room. Ivan stood next to me, also watching her on the stage. Other Dubinin men were stationed throughout the building. Several others were posted outside, to surround the theater. Even though she'd asked—sarcastically—about my letting her out of the confines of my fortress of a home, I had no worries that she would run.

It seemed to be on Ivan's mind, though.

"Are you sticking around because you worry she'll run?" he whispered as she moved from one sequence of graceful and complicated steps, jumps, and turns on the stage.

I shook my head slightly, not lowering my guard and still looking around, too *on* to relax. "She wants me too much to leave."

He huffed a wry laugh.

"She wants this audition and all these chances to better her skill to leave."

I couldn't be sure that would always be true, but it was right now.

"I'm staying to watch because she's too breathtaking to miss."

I wasn't telling him that in the vein of appreciating how

sexy and gorgeous she was on the stage, alone with the spotlight tracking her as she performed for the judges. I meant it in the manner of admiring her skill. Her courage. Her cool confidence to prove she was truly this talented. She wasn't merely going through the motions of a hobby. She had real skill and experience, and it showed. Dancing like this, she was a living work of art in action.

"I won't claim to be an expert on dancers or anything," Ivan whispered back, "but she is pretty good."

Pretty good was an understatement if I'd ever heard one. She was a master of the music, a ruler of those moves. Gabriella was a damned talented dancer. Ivan and I weren't the only ones to realize it, either. Another glance at the small panel of selected judges showed they nodded along and smiled. A couple leaned in to whisper, their brows raised in praise and surprise.

She was killing it. Not a single flinch or mistake. No pauses or hiccups.

I exhaled slowly, relishing the steady elation of witnessing her passion coming to fruition. Her skills were honed with my help and what I provided. It always felt good to care for a woman, but I was too stubborn yet to consider her *my* woman, not in a permanent sense.

She'd gotten better at not locking down in a trauma response whenever something scarier happened at home. Yet, she wasn't a tried-and-tested Mafia woman I could count on in any other way.

"Almost done, right?" Ivan asked once the hour was almost up. "If so, I'll have the security detail move into place outside for us to—"

The sudden burst of gunfire cut him off. Triggered by the sound, I reached for my gun and scanned the theater. No other audience was in here. It was only the one row of a handful of judges. They all screamed and ducked down for cover, their hands up to shield the backs of their heads as if that would stop a bullet.

Dubinin soldiers and guards rushed down the aisles to secure the entrance and exit points that led into the darkened performing space.

But it was only Gabriella on the stage.

She'd stopped suddenly, dropping into a low crouch, as if to make herself as small as possible.

It wouldn't make a difference.

With only her on the stage and those blinding spotlights on her to emphasize her lone presence up there, she couldn't have been more of a target.

"Get down!" I shouted, running forward as Ivan sprinted toward the double doors where the armed men broke in.

Too many questions hit me at once. I'd deal with them later. Finding out how they'd gotten in past my guards, why they knew to come here tonight, and who the fuck they were fell under the list of imperative details to analyze later.

Right now, as I ran as fast as I could for the stage before the assassins could reach it, I only focused on getting to Gabriella and saving her.

Breathing hard and fast as the adrenaline rushed through me and fueled me to get to her, I stared ahead with tunnel vision.

All that mattered was saving her. Protecting her. It was too cruel to be taken from the beauty of her dance to this fear of her being harmed, this threat of violence and danger that crept too damn close at the wrong time.

At the edge of the stage, counting on Ivan and the other Dubinin men to have my back amid the continued gunfire, I ignored the echoes of shots. I dismissed the judges screaming and hurrying to escape.

I grabbed hold of the stage edge and hauled myself up. Leaping onto the polished surface, I skidded into a slide. The second I was fully on my feet, I ran for her. Men— Cartel, from the instant first impression I allowed myself— raced forward to reach her too. I fired at them all. With this close of a range, they had no odds of surviving my hits. Every time I pulled on the trigger resulted in a man dropping down. Blood was shed. Lives were lost.

No. Lives were taken.

By me.

Powered with the need to kill anyone who would harm this gorgeous innocent, I shot at them as I ran toward her. Yards parted us. Feet.

Then I was there. Clutching her into my arms, I shielded her and blocked her. She tucked against me immediately. Her slender, smaller frame fit against me. As I spun us, still firing at the Cartel assassins who'd trespassed this opportunity, I killed another.

Ivan and the guards were right there with me. They scaled the stage and surrounded me. Practiced training had them forming a solid wall and unit around me, around me and Gabriella.

My chest heaved and my throat burned. Going from a hard run in panic to stopping short as the backup kept us safe, I stared down the men who dared to take something of mine.

"Go. Go, Uncle. Go." Ivan dismissed me with a hard look. Both hands stayed on his gun as he ordered the men to check the ones who'd been shot.

It wasn't his place to tell me what to do, but this wasn't the first time I'd been in the line of fire with him. The priority would be to secure my safety, and at this moment, that meant transporting Gabriella out of here as well.

I didn't linger. I didn't wait. Those answers would come later.

Tucking Gabriella into my embrace, I kept my arms around her and steered her to dash off the stage with me. She moved with me, meeting my stride. No argument would come from her now as she fled.

This wasn't how it was supposed to end. This wasn't how her audition was supposed to conclude, my whisking her off stage and rushing to safety.

Having to respond to violence like this and giving her a firsthand view of what kind of a ruthless monster I was shouldn't have happened. Not like this.

But there was no rewind button. There was no redo option. It was done.

She was safe. I got her. The Dubinin men would protect us both.

Yet, with every step of the way to get her back into my car and on the way home, I scolded myself. I damned myself for being so eager to please her and make her happy. I kicked myself for focusing so hard on earning a fucking smile from her that I risked her safety like this.

I never should have risked bringing her out of my secure home. Not before knowing with more confidence that she'd never be a target.

20

GABRIELLA

It's okay.

I'm okay.

Luka didn't let go of me once. Not as we ran toward his sleek black car. Not as the Dubinin men flanked us. The sight of the guns in their hands should've scared me. Feeling the cool metal of Luka's firearm against me as we bolted out of the theater should've terrified me.

They're gone.

Those thugs are not coming after you.

They're not chasing us.

I jerked to look past Luka before we got in the backseat, having to see with my own eyes that those armed men weren't chasing us out here.

They're not coming.

You got away.

We got away.

As I slid into the backseat, I had to cling to that fact the most.

I wasn't alone.

This was not like when Tony tried to rape me in the

apartment I shared with my dad. This was not another episode of random street violence.

I was *not* alone. The smoky, masculine scent of Luka reminded me of his presence when all my other senses were skewed. Frantic, panicked, and scared, I couldn't think straight at all as the door was closed on us.

Darkness followed.

Silence was our soundtrack.

The rumble of the engine felt as throaty as ever, but it was a comforting purr because it meant this expensive vehicle was speeding us further away from the danger.

Danger.

Life-or-death danger.

Trying to catch my breath and not wheeze from the adrenaline rush, I curled my fingers in the front of Luka's jacket.

Life.

I'm alive.

It's okay.

It was only okay that a group of thugs burst into my private audition with guns blaring because of this strong, powerful man keeping me in his embrace.

Luka. My God, Luka. Thank you.

I struggled to swallow, wishing my heightened senses could fade and I could relax long enough to think. To be coherent for more than a second. Too jumbled up and racing along this ride of a trauma reaction, I couldn't slow my thoughts. I couldn't force my heart to take it down a notch. Air just couldn't fill my lungs fast enough.

"Gabriella." Luka shifted only to put his gun away. He kept me in his arms, practically draped over his lap as we sped away.

I had no reply. I could only snuggle in closer, tucking my

face against his shirt so I could inhale deep pulls of his scent. Authority and testosterone. They didn't make sense together, but it was just *him*. I was familiar with how he smelled. I was getting more used to his hot, callused hands on me. And I was tuned in to the sound of his husky timbre, always full of command.

"Gabriella." He repeated it as he reached to get his buzzing phone out of his jacket pocket. As he moved, he tipped my chin up. "Are you hurt?"

I shook my head, too off-kilter to speak yet. Besides, he was directed to his phone.

Seeming content with the gesture that I wasn't harmed —all thanks to him and his brave men—he urged me to lean against him for the rest of the ride while he spoke to his men. Ivan. Allen. Others I forgot the names of. Emil, too. I wasn't listening in. He didn't say much, either, more like he was being reported in to.

All I focused on was him holding me close. Anchoring me. Grounding me. Securing me until we reached his fortress of a residence. The tall walls didn't seem foreboding and looming too tall. The guards at the entrance didn't look threatening. The thick material of this massive mansion in the city only gave me the impression of safety, of security, and my heart beat steadier with the fact that I was here again. That I would be sheltered and safe within these walls once more.

But nothing calmed me as much as Luka's touch did.

Without my having to say anything, he seemed to understand. The door was opened for us in the garage, and he got out first, only to extend his hand to me and help me out. Then as we entered the building, he clutched my hand in his big one, not releasing me one bit.

Inside, he nodded at Allen who rambled a summary of

whatever must have been pertinent for Luka to know now. Towing me with him and keeping me at his side, Luka seemed on the go, not ready to slow or stop for anyone.

Sticking with me, he led me straight up to his private wing.

I was still in my dance apparel, my tights, shoes, and leotard. My hair was still up in a tight, unforgiving bun. Makeup still coated my skin. Sweat, not from the dance but from the fear, slicked my flesh.

Throughout it all, this escape from the theater didn't truly register with me. I was there. And now I was here.

My audition was done—prematurely. Yet, I couldn't summon the stubbornness to care right now.

All I could feel and experience was the soulful gratitude that Luka saved me.

He'd *killed* to save me.

Questions would haunt me. I didn't know why that had happened if it was guarded and secure. I wasn't sure why I'd be targeted, what those men wanted to accomplish, who they were and who they worked for.

Nothing made sense.

Only being here with Luka did.

"Are you all right?" he asked, checking again as he loosened his tie with one hand. With his other, he steered me into my room, almost as if he counted on my getting in the shower.

"I'm all right," I replied, hating how shaky my voice sounded.

"I won't coddle you, Gabriella." He shook his head as he caught me watching him. "I can't."

I shook my head, uninterested in what he said. I wasn't in the mood to be babied and coddled. "I know."

"This world isn't for you. I know that. The death and

violence aren't something just anyone can get used to, but I can't coddle and sweettalk you into accepting this way of life."

I furrowed my brow, letting the spark of annoyance keep me rooted in this moment. "I don't want to be coddled."

Of course, I was an outsider looking in. I wasn't born in this lifestyle of gun-toting, lawless men who ruled through a conduct system of their own making. I hadn't handled the hints and experiences of danger smoothly so far. Right now, in the aftermath of seeing Luka confidently gun down five men to reach me and protect me, all I needed to keep my wits was *him*.

"I don't want to be coddled." I blinked, trying to reconcile the image of this strong brute wielding his gun without pause, taking lives like it was his business, with the idea of him holding me and smoothing my hair from my face as he whispered sweet platitudes.

"I don't want—" I shook my head, rushing toward him. "I don't want to be coddled. Just make me forget. Make it stop." I cringed, hating the flashbacks circling through my mind.

I could breathe easier here. The panic attack after the trauma couldn't be as acute now that we'd distanced ourselves from the dead bodies.

But I needed him.

"Fuck." He gripped the back of my neck as I lifted my hands to set them on his shoulders.

"Make me forget," I begged before reaching up on my toes to kiss him.

The first touch of his hot lips on mine scalded me, but the fire of his desire for me made the burn worth it.

He growled, squeezing his fingers around the back of my neck. He parted my lips to taste me, to devour me. He lowered one hand to lift my thigh, prompting me to lean up and into him.

I gasped, parting for air as he lifted me fully. Like this, torn from trauma and the reaction to such violence at a pivotal time of my dancing career, I shifted into something else entirely.

Letting him carry me to my bed, I surrendered all thoughts of my steps and choreo. Sucking in a desperate breath, I gave in to the free-fall sensation of him dropping me onto the mattress.

"Luka." I reached up to frame his face as he slanted down, already so busy with his hands. Fingers grabbed at my clothes. His nails scraped on my skin in his rush. His palms smoothed over every inch of my flesh that he bared. Kissing me as he stripped me on the bed, he gave me no pause. He showed me that even in this, he'd take what he wanted. He demonstrated with needy growls and urgent thrusts against me that he wasn't about to disappoint me.

"Luka, please." I uttered it once the cool air kissed my skin. Nude and willing on the bed, I was his for the taking. But as he straightened to shed his clothes, I couldn't stand that gap between us. His body heat was a necessity. His lips were a demand to fulfill. While he frantically tore his clothes off, I assisted. First, I got onto my knees to return my mouth to his. Then, I wrenched at his garments to help. His tie, that jacket. Then his shirt and pants.

Only once he was naked, baring all the dips and ridges of his muscles, did he claim me again.

"Oh, fuck," I whispered as his erection rubbed between my legs. Long, thick, and rigid, it probed at where I dripped for him already. Hard like velvet-covered steel, it pointed at my pussy.

"Gabriella," he growled as he lowered me back down on

the bed. Taking hold of my chin, he forced me to stare right back at him.

Was he going to walk away and retreat?

Was he having second thoughts?

Was he rethinking this because it looked like I was intimidated at taking all of him inside me?

"Please," I begged. I'd whine. I'd cry it out so loudly until the rest of the whole house heard. He could *not* lead me on like this. I needed him too much. I was that desperate for a distraction from the violence that stunned me, the shock of my audition being ended too soon.

Crushing his lips to mine, he lined himself up and pushed. The stretch of his wide cockhead taunted me. Then the next inch inside startled me. More and more, he steadily thrust into me. Not stopping once, he rammed and rammed, stuffing that big dick into my cunt.

Just like that, he took me.

He took my virginity. As he seated himself, pausing his kiss to stare into my eyes, I knew it couldn't have happened in any other way that would feel this good.

This magical.

This wickedly hot and sinful, yet... *right.*

"Oh, fuck. Fuck." I couldn't catch my breath, feeling split in two by the most thrilling sensation ever.

He withdrew, watching my face before he slammed all the way back in.

"Oh, fuck!" I couldn't think. I couldn't speak. Only those brief shouts. Watching me all the while, he withdrew and pushed right back in, setting up a dizzying rhythm that had me hurtling too quickly to an intense orgasm.

Relief waited just right there. Bliss was within reach. Ecstasy would be mine.

"Come." He gritted his teeth, seeming ready to shoot his load in me. "Come for me, Gabriella."

I nodded, accepting his wet kisses up along my throat as he ravaged me with his hard dick. Like a sword plunged in and out without a break, he coaxed me closer and closer to letting go.

"Gabriella. Come for me!" He tightened his fingers on my hands that he'd thrust up over my head.

I wanted to. I was right there. Under him and full of his hardness, I couldn't even think of anything else.

When he lowered his lips to mine again, sucking on my tongue as he whipped his hips faster, I was done for. I was gone.

Soaring then drowning, all in the same intense moment, I came. Unlike when he'd gone down on me, there was no recovering from this. I screamed, only to be muffled by his lips. I bucked, arching up to meet him, just to feel every sinful second of him making me climax.

I came—just for him.

My hero. But also my captor.

My savior. But also my enemy.

Luka. He'd taken my virginity because I'd asked him to distract me and make me forget how he'd ruthlessly murdered men who wanted me dead.

Sinking under the weight of such utter bliss, I braced for him as he followed after me. With two more deep, hard, pounding thrusts that would no doubt leave me bruised, he came. His dick twitched deep inside me as he flooded my womb. His thighs tightened as he lay over me with all of his weight. His arms shook as he kept my hands high up above my head. Plastered over me, he gave me a chance to experience the all-body sensation of his orgasm as he groaned then rolled.

Holding me close so I'd drape over him, he exhaled a long, hard breath that fluffed my hair off my face. I couldn't care. I couldn't move. So spent and sated, I could only lie there, limp and numb from bliss and a kind of gratitude I'd never felt before.

Because I wasn't alone.

I couldn't be ever again after knowing what it was like to be with him like this. He'd taken my virginity and stamped himself on my soul, to always be connected and remind me that at least physically, I belonged to him now.

21

LUKA

Sleeping in with a woman was a leisure and luxury that I never allowed myself. Even when Maria was alive and we were newlyweds in love, there was always something for me to hurry off to. That was the nature of being the Dubinin boss. There was no shortage of some type of dilemma or problem to solve, some kind of argument or fight to referee. Work was just there, always waiting for me. In the beginning, when I was younger, I was expected to be more hands-on more frequently than I was now. Now, my men could handle everything. I trusted them all. Even for the bloodbath left at the theater, I could count on the Dubinin forces to handle it and clean it up.

Still, waking up next to Gabriella was different.

She was different.

What I was trying to do with her was different. Because in any other ordinary way, I should've treated her just like any other woman, a common, no-strings-attached fling to dismiss once I was through with her and had taken her.

She stirred, as if the weight of my stare was enough to

rouse her. Rolling over, she blinked her eyes open until she gazed at me.

I waited for her reaction.

I'd killed men in front of her last night.

I'd also taken her virginity.

But it was a guessing game which would've made more of an impact on her in the light of this new morning.

She didn't give me a reaction, though, merely watching me calmly and meeting eye contact levelly.

Fuck, she was gorgeous.

Serene and sleepy like this, not already at arms with me and stubborn or combative, she looked like a rare and unique creature I'd want to try to tame over and over again. Relaxed and present in my bed, she was the ultimate temptation.

Looking at her was enough to get my dick waking up, too.

She was a temptation I wasn't feeling ready to pass up on yet. "How do you feel?"

She let out a long, lazy breath. "I feel like I want to not be coddled again."

And then she did it.

She gave it to me.

That elusive smile. It was as bright and sexy as I imagined it could be. Unlike the shy expressions she'd given me before, this one came with the full punch. Without looking away, she dazzled me with her bold gaze, so warm and intoxicating, like I might never learn all her secrets. Her lips curled up in a mischievous grin, and I couldn't hold back.

Lunging for her, I rolled her until she was beneath me, all warm and naked, rubbing against me from head to toe. Kissing her first, I showed her how much I wanted her again. Then, grinding my growing erection against her as she parted her legs and whimpered with need, I proved that I wasn't anywhere near done with her yet.

"Oh, fuck. Luka. How can you be so hard again?"

I chuckled, kissing a path down her neck until I could suck on her breasts. Her nipples. The swells of her tits. I was hungry to taste it all. Not stopping the slow pushes of my dick against her, I felt the smear of her arousal.

"I'm always hard for you." It didn't matter that she was half my age. She was a full-bodied woman I couldn't resist. "Are you sore?"

"Not sore enough to want you to stop." She moaned, closing her eyes as she threaded her fingers through my hair to keep my head where she wanted it. It seemed that licking and sucking on her nipples turned her on even faster, but I was determined to prolong it for as long as I could. I had to, if not to keep up the novelty of it all, then to cherish her innocence she so freely gave to me.

Hours later, after we'd come and showered, I suggested that she move more of her things into my room.

"That fast, huh?"

"I've been putting off fucking you for over two months," I growled. "That's about as far as my patience was going to last where you're concerned."

She smiled, teasing me again with her mirth and amusement.

No one in the house needed to be updated that my relationship with Gabriella had shifted. It was evident in the amount of time I spent at home, often with her. On my lap as I kissed her. Clinging to me as I felt her up in the kitchen. Fingering her under the table when we had dinner.

At first, I tried to be as gentle as I could manage. She was a virgin when she arrived. As time passed, she showed me how much she favored my rougher side. Going from completely vanilla to a little more kinky revealed more layers to the exquisite woman she was.

And still, I didn't tire of her.

No matter what, in the weeks following her botched audition, I only wanted her more.

She didn't pry or ask about that night, but it was Emil and Alexsei who shared more details about it at lunch one day.

"They were from the Viper Cartel," Emil remarked.

"And they were coming for me because...?" Gabriella furrowed her brow and glanced at me. "Because of my dad?"

I covered her hand with mine and squeezed her delicate fingers. "Perhaps. We're still investigating it. Miguel seemed disloyal to all organizations."

That night, as I stripped her slowly so I could fuck her in the shower, she asked more. I couldn't tell whether she was nervous to know the truth or afraid to seem nosy.

"Was my dad disloyal to you?" she asked.

"He was." Under the heat of the water in the shower, I explained how he'd lied and two-timed the Dubinin Family as well as the Riveras. "Traitors are common."

"I'm sorry he did that." She kissed me tenderly. "But I'm not surprised that he did. He's not loyal to anyone. Not even me, his own daughter."

For that, I was eternally grateful. Otherwise, I might not have ever known she existed.

With her settling in as my woman—for now—I granted her more freedom within my home. She could go wherever she wanted except for the holding rooms. She had free rein to explore and pursue whatever hobbies she wanted. Like this, she was more of a guest than a captive, but there was always an undercurrent of expectation.

She would be here per my order. She wouldn't leave

without my consent. While she didn't express any desire to leave, I was suspicious that her freedom was still in the back of her mind.

With how her audition ended abruptly, I almost wondered if she'd push for another one. To try again. But she didn't. Dancing was still her routine. Day and night, she'd be in the studio I'd built for her, practicing and staying consistent with her choice of art. Yet, she made no mention of what she would do with her dream, her passion.

"Maybe she's too scared to go back on the stage," Allen suggested one day when I was watching her. He'd passed me in the hall and offered his comment about my question of her not auditioning again or mentioning it. A greedy part of me wanted to believe she no longer had as fervent of an interest in her dreams to be on stage because she had changed to see *me* as her dream.

He might have had a point, but even in that regard, I saw the changes. She was more confident. She didn't flinch at mentions of attacks or deaths. There was no way she was hardened enough to handle any form of violence, but she seemed to acclimate.

She had to. Because the longer she stayed in my bed, in my room, and in my life, it was so painfully clear to me how badly I needed her.

She was the light to my darkness.

She was the salvation for my crimes and bitter soul.

And even though she wanted me, she could respect that my world was a cruel one, not all hearts and flowers.

Despite our differences, we grew closer. We became almost inseparable, addicted to being with each other as much as we could. It even came to the point where Ivan and Emil questioned whether I was too distracted by her. News of challenges and threats reached us daily. That was nothing new. So long as the Dubinin Family remained at the top of the food web and as apex predators in the criminal underworld we operated in, someone else would always covet our wealth, our land, and our power.

"I'm just saying..." Ivan shrugged as we walked away from my home office after a meeting. "You seemed very distant when we checked in with the supervisors about the Rivera sightings near the docks."

"I wasn't distant." I shook my head. "I was there, hearing the same things you did." *Including that bullshit about the Vipers planning another attack.* They had yet to take credit for the shooting and ambush at Gabriella's audition. No one was stepping up to take credit for those Cartel men, and it infuriated me to lack the direction to strike back appropriately. Justly.

"But you're so busy with—"

I held up my hand to cut off Emil. My son and I were close, but in this, he would not win the argument.

"I am not too busy with Gabriella. Trust me, Son." I stared him down as we walked along the lengthy hallway. "I will never lose my edge. I had once before, and I never will again."

By being too in love and addicted to enjoying Maria in my life, I'd lowered my guard and had been too slow to prevent her death. I'd been caught off guard then.

And I vowed to never let that happen again.

It couldn't happen with Gabriella. No love was bonding us.

She was a temptation, a distraction that I'd sorely needed.

But nothing more.

Not anything that would be lasting.

22

GABRIELLA

Nothing was the same anymore.

I no longer had to clean and act like a maid for my dad just to "earn" his paying for dance lessons. That felt like another lifetime ago, a whole existence that ceased to be.

I never had to worry about missing or falling behind with my skills. Being privileged enough to have those tutors solidified my intent to be the best dancer I could right now.

But it was how swiftly my dreams had shifted that stunned me.

My passion to dance was still there. My hopes of being on the stage burned within me, and that fire wouldn't be extinguished.

Yet, after how violently my audition ended and how intimately my relationship with Luka had advanced, I would be a liar to say that *all* I wanted to fight for was getting into Juilliard and being on stage.

Someday, it would be nice.

The fantasies of performing for an audience like that still played like a movie in my mind.

I had to incorporate new dreams. Luka dominated my thoughts, and I couldn't deny how he'd been slowly but surely transforming my desires and wishes to center on him and him alone.

But what is the point?

What's the endgame now?

Those questions were the only thoughts I could count on to keep my head on straight. Being here was like a nightmare that had corrected its course. I felt like I was swimming beneath the surface, suspended in a fantasy. A delusion, even, that this could be my life.

I'd given up my fierce insistence to escape or get out of here. I was outnumbered. Too many guards remained at posts. Locks held me inside. Now, though, it was more than the hardware on the doors and windows that had me trapped. It was more than the Dubinin security force always watching for anyone coming in or out.

It was Luka.

My desire for him was enslaving me to stay. My lust for him never abated, always simmering my hunger for him and his touches. And my enjoyment of this exploration we shared ensured that I'd be a fool to ever voluntarily leave.

He was keeping me here.

I spun through a move, focusing on staying engaged physically as I danced into the night while my mind was preoccupied on the heavy thoughts that I might've finally succumbed to him. That he'd won my submission after how valiantly I'd said he wouldn't ever have it.

It's not like it would be safe to leave now.

That was a fraction of my survivalist instinct. The one time I'd left the safety of this house, members of the Viper Cartel came to kill me. If I were to try to take off, to just leave and start my life over like I'd wished I could when I felt so stuck in my life with my dad, I would be hunted. Luka's enemies would target me. They'd try to kill me. Why, I still didn't know. The best that I could understand of it after a discussion with Emil was that I was now collateral damage. Others viewed me as Luka's prized possession. Maybe they assumed I was his official partner and not his plaything of the moment. And for that, they'd attack me and use me as leverage against Luka.

In essence, I was *still* a pawn.

When it was just me and Luka, though, I wasn't a thing to place somewhere and lock up for security. I wasn't a pawn or transaction. I was the other half of a different sort of dance, one where we'd come together like one. I couldn't tell where I started and where I ended.

As I turned back from the wall of windows in the studio, segueing into a lower position that would lead up to a jump, I stopped short.

I didn't understand how I'd missed feeling his stare on me. But there he was.

Luka had returned. I never knew his schedule and I realized that his "job" wasn't conventional or traditional like a nine-to-five. And I knew better than to ever ask about it.

He stood there now.

Haggard but stern. Exhaustion oozed from him as he leaned against the doorframe. That suit, one like all the other finely tailored ones he wore day in and out, was ripped, dirtied up, and showing blood stains. His face was swollen in spots, like he'd taken more than a couple of hits in a fight. Small but visible, a thin cut showed on his lip where it had been split.

It was the severe intensity in his eyes that captured me and had me furrowing my brow.

He stared at me like I was the drink he needed in the desert.

He watched me hungrily like I was the only decadent nourishment he wished to devour.

As he stalked further into the room, limping slightly like he'd been wounded in his left leg, he gazed at me with that addictive energy I could only hope to match. Like he'd been made for me, and I for him. As though we were the only two souls that could matter when we were pulled and drawn together with this sizzling chemistry that had yet to fade.

Even now.

Now, as he looked filthy and injured, tired and mad, I wanted him. I *still* craved him, and I wondered if the allure of being the object of his affection would ever cease or wither away.

"Luka, what—"

He held up his hand, quieting me. Reaching me, he lowered his fingers toward my elbow until he could smooth his touch all the way up my arm, then higher yet, caressing my neck with a rough grip. At last, he threaded his dirty fingers up into my messy bun, coiling the strands tightly so I'd feel a sting on my scalp.

Possessive. That was the mood he gave off right now.

And I was all for it.

Falling against him as he hauled me toward him, I sighed and braced for the perfection of his famished lips against mine. That hard and brutal press of his mouth was a kiss that would leave me weak in the knees.

I grunted lightly at the intensity of him kissing me, parting my lips and tasting immediately. Under the increased pressure of him pushing me to meet him in the middle, I moaned. Already, I was embarrassingly wet. Even now, I was desperate for him.

He'd startled me, showing up like this. But the almost feverish pull he seemed to claw at me with was something else.

What happened?

Who did this?

What's wrong?

What went so badly tonight?

Are you really hurt?

None of those questions left my lips. I couldn't ask a single one of them with my mouth so preoccupied. The more that I gave in to this mutual desire, the less I cared.

He picked me up effortlessly. Held tightly to his chest, it was instinct to wrap my legs around his waist. Like this, with his bloodied lip sucking at me, his cut-up hands gripping my ass cheeks, and his dick already hard and poking at me, he carried me out of the studio.

Feeling the limp in his gait reminded me that he was hurt. Tasting the metallic tang in his kiss was a show of how he'd been injured in another round of violence.

It all pointed to the fact that he was a dangerous man. One prone to fighting, to killing. To taking whatever he saw fit, including me. All those details should've had me running, terrified and logically wanting nothing to do with him. But that was the old me. That was the old reality.

Now, I knew better. I was aware of how right he was for me despite being almost twice my age. I'd realized how perfectly he'd keep me safe and sated.

Keeping my eyes closed, I framed his face and let him take me to bed. To his bed, the one we shared as though we were a real couple.

Instead of lowering me to the mattress, he sat. I strad-dled him, not letting up on this seal between our mouths as we continued to kiss. The rub of my breasts against his rock-hard chest was the ultimate tease of friction. But when I ground down, moving my pussy over his erection, that had me gasping for air and crying out in need.

"Fuck me."

He growled it so gruffly that I couldn't tell if it was a gritty expletive of awe and marvel or if he was ordering me.

"Fuck me, Gabriella." He gripped the hem of my shirt and shoved it upward. "I need you."

My pulse skyrocketed. My pussy dripped. Between my aching nipples and this tension banding within my stomach, I was so ready to ride him and appease him. When he was hungry for me like this, it was impossible not to view him as my beast to tame.

"I want to see you." He wrenched his hand upward to rip my shirt partway.

Giving up on kissing him just so I could acquiesce and get my dance gear off, I stood and stripped while maintaining eye contact.

"I need to feel you."

My shirt and bra were gone, but I wasn't fast enough.

He leaned in, hooking his arm around my waist as he pulled me closer until he took my nipple into his mouth. Biting my lip at the deep suction there, I squirmed and hurried to get my skirt and panties off. My tights. Socks. All of it. He didn't give me much leeway, no slack to move with ease. But that was all part of the thrill. Being held and trapped, to submit when he was in this dominant mood.

He ripped his mouth from my breasts. The wetness left there from his tongue taunted me as it cooled from the air. Goosebumps spread over my flesh. I couldn't help but shiver from the delicious anticipation of him taking me.

Standing abruptly to tug his clothes off, he narrowed his eyes and growled. "Fuck me, Gabriella. Fuck me *now*."

I nodded, but before I could ever reach for him, he'd spun me around and I fell toward the bed. He crawled onto it after me, spanking my ass once as I faced him. Then we were united again.

Pushed to kneel on my hands and knees in front of him, I thrust my ass up and waited for him to enter me.

He didn't delay. Lining up his dick to my pussy, he pushed the head in and stretched me. Full and wide, I was split open for him. Just like every other time he took me hard, I moaned and pushed back into him.

"Fuck me." He grabbed my hips and pulled me backward until he was seated. "I said fuck me."

Another spank landed on my ass cheek. Warmth radiated from the strike. So taboo and naughty. I felt ready to come from that alone.

"Fuck me now," he ordered as he pushed me.

Even though the position was one where he'd do much better at ramming into me, I wasn't going to turn down the challenge.

He was in a mood. Mad. Hurt. Impatient. I didn't want to know what had gone down earlier. All I could focus on was that he was here right now, with me, seeking solace deep inside me.

I rocked back and forth, fucking him and trying not to lose my control. Having his dick deep inside me was the ultimate race to an orgasm. When he added his fingers to my clit, I damn near dropped and gave up then, trembling with bliss.

I resisted it, determined to please him, too, to submit and do as he wanted when it seemed like some days, he'd given me the whole world, the best of the world I could've ever dreamed of with all my needs met and my dreams encouraged.

"Fuck me with that sweet pussy," he ordered with a filthy growl. The sound of him sucking on his fingers followed, and then the pressure came at my rear hole. He'd only started playing with other varieties of kinks. I was proud to move past my virginal naïveté and explore with him. To learn from him and appreciate how good he'd always make me feel no matter what we tried to introduce.

So far, I'd already learned how much faster I could come with him giving me some light anal play.

Between the furious need to rock back and take his dick as far and fast as I could and the pressure he gave me on my clit and ass, I was lost. I couldn't hold on. I *was* fucking him, submitting to pleasing him like this, but it just felt too damn good for me, too.

"Luka!"

As the first waves of my intense orgasm came, he spanked me once more, harder, and roared his pleasure.

I sucked him in. I quivered and nearly collapsed. But as he twitched inside me and shot his hot cum up into me, I knew that I'd won this round. I was milking him dry, earning every one of his guttural sounds of relief as we came together.

He only had to ask now.

And I would agree to be his anything.

His thing. His woman. His lover. His partner.

Just so long as it would always be me and him coming so brutally together like this, spent and weak until we dropped onto the mattress and had to fight to catch our breath again.

23

LUKA

I t wasn't supposed to feel like this.

It wasn't supposed to ever be this fucking perfect.

Gabriella had come into my life as a payment. As a punishment and payment for her father's sins.

And now, as I helped her upright so we could go shower together, I had to admit that she'd become so much more than that.

My son and nephews were right to call me out on being distracted. If I wasn't touching this delectable woman and making her sigh with pleasure and reward me with her smiles, I was thinking about how I could pull it off.

She had well and truly become my fucking kryptonite. I had no clue how to navigate the situation of needing her all the time this viscerally. As if my soul would be too dark and dull without her light.

"Easy," I coaxed as she moaned. Leaning with me and getting upright, she gave me a sleepy smile. Like that little gesture took so much energy, she'd much rather stay put and pass out.

"No, come on. Let me clean you up."

"Okay," she agreed sleepily. Once she slung her arms around me, I could pick her up and carry her into the bathroom. Every step I took reminded me of how sticky I was from our combined juices. She'd come so hard, like always. I'd emptied myself into her, but now, all our cum dripped from my dick and her body.

I had to will away the temptation to push it back in with my finger.

To keep it in her.

So she'd feel me like that just a little longer. Full. Stuffed. Owned. Dominated.

"Mmm." She moaned long and low as I started the water. Steam filled the room immediately, and together, since we were both sluggish and weak, we got into the stall.

"No, no," she protested mildly when I started to soap her up and wash her. "I can manage. Let me take care of you."

I wouldn't turn that offer down. Standing close so I could catch her if she slipped or fell, I rested my brow against hers. Mesmerized by her dark, inviting gaze, so full of strength and concern, I sighed and let her have her way with me like this. Over and over, she scrubbed my skin, but as she went about it, it seemed like she was also taking an inventory of my wounds. All the scrapes and gashes, the bruises and swollen contusions.

"Don't ask," I warned gently but seriously.

She shook her head. "I won't. I know better."

She truly did. In these few months she'd been with me, she had definitely passed a crash course in learning to look the other way. She excelled at minding her own business, clearly aware that many things I did were illegal and dangerous.

And she still wants me.

She still covets me.

After we showered, I carried her to bed and held her until she passed out. It should've put me to sleep. Feeling her warm, naked body flush against mine was the ultimate calming variable I could count on. Hearing her soft breaths so steady like a familiar rhythm should have been the soundtrack to lull me into resting.

But I was too awake.

I couldn't tell if I was wired from the violence I'd endured earlier. Fighting those Cartel fuckers hadn't been part of my plans for the night, but that was where the evening took us. Even hearing a mention of the Vipers assisting the Rivera Family was enough to make my blood boil.

More than that, though, it was this belated realization that I could be falling too quickly for Gabriella.

I dismissed the worry that I had to prolong everything and go slow with her to better savor her newness. The adventure hadn't stopped yet, and I had a hunch that I would never tire of the pleasure of calling her mine. Of knowing she would be here, waiting for me alone.

I can't be...

I sighed, easing away from spooning her. As if putting physical distance between us would help me fight back the nagging suspicion in my head.

I couldn't be falling in love with her.

Love wasn't part of this equation. It wasn't supposed to be a possibility. After I'd loved and lost my wife, flings and affairs were all my heart could handle.

Or is that not true any longer?

I stood, wrapping a robe around myself as I stared down

at her sleeping so innocently and peacefully in my bed. Her face was smooth without a single worry. Merely witnessing her lowering her guard and being so serene because of all that I gave her was the highest reward.

But is it only about giving her what she wants?

Not taking what I want?

I shook my head, annoyed with how awake I was after fighting and then fucking her like that.

Turning to let her be, I left my room and headed down to the study.

Finding my son and nephews there didn't surprise me. They'd likely stayed to talk about all that had gone down tonight. A meeting in the study wasn't out of the norm for them. Most times, I was there as well, double-checking reports and following up on loose threads.

Tonight, I'd needed Gabriella's light. I'd been too addicted to the possibility of venting out my anger in her that I hadn't stayed to talk to Emil or the others at all.

"That was fast," Emil taunted as I entered the study. He tipped a glass of vodka back then sighed.

"Fast?" I asked with a scoff.

"Never mind," Ivan said, lifting his hand as if he'd be the mediator here. "Never mind that."

"No." Emil shook his head as he cleared his throat and sat up more. "I'm not talking about how fast he hurried upstairs to fuck her." He huffed a wry laugh. "I'm talking about how fast she became so important that she'd be your..." He rolled his hand in the air abstractly, as if manually summoning a word to hit him.

"Thing?" Ivan asked.

"No, his woman," Alexsei said.

"No." I shook my head and took a seat. Emil poured me a

drink but I didn't rush to pick it up. "She's not either of those anymore."

"Then what is she?" Allen asked, coming into the room and bringing a tray of more vodka.

"My..." I sighed. "She's mine." I wasn't in the mood to talk about fucking feelings and sappy emotions at the end of such a grisly and violent night. But they would be the ones I'd trust with a conversation like this. Maybe I needed them to put me on the spot like this to force me to admit what I was feeling about this woman I hadn't planned to keep here for long at all. "That's all you need to know. She's mine."

I lifted my glass and glanced up at them. All four of them stared back at me, nonplussed. Emil's smirk of amusement peeved me. "What?"

"She's yours?" he replied. "No shit. You're fucking crazy about her."

I wouldn't necessarily use that wording, but he had a point. The way she made me feel just before I came apart inside her was an out-of-the-world experience.

"Would it be so bad if I allowed her to be mine?" I asked. In my head, I intended that to be a rhetorical question, but as I let the words leave my lips, I wanted their opinions. "Would it be such a trouble if I let her stay?"

Allen raised his brows. "I wasn't aware that she had to have an expiration date."

"She doesn't," I said. But I had taken her on the premise that she'd be the product of a transaction. An asset I could unload for the best profit.

"I don't think it would be the end of the world if you committed to her." Alexsei shrugged, glancing at his phone where the camera feed showed the room of his son, Misha, back at his house. Even when he was out on a mission with us, he'd have a link to watching over his child. "I mean, if you proposed and—"

"No." I barked a laugh. "What the fuck are you saying? Propose? No. No fucking way. I'm not *marrying* her."

A housekeeper kept her head down as she collected the empty glasses to take out.

"I'm not fucking marrying Gabriella. Ever." I slashed my hand through the air to make that a fact. "She's just here for fun. For now. That's it."

"Why?" Alexsei set his phone down and sighed as he faced me. "Why can't you marry her? We can't all be bachelors forever."

I rolled my eyes. "I'm a widower." Although, as I said that, it felt untrue. Maria had died so many years ago. "Or I was."

No one had to remind anyone that Alexsei was the more recent widower. His loss was too tender to bring up.

"Besides," Emil said, swatting his hand at Ivan's upper arm. "He's still so lovesick about his fiancée that he'll never marry anyone else."

Ivan scowled, cutting my son a stern glower. "Shut the fuck up."

"It's true," Emil insisted of Ivan's former lover he'd left suddenly and never gotten over.

"Hey, maybe you could try again to find her," Alexsei suggested, "then marry her when you're older."

Emil laughed as he stood, then stretched, showing similar signs of a hard fight like I had when I walked into Gabriella's studio. "Older? Don't wait too long and be old like this one." He set his hands on my shoulders and squeezed lightly, teasing me.

"Joke all you want," I replied coolly, letting a smile lift my lips. "Gabriella seems to appreciate how much older I am. She has never complained about how knowledgeable I am to pleasure her."

Emil rolled his eyes and bade us goodnight as he left on that note.

Once the others left as well, I finished my drink and returned to my bedroom. To my bed.

To my... woman.

For now.

24

GABRIELLA

When my period didn't come a week after I expected it, it put a twist on the concept of my life being completely changed.

I can't be...

Pacing in the bathroom, I tried to dispel the growing worry that the pregnancy test I had yet to take would damn me to another new identity.

It was one thing to forget about my past, to leave behind those days of wishing I could further my lessons in dance and not have to put up with my dad. Or not knowing anyone influential to help me change my life. Or not wondering when money wouldn't be so tight and I wouldn't go hungry.

But to think ahead and envision being the mother of a baby I'd share with a Mafia boss like Luka? That terrified me.

It was just too big of a change to accept.

I can't be.

Life couldn't be that wicked, that cruel.

I just couldn't be pregnant. As if willing it not to be true,

I delayed taking the test and paced. And paced some more, like more movement would keep the likely truth and reality further away.

Physically and biologically, yes, I had high chances of this happening. Luka hadn't once used protection of any kind with me. No protection at all. With that wild card, it was as though we were playing with the unknown.

Slumping to lean against the edge of the vanity, I stared down at the test kit again. Willing myself to just take it already wasn't helping. The need to know burned inside me, but the fear of what could happen afterward intimidated me. My chest hadn't been this tight with anxiety since that day Alexsei and Emil showed up to kidnap me for Luka, snatching me right out of the crummy apartment I'd shared with Dad.

Just take it.

Knowing would help.

It was the unknown that loomed so hugely and scarily.

I blinked, watching my trembling fingers as I opened the box slowly.

Yes, I was *that* nervous. No, scratch that, I was petrified.

But what did you expect? Huh?

To just fuck all the time and magically never have this happen?

Luka had his cum in me all the time. Constantly. At the rate that we couldn't keep our hands off each other, it was almost like we were testing fate to see when, not if, I would become pregnant with his baby.

I set the box on the vanity and drew in a long, shaky breath to steady myself.

Clearly, he can't be opposed to having a baby. If he didn't want one, then he would've insisted on protection.

Right?

I swallowed hard as another, even worse, idea hit me.

Or...

I moved toward the toilet to take the test, determined not to consider the alternative. Once the test was done and I'd washed my hands, I lifted my head to stare at my reflection in the mirror.

Or... I grimaced, putting my hand on my stomach that had been off lately with most mornings presenting nausea.

Or he could just not care and plan to make me get rid of it.

Tears burned at my closed lids as I fought the idea of losing a child. To give up a baby, a new life.

I'd lost my mother far too young. My dad was never a parent to me. He'd given me away so easily, proving how little I'd ever mattered to him.

A family was one thing I never thought I'd have. A *real* family. It had been so deeply entrenched in my soul that I'd always be alone and never have anyone to count on.

That's not true.

I have Luka.

He'd killed to save me. He'd spent so much time and money to provide for me and show me the wonderful world of intimacy.

If I didn't dwell on it and think too hard about it, these Dubinin men were becoming something like a family. One I'd found, rather than been born into. But if I were to actually have a baby and grow my own little family here with them...

Oh, God.

Dread claimed me again. I had to know. I glanced at the timer I'd set and resolved to wait the full time for the test, to ensure it could be as accurate as possible.

"One more minute," I whispered to myself, as if hearing my voice would steady my nerves.

I had to know. Then I'd react. Whatever the results were, I'd survive. That was what I was best at.

While it was becoming easier to adjust and see Luka—and even the others like Emil, Ivan, and Alexsei—as family, that was it. Allen, too, I supposed. He was all right. But past that group of men, the rest of their organization consisted of a bunch of strangers to me. Nameless yet there, always in the background and never for me to deal with personally.

Especially them.

Narrowing my eyes at my reflection in the mirror, I listened to the telltale sound of one of the maids moving throughout the hallway. Luka was the boss of a huge organization, and that included a hefty house staff here at his house.

I realized within my first month of being here that they'd never welcome me.

The maids. All the housekeepers. Even a couple of the cooks. They'd made it clear that I wasn't a distinguished guest. With slight smirks and side-eyes, they'd given me the impression that I was a nuisance here, unwanted and rejected no matter how much I'd practically moved into Luka's bed and stayed in his room with him.

I wasn't eager to explore why they had such antagonism to me. From the gossip I overheard, when they assumed I wasn't near to hear anything, they counted on my being gone soon. That I was just a pastime, a temporary fuck toy for Luka before he'd tire of me and get bored until he got rid of me.

They'd talk without a care when Luka and the others weren't in the house. I heard it all, filing it away to better know who my enemies were and what I'd need to look out for. It hadn't seemed to matter when Luka spent more time with me here. Near him, they'd be obedient. With him around, they wouldn't dare to talk shit about me.

Like that, they were proving to be catty, mean girls. Jealous, perhaps, that Luka wouldn't pay attention to them.

For the first couple of months of sleeping with Luka, I hadn't thought much about it. I dismissed it, secure in Luka's desire. I felt safe with even Emil's tentative approval. Ivan and Alexsei seemed to assume I was here to stay for now, and I could fit in.

But the house staff were something else. They'd never be my family. I still didn't have a friend here. And I could've used one with this panic that I could be pregnant. Instead of being able to ask one of the maids for a pregnancy test, I had to spend a couple of days hunting down a test kit in the guest bathrooms.

They had to be suspicious of even that. I knew they'd noticed me snooping.

So what? Fuck them. Find out what's going on in your life and ignore them.

Pushing out a deep exhale, I straightened and reached for the test. The time was up. I held my breath as I turned the plastic stick over and saw that my life was definitely going to be different.

Pregnant.

I set my hand on the back of my neck and fought through the instant adrenaline rush.

Calm down.

It'll be okay.

You'll figure this out.

I staggered down to the floor, sliding against the wall of the vanity counter. Seated as my heart raced, I dropped the test and hugged my knees. Tucking my head against my folded arms wouldn't hide the reality from me.

And I should've suspected sooner.

Last month, I spotted, and I assumed that was my period, out of whack from the stress of being here and how I'd nearly been gunned down at my audition.

Then this month, I was waiting for my period to show. As an athletic dancer, it wasn't uncommon for me to skip a month here or there.

Luka knew when I'd spotted. But he hadn't followed up to ask anything lately.

He has to know.

Or assume.

Or, fuck, I don't know. Maybe he's too busy to realize I could be skipping my periods. It hadn't come to the point that he wanted sex and I had to explain that I wasn't able to.

I'm pregnant.

I sat there, zoning out as that line of truth replayed in my mind like a mantra. It was just so shocking, so surreal, that I struggled to accept it. With time, though, as I steadied my breath and tried to calm down, I knew that panicking wouldn't be wise.

I have to hide it.

Telling Luka felt like too much of a risk. It would be an enormous risk when I had no clue of what he saw happening with me in the long term. As the plan to hide this pregnancy formed in my mind, I battled the self-loathing and annoyance that I could've been this careless too. I was a virgin when I'd arrived, and I was obviously less experienced than Luka. But I could've asked about a condom, too. It was stupid of me to be so hung up on him that I neglected that all-important detail too.

Hide it. Wait and see if you can bring this up to Luka and go from there. It felt so clinical, like it was a mission, rather than the discovery of a new life to celebrate.

Just get up. Wait and see. And survive. You can do this.

I'd even do it alone if I had to.

Once I wrapped the test in paper and shoved it way down in the trash can to cover it up so the nosy house-keepers wouldn't see it, I left the bathroom.

Two women in maid uniforms looked up when I entered the hallway. It seemed that I'd caught them mid-gossip. In this context, though, I couldn't spare them a worry. My head was jumbled with this revelation that I'd be a mother.

That I'd bring a baby into this world.

Into this building, locked up and secure because the men who ruled here were ruthless killers and powerful leaders of crime.

Over the next couple of days, I tried my best not to show how severely this secret was eating away at me. Luka was busy, fortunately, and he didn't seem to notice how quiet I was. I tried not to act any differently, but inside, I wasn't the same. Instead of just dancing and looking forward to spending time with him, I was doing calculations of how far along I was and if I could ensure a healthy life for this child.

I spent time fantasizing the best- and worst-case scenarios of where I could live, how I'd raise this baby.

With Luka?

Or would he kick me out?

I refused to even consider the idea that he'd make me terminate the pregnancy. I'd run before he'd see to that.

Maybe he wouldn't mind. After all, he does have a son. He loves Emil.

What didn't help was the increase of gossip I overheard from the house staff. When they were near the serving quarters, in the kitchen they used, they didn't hold back on any juicy Mafia secrets. Most of what they said didn't matter to me. It was all irrelevant rumors about people I didn't know. But when they talked about other crime families and how they stuck with the principle that sons were worth more than daughters, I had to cringe.

I was horrified how these people would talk so freely of how the criminal families worked and were structured.

I didn't want my son to be a pawn or a token of leverage, expected to grow up as a killer.

I didn't want my daughter to be raised with the expectation that she'd be sold or traded, worthy only as a virgin before being bred to have babies and heirs.

Late in the evening, when Luka was still gone with work, I did my best to stifle the tears that threatened to leak. Sitting in my room, hugging a pillow to my stomach as I watched the rain fall outside, I thought back to all I'd overheard. I ruminated on how I could figure out *my* future.

I can't stay.

I couldn't bear to risk the slight possibility of Luka welcoming a child with me, only to use him or her.

I have to get out of here before he can find out.

He couldn't know. I had to escape once and for all, no matter how much I was coming to lo—

Stop it.

Shaking my head, I squeezed my eyes shut tighter. That couldn't be it. I dismissed this stupid idea that I could *love* this Mafia boss who'd taken me.

He wouldn't love me.

The longer I waited for him to come home from another lengthy night of him delivering violence and justice as he saw fit, I knew that much.

He didn't love me.

Lusted for me, yes.

Desired me in his bed, of course.

But love wasn't a part of what we shared. Since the moment I arrived here, he'd emphasized that I was a *thing*, his thing. Here to be owned.

Not loved.

25

LUKA

The biggest sign that I was torn in two was the guilt that came to me when I was busy in the office. Those moments when I was out with the men and I'd think about Gabriella. It didn't matter what time of the day or night it was. She was creeping into my thoughts nonstop.

I wanted her.

I lusted for her.

And with how difficult it was to shut off this need to be near her, to feel her warm, silky skin rubbing against mine or her lips pressing with demand on mine, I was addicted to having her in my life.

Emil ceased to give me shit about it. He seemed smug in knowing I'd found "my match". Ivan didn't comment either. At times, I had to wonder if he was jealous of my finding a woman to possess and concentrate on like this. He'd had the sorriest story of us all, losing his former love, but there wasn't anything I could do to convince him to seek her out. He had already tried to find the woman he'd walked away from, but she was hiding too well for him to locate. Alexsei, too, reacted to how connected I was with Gabriella. He was the most welcoming of the men, already that quick to assume that she fit with us.

Yet, as time drew on and I became busier with the fucking Cartel and Italians, both of those enemies never content to allow any semblance of peace, I hated how my duties kept me from spending time with Gabriella.

While I always made sure to end up in bed with her after even the longest days and nights, it didn't feel like a boring routine. It wasn't the same old because every kiss and every touch was better than the last. It was a consistent exploration of learning about her, and I never wanted it to stop.

Being this attuned to her also gave me an immediate heads up when something seemed off.

She was distant. It started with slight signs of her pulling away. At first, I chalked it up to her being grumpy that I was so busy lately, always away and doing the leadership tasks expected of me as the *Pakhan* of the family. She was still with me, still in bed with me, still eager to take my dick. I hadn't scared her off, but the suspicion that something was wrong lurked beneath the surface. It was enough to caution me that I would do better to balance my time with the family and with her. Those seemed exclusive and apart, but I wondered how different things would be—for the better— if I simply made her part of the family.

Like my son and nephews had hinted, it wouldn't be the end of the world if I took her for a wife. If I made it official that she was *mine*, publicly.

Besides, it was already a given that she was. Otherwise, those Cartel fuckers wouldn't have targeted her at her audition. She was viewed as mine. She did fall under the blanket of Dubinin protection.

Waking up with her this morning, I was annoyed to find her sleeping on the edge of the bed. She *was* pulling away. But that didn't mean I had to throw her a bone and offer her more commitment. I took. That wouldn't change. I was the boss. I would always be in charge. She didn't dictate the terms between us, but as I urged her to roll toward me, I marveled at how I wanted her to be happy with me like this.

"How about I take you out for lunch?" I asked between kisses I placed on her bare shoulder.

She smiled, slowly and lazily. "Lunch? Isn't it still morning?"

"Brunch, then." I tugged her out of bed with me, determined that taking her on a little outing would smooth out any issues that might have been the cause for this distance between us.

Instead of staying close to the mansion, I had the driver bring us to one of the properties the family owned near the water. Coastal land was significant in our portfolio for many reasons, namely the ease of transportation for goods. This resort was a newer acquisition, though, a ritzy, five-star destination where celebrities and politicians rubbed elbows and tried to avoid the public's eye.

After we ate, I led her to the balcony of the penthouse suite. Even though the sky was still stormy, it wasn't raining yet and we could admire the view of the ocean and the city not far from this area.

"I'm surprised you don't need to hurry back to the office," she admitted softly as she stood at the railing. With her hands on the ledge, her legs crossed at the ankles, she presented herself as at ease and relaxed. We'd talked throughout our brunch and she hadn't seemed as standoffish or distant. Now, she seemed open to caving to me and welcoming my company again.

Fuck, maybe it's all in my head and nothing is wrong.

Women can be like that. Hormones and all. Whatever.

I approached her from behind, pressing my chest against her back. She reacted with a sigh as she leaned back toward me. Resting her head on my shoulder, she seemed to curl into my embrace. Starting with my hands on top of hers, I caressed up her arms, then traced my fingers down her breasts until I could hug her snugly to me.

"No. No need to hurry to anything," I said.

"Hmm. So I've got you to myself today?" she asked, tilting her head to the side to give me better access so I could kiss up along her neck.

"For now," I admitted, focusing on tasting every inch of her. When she relaxed against me, I tugged the low scoop neckline of her shirt down lower. Those generous globes spilled out, barely contained by her bra.

Her lips lifted in a smile as she pushed her ass back to me. "For now?" she replied teasingly.

"Yeah, right now, I'm all yours." Kissing her as I unclasped her bra, I felt her slip her hand lower and back, aiming to stroke my erection through my pants. She was mine, too, a vixen I couldn't get enough of. Having her touch me like this was proof she'd still cave to me. No matter her moods or whatever she was working out in her mind, she wasn't giving up on this connection we'd forged.

"I won't apologize for being busy," I warned her gruffly as I played with her nipples, baring her to the world as we stood so high up on this private balcony where no one would see her directly. "I am the boss, and duties will always call me."

"I know," she admitted.

I bunched up her skirt to tug her panties off. She caught

on quickly, shimmying to help me get them off before she reached back to unzip me.

"And I won't ever apologize for how badly I need you," I added before lining my dick up to her sweet pussy so slick with her arousal.

"Oh, fuck. Don't. Don't ever stop," she got out between panted breaths.

Lowering my hands, I moved them to hers. I instructed her to hold on to the railing and lean forward so I could ram into her harder and faster like I wanted. She didn't protest. Instead, she rushed to slant to accommodate us both.

Gripping her hips as I fisted her skirt to keep the fabric out of the way, I stared at my glistening dick sliding in and out of her. Over and over again, I stuffed her with my cock, then withdrew to see the evidence of how much she wanted me. How much I needed her.

"I don't think I can stop," I replied belatedly. Not now. Not ever. She was burrowing under my skin and tricking me to confuse this relentless physical desire with love.

"Oh, Luka. Luka!" She lifted her ass, thrusting it out at me as she neared her orgasm. Already, she was so close, a puppet under my mastery. I owned her, body and soul, and as I leaned over her to cup her bouncing and swaying tits to pull at her nipples, I wondered how bad it would be if I admitted to myself that I wouldn't mind owning her heart too.

If she'd give it to me.

She'd submitted to me. Here and now, she was caving to me on this balcony as I fucked her senseless. I was aware of how seldom she fought with me now, adjusting to living with me, but I wouldn't be deluded to think she couldn't be stubborn again.

After a couple more hard thrusts, she gave me her

release. Coming so hard that she cried out and slumped forward to drape over the railing more, she proved how helpless she was to withstand my dick stretching her and stuffing her. Feeling her inner walls clench around me and glove me so tightly, I was helpless to hold out and wait.

I came, digging my fingers into the heavy weight of her breasts as I pulled her back to me. Not a single millimeter of space could be allowed between us.

It was impossible to count on any gap. Like this, we were one, two halves stitched together. Because I hadn't been looking for someone to love, it still struck me with a blinding punch of awe.

I loved her.

There was no use trying to deny it.

But as I closed my eyes and hugged her to me, catching my breath, I wondered if it would be the biggest mistake of my life to admit it to her.

I didn't only love.

I destroyed.

One came with the other, and I wasn't sure I wanted to risk bringing any more danger to her. Because loving me required the potential sacrifice of so much more than merely taking my cock.

26

GABRIELLA

L uka was right.

As I rode the thrill and exhilarating elation of coming so hard, I knew he had a solid and valid point.

Right now, he was mine. I had exclusive rights to enjoy his attention, and boy, did he give it to me. He didn't hold back in pleasuring me, already so wise in how to use his body to fit with mine so we'd both shatter from intense orgasms.

However, in the back of my mind, I knew how wrong he was too.

We could enjoy this moment. Living in the present had always seemed like such a stupid, illogical line of advice. With him, I tried to. Focusing only on how good he felt rutting me like this, high up on a balcony in the open air before a storm would crash down on us, I felt like I was the star in an epic adventure, at the top of the world. Physically, he could commandeer my thoughts until they ceased to bother me. He could distract me like this.

Yet, as he withdrew then cleaned me up, wiping me gently, I had to return to earth.

The present was fine.

But it was the future that consumed my worries.

I had Luka right now, here, as a sexy, sinful lover.

What would he be tomorrow? What would he be in approximately six and a half more months when I'd probably be ready to have this baby?

Would he be with me, excited to be a father again?

Would he order me to get rid of him or her?

Or would I be gone, too scared to trust his reaction or the chance of raising this innocent new life in the grip and context of all that came with a violent criminal family?

Hanging my head as I pulled my bra and shirt back up and together, I wrestled with the need to come clean and just tell him. To be brave and simply confess.

Luka, I'm pregnant. I'm not giving this baby up.

Take it or leave it.

Rehearsing those bold lines in my head threatened a panic attack.

Hey, Luka? What would you think about my being a mother? I'll handle it all and go.

Thinking along that path didn't make me feel any better. For one, I doubted he'd just release me. He'd made it crystal clear that I was his until he saw no worth left in me. Secondly, I didn't *want* to leave him. I wanted to stay and bask in the comfort and security he offered me. I only wished to know if I could have him but not dread my child being shipped away to be a soldier or a token in a trade.

"Come in before it rains," he said, reaching for my hand. "Unless you'd rather shower out here with the storm."

I smiled slightly at his sarcasm, following him inside so we could shower together. He never failed to care for me and comfort me in a warm, steamy stall until we'd both be tempted to start round two of more intimacy.

Before I fully entered the penthouse, this extravagant and expensive floor I never could've imagined setting foot in with my previous life as a nobody, his phone rang.

He sighed, perhaps daunted by how he'd be in demand already. No breaks for the boss.

Without letting go of my hand, he extracted his phone from his pocket and answered. "Yes?"

I couldn't hear the other line, but whoever the caller was, they spoke loudly and with urgency. It was an urgency that transferred to Luka. I felt the tension in him right away. His fingers tightened on mine. His knuckles turned whiter as he gripped his phone and held it close to his ear. Those dark eyes narrowed. Anger lit the glitter of power in his gaze, but it wasn't a fury directed at me.

"We're leaving now," he growled after a few more seconds of listening to the caller.

Something was up.

Or something was going down.

I didn't know and I didn't want to, preferring to mind my own business as I lived in the world of these criminals.

"Yes," he said into the phone before disconnecting in a hurry. Staring at me as he led me toward the front door, he explained what I could already guess. "We need to go. Now."

I nodded, but I doubted he even registered my agreement. He had already turned to face forward, practically dragging me out of the penthouse and racing toward the elevator. A pair of Dubinin soldiers were standing out there, always ready to protect the boss. They, too, must have heard the same urgent news in the comms units they wore in their ears. No confusion showed in their serious expressions as they flanked us toward the elevator.

"Go down in the freight," Luka said as the metal panels slid open. "Petyr said they're surrounding the building on the west side."

Both men seemed hesitant to leave the boss, but they nodded anyway.

"I'll meet you in the garage," he added. Still holding my hand, he used his other one to get his gun out. "We'll be able to move and evade them if we're not together."

His argument ended there, giving him the last word. The panels slid shut, and as he pushed the button to go down, he glanced at me.

"It will be okay."

I nodded, licking my lips and worrying whether this suspense and fear would be bad for the baby. I was doing my best to get used to the violence, but still, I felt like such an outsider, a foreigner to his world of danger and death, of fighting and guns. Anxiety was becoming too common, and as an expectant mother, I couldn't convince myself that everything *would* be okay.

This wasn't the kind of world I wanted my baby to be born into.

Always on the cusp of life-or-death concerns.

"I will protect you," he added. Even though his words to me were ones of compassion and protectiveness, I didn't miss the anger and tension that laced them. He was furious.

"Men are trespassing on our turf here, but we will get back home."

I nodded again, too numb and mute to offer him anything else. I'd follow his lead. He'd proven to keep me safe before, and I wanted to rely on his doing so again.

But wouldn't it be better to just be far away from all of this?

To raise this baby outside this cycle of never-ending violence?

Elevators weren't supposed to bend time, but this ride

was such an elongated blur that passed like an eternity of anxiousness and suspense. But then before I could be ready to acknowledge it, we were there. The car stopped at the lowest level, in the garage. Sliding slowly, the doors parted to let us out.

I held my breath.

I didn't let go of Luka's hand gripping mine securely. He blocked me with his body, shielding me as the panels opened.

And still, I remained tense, unsure if men would be waiting out there to ambush us, guns at the ready to fire at us both and kill us.

This was the risk of being with a killer like Luka.

I had all faith that he'd take every step to protect me. His men were trained that well. They were that strong and quick. But I was the only one who knew about the new life inside me. I was the only one who could know to protect this baby.

"Luka?" I tugged on his hand, suddenly too nervous to exit the elevator without him knowing, without anyone aware of what we'd created in this forbidden passion we'd found.

"Just stay with me, Gabriella." He glanced at me once, then focused on the garage coming into view as the elevator opened.

That's just it, though.

If I stuck with him and stayed in his orbit, I'd be that much closer to danger. Always. He'd never change who he was. But I was being changed, from a thing he could own to a protective mother.

We stepped out, with me following behind him. I wished more Dubinin men were waiting right here to give me the impression of safety in numbers, but they were over by the car. Those two guards were still at the other side of the building, per Luka's orders.

"Let's go," he told me as he dropped into a jog.

I ran with him, scanning the seemingly calm and empty garage. No one was here to stop us. It was just rows and rows of parked vehicles.

Once we rounded the line of the nearest lane of stationary cars and limos, two men approached. At first glance, they appeared like those thugs at my audition. Guns up. Faces scowling. Clothes tacky but clearly newly purchased. Bling had never impressed me, but it seemed these guys didn't follow that logic.

"Ah, and what do we have here?" one, a taller man with a severely receding hairline boasted. He sounded too jovial for someone aiming a gun at us. His smile was too fake, belying his true mood.

He cut us off with his buddy, raising his arms to let his gun twirl on his finger. It wasn't a combative pose. But it wasn't a move to suggest he was actually surrendering his intention to shoot or harm us.

I tucked back behind Luka as he stepped forward, blocking me again.

"Fuck off," he snarled, not lowering his gun.

"Hey, hey, now, Mr. Dubinin," the other, shorter man taunted with a smile that grew to match his buddy's. "We just came here to collect."

"Collect?" Luka scoffed. "What the fuck are you talking about?"

I tensed as they chuckled, glancing at each other.

"Come on. You know," one replied cockily.

"No. I don't. I don't have anything that could belong to you. Or are all of you Rivera dumbasses too slow to make sense?" Luka lifted his gun higher, ready to fire.

"Easy, man. Easy." The shorter one straightened his arm, aiming his gun back at us. "We're just here to collect her."

Me? My heart hammered against my ribcage at his words. It couldn't be true!

"She's mine," Luka growled. "I don't know or care why you're confused about that fact, but she's not going anywhere."

The balding man sneered. "That ain't how we were told to interpret it at the Rivera headquarters." He tilted his head to the side, narrowing his eyes. "According to Mr. Miguel Lopez, he's reconsidered his business with you and is willing to sell her to us."

I clutched the back of Luka's jacket. Fear filled me. Rage fired me up. Locked in shock, though, I couldn't even think straight.

"He didn't *sell* her to me. I took her. She was given," Luka argued. "She is *mine*."

"Well, it sounds like he's giving her to us," the short man replied with a shrug.

"She's not his to give," Luka bit out.

Every word they said sliced at my heart. I wasn't a thing. I wasn't a product or item to negotiate like this! Alarmed by the fact that they'd barter with my life like this, I resisted the urge to sink into complete hatred for the man I was supposed to call my dad.

He gave me to Luka, and that had been a godsend.

But now he wanted to sell me? Again?

"She is mine," Luka repeated. "I own her."

His statement was bold and true, but the meaning behind it chilled me.

I wasn't *someone* to him. I was *something*. Still, he would objectify me.

Scolding myself for ever trying to see him as a lover and

duping myself into believing we were really together despite the tumultuous way we'd met, I had to remember that he was a criminal. He was okay with owning lives. Taking them. He'd captured me, and it was only some sick sense of fate that we'd bonded like we had.

"She is mine," Luka declared.

"Yeah," one mocked. "For now. But the terms have changed. We're here to take her and that bastard in her belly."

Oh, my God!

He'd announced my secret.

These Italian Mafia men knew I was pregnant!

Luka opened his mouth to reply, but right then, his car pulled up, intercepting us.

Ivan exited the backseat, opening the door and urging us to get in.

Another Dubinin got in and began firing at the Rivera men who ran away, darting behind parked cars.

I was desperate to know Luka's reaction to what that man said, but right now—living in the damn present—I concentrated on following him into the backseat of his car and taking his offer of safety and security, no matter how short-lived it might turn out to be.

27

LUKA

id he just say what I thought he said?

Is she really—

Gabriella settled against me as the car sped off. She scrambled to sit upright, clutching at the armrest. Rocked by the shocking bombshell of what that Rivera asshole said, I was too slow to react and assist her. To help her.

Is that true?

Is she carrying my child?

How the fuck—

I didn't have the time to ask her. With those Rivera thugs trespassing on my turf, I had to handle the issues of an enemy too close for comfort. My phone rang. Of course, it did. I was always on. Instead of demanding an answer from Gabriella about what that man said, I answered Emil's call.

"They started trouble at the back of the resort," he said, reporting in like I trusted him to always do.

Everyone in my organization was held to the same expectation to be quick to share intel.

They were held to the standards of honesty, too.

Something I had a nasty and sinking suspicion Gabriella
hadn't thought to consider.

She's been lying?

All this time?

How long?

With half of my attention on what my son reported, I
tried not to get sucked in and carried away by the tidal wave
of confusion. Thinking back to when I'd first slept with
Gabriella, then when she'd seemed to have her menstrual
time, something I would only know because she'd tell me
before we fucked, I realized she hadn't had her period.
Maybe that one time, which hadn't lasted long, now that I
thought back to it.

When I was married to Maria, she'd been so eager to
start a family with me. We'd tracked her ovulation and
cycles to better ensure the beginning of having kids. That
was how she'd given me Emil so quickly. I'd knocked her up
on the first try. We'd been expecting a daughter when she
was killed.

But with Gabriella and how I hadn't focused on
anything long-term with her, it hadn't even crossed my
mind. All I'd homed in on was teaching her how to please
me and how she could take her own bliss from my touch. I
hadn't slowed down to consider protection since she was a
virgin and wouldn't have any diseases to give me. I hadn't
paused to consider not knocking her up because I'd been so
impatient to have her after taking a gradual approach to
getting her submission.

All while Emil talked, filling me in on the latest trouble
the Riveras planned at that location, I steamed and stewed
over this revelation.

She's fucking pregnant?

And didn't think to mention it to me?

Rage and fury built and mixed within me on the drive. Once we arrived, I was too shocked and disappointed to face her.

I got out, waiting for her to exit. Giving her only a stern glower, I directed her inside with a point of my finger. "Go. Wait inside."

Still on the phone with Emil, who was back at that resort property handling the aftermath of the Rivera attack and ambush, I nodded and exhaled a long breath. "All right. We are back now and I'll speak with you when you get here."

Ivan strode toward me, face serious and eyes narrowed. "Is she all right?" He shook his head. "I was just updated about the ambush."

"She's fucking pregnant?" I roared.

He went still, staring at me like I'd spoken another language. "What? What the hell are you talking about?"

"She's pregnant."

"Are you asking or telling me this?"

I huffed, stalking through the house with him at my side. "Oh, so it's news to you, too?"

"I have no clue what you're talking about." He didn't miss a beat, matching my stride and not slowing until my office door was in view at the end of the hall. "Allen!" Facing me as we entered my domain, he shook his head. "Uncle, what are you saying? Gabriella is pregnant?"

"It fucking seems that way." I paced, too worked up to sit still.

"With your child?" he asked as Allen appeared.

I narrowed my eyes. "Yes, with my child. For fuck's sake." She was a virgin when she came here, and she had no freedom to be anywhere without me. Of course, it would be my child.

"All I know is what was reported moments ago. Lopez is

stirring shit, trying to tell the Riveras that they can have her, which is ridiculous since she's here, with you and—" He ran his hand through his hair, furrowing his brow. "What—"

"The fuckers who came to try to take her said she was expecting. That they'd take her and her child. *My*—" I gritted my teeth, pacing once more and so furious at this sudden change of events that was throwing me off balance.

"*They* told you that she was pregnant?" His brows hiked high. "And you believed them?"

I shook my head. "It's not a matter of believing them. It's a matter of her never having her cycles. Of her—" I growled, pissed all over again that she'd kept this from me.

"Wait." Allen lifted his hand. "Did you ask her? Did she confirm?"

"No." I shook my head. "I haven't asked her." But it was all too telling how quiet she got and how she didn't rush to tell me that wasn't true. I hadn't given her the chance to speak up since I was focused on the phone the whole ride out of there, but as soon as I had everything under control, she'd be fucking answering me.

"How could they know?" Ivan asked, keeping a clear and level head despite the heightened senses and rush of this news. "If she hasn't told you or anyone here about her being pregnant, how the fuck would the Riveras know?"

Allen shook his head, just as confused.

"How would Miguel know?" Ivan asked, more like he was postulating out loud instead of expecting a reply.

"She hasn't been in contact with him," Allen said. "She's never tried to contact him. Or anyone else." He would know. I put him in charge of surveillance in my stead. Nothing got past Allen in this household. But now, he arched one brow, lifting a finger to indicate that we should wait. "Let me go speak with the housekeeping staff."

I rolled my eyes. "I don't give a fuck about them being catty right now." They'd always given her a hard time. I was aware of it. So was Allen. All that had mattered to me about that was the way Gabriella ignored them and never let the jealous house staff's attitudes bother her.

"No, no." Allen shook his head, backing up to exit the office. "One of them was acting strange the other day. Secretive. It made me suspicious but not overly so. Now, though..."

I flicked my hand at him, dismissing him. "Go. Go bring her to me." If this maid had a clue about Gabriella's secret, I wanted to hear it now.

"She didn't give you any hints? Nothing?" Ivan seemed determined not to assume the worst of Gabriella for lying to me.

"Nothing," I growled.

"You have been away and busier than usual lately."

"But not so much that she couldn't fucking tell me if I'd knocked her up." She shared a bed with me every night. She could've had every chance to mention this detail.

Allen returned with the maid. At the first glance of the nervous, crying woman, I knew it.

It was all I had to see.

She was guilty. Scared. And probably regretting her mistake in this matter.

"Speak."

Allen pushed her until she fell to her knees. Sobbing and trembling, she lowered her head.

"I won't repeat myself," I growled.

I'd had it with liars and rats. Traitors would never belong in my sphere. If she thought tears would help her case, she was mistaken. My patience was running thin.

Ivan stepped up close and pressed the end of his gun to her temple. "Start talking *now*."

She vibrated, shaking like a leaf. Yet, she looked up at me and licked her trembling lower lip. "I wondered why your guest was seeming so ill in the mornings."

It was none of your fucking business.

You're here to serve my household, not wonder about fucking anything.

My expectation to count on my organization included those in my home.

"Then one day, I caught her snooping in some of the restroom closets to the other guest rooms."

I narrowed my eyes, suspicious that this was a lie. Gabriella never asked questions, never snooped or pried. She had a healthy respect for ignorance being bliss.

"When I checked back through the closets, I noticed that a case of pregnancy tests was messed with. I knew she'd taken one. I waited until after she seemed to have used it and found the test stick hidden in the trash."

Hidden.

That was the one word that stood out to me. Gabriella had tried to hide this from me. This maid did as well.

I had no patience for liars.

None.

"Go on," I ordered.

This confirmed that Gabriella was pregnant and that she'd hidden it from me. It proved this maid thought she could be deceptive about it as well, not reporting to her superior or even Allen about this if she couldn't face me directly.

But it didn't answer why Miguel or the Riveras would've been informed about this pregnancy.

"Then I..." She lowered her head again, crying. "I'm so sorry."

"Tell me!" I roared.

"Then I..." She sniffled, taking a few seconds to gather herself to keep talking. "Then I talked to one of my friends. Someone I know who works for the Rivera Family. I... I mentioned it to her, and they were interested. Mr. Lopez approached me when I walked home one night after my shift here. And he paid me for the pregnancy stick. He gave me extra for telling him that I wouldn't tell anyone else. I need..." More sobs broke her speech. "I just need the money to get out of debt and all. I just needed some money."

I didn't give a shit. What she wanted or felt like she needed wasn't my concern. The second she decided to turn against my interests, she was gone to me. She was nothing but a waste of space to get rid of.

Meeting Ivan's gaze over her head, I nodded once. He acknowledged me in kind, dipping his chin in reply.

She was dead. This maid would be replaced, killed for her sins. Not for keeping things from me, but for fucking selling a secret to the enemy that I had another heir on the way.

Allen and Ivan gestured for another guard to drag the woman out of my office. Defeated and knowing it was game over for her, she didn't scream and fight to get free. Crying silently, her face etched with lines as she sobbed, she let them remove her from my office.

"Leave me," I ordered. Ivan was a confidante. I could always rely on him. He was, almost like Emil, a good man to speak with about difficult or challenging issues. Right now, though, I didn't welcome his presence. Nor Allen's.

Furious with Gabriella's deception, I wanted to be alone to think this through. To walk myself through the steps of how I could accept this news and move on with it, adjusting to the fact that I'd be a father again.

It wasn't that surprising. We never used protection. It just hadn't come to mind.

Now, it was the big boulder weighing down on my conscience. Consumed with the reality that Emil would have a half-sibling, I tried to envision this future.

Gabriella, vulnerable and her stomach swollen with my child.

This baby, another asset and part of the family.

My child.

Rage wouldn't leave me, because each time I thought back to these recent moments of her pulling away from me, I damned her for trying to hide this from me.

She was *mine*, goddammit, and that meant all of her. All her secrets. All her troubles.

Her blessings too.

After a long while of thinking about how the woman I was coming to love could've done such a shitty thing as hiding her pregnancy from me, someone knocked on my door.

I glanced up in time to catch Emil and Ivan entering my office.

Word had to have spread by now. Ivan would've told Emil that he would no longer be my only child. But I wasn't in the mood to talk it out with him. Business matters still had to be dealt with first.

"I want you to figure out what the fuck Miguel Lopez is plotting by aligning with the Riveras." Those Italians would forever be a thorn in my side, but I required more intel before planning any retaliation. I had to know what the end game was here.

"Of course," Emil replied, nodding at me before turning to leave.

"Anything else you need at the moment?" Ivan asked, hesitant to go.

They'd likely just come to check in with me. I appreciated the support, but there wasn't anything else that could be done for me at the moment.

"I need to speak with her." I stood, letting all my anger simmer and fuel me to seek her out.

Only after I'd heard her explanation for why she'd fucking lied to me would I be closer to deciding how to handle this grievance.

In turn, it would most definitely push me further from falling into this idea of loving her.

28

GABRIELLA

Luka hadn't dismissed me like that since I'd gotten here. No matter what, he infiltrated my space and my mind until I had to cave. Until I would cave and give in to him and accept that he was my owner. My master. It later turned to accepting him as my lover.

Or so I thought.

Being sent to my room like that was a cruel punishment. The fact that he wanted to put distance between us was enough of a sign that he had heard that Rivera man. That he was clued in to the fact that I was pregnant.

And from the stern set of his jaw and the cold anger in his dark eyes, I could only believe he was furious.

Of course, he's mad.

He was surprised in the worst way imaginable.

I should have just come clean and told him!

These past few weeks of hiding my pregnancy had been hell. Now, it was all out of my hands. It was beyond my control how he might perceive the situation. With him busy elsewhere and not even slowing down to ask me about it, he'd made it clear that he didn't want to hear me out. He wasn't interested in what I could say to elaborate about the fact that I was expecting his child.

All I could do was pace.

Back and forth, I walked in my room like a caged animal. This feeling of being trapped and stuck wasn't anything new. I felt like this back when I first woke up here, lost and confused when this big brute of a Mafia boss came in here to tell me that he owned me because of my dad's problems.

All I could do now was vent this nervous energy.

Because that was all I could embrace. The anxiety. The unknowns. The threat of his anger being funneled toward me and no one else. Being the enemy of a Mafia boss was an incredibly stupid thing to let happen, but there was no erasing time now. I couldn't go back and clarify.

Nope. He expected me to stay in here and stew. To wait for him.

When he at last appeared, entering my room without so much as a knock, fear claimed me. My nervousness escalated to outright trepidation as he walked in, closed the door behind himself, and stared me down.

His hands were shoved into his pockets, but that seemingly relaxed and casual stance wasn't fooling me. That intense look warned that he was livid. The tension in the air between us proved he was still mad, here to expect answers that would probably not appease him in the end.

A fleeting conviction rolled through my mind that I was in the wrong. That it had been my fault to hide my pregnancy from him. But I wouldn't take back my actions. I wouldn't apologize for acting out of fear and dealing with this the best I could.

He wasn't some standard, upfront kind of guy. He wasn't an ideal book boyfriend of a fictional hero I could lean on.

Luka Dubinin was a cruel, hardened, lethal Mafia boss.

But he was also the father of my child.

And that had to be what he'd come here to talk about with me. Not that fact that my dad was trying to figure out a new, illegitimate deal that would allow the Rivera Mafia to have me, but the fact that I was pregnant.

"Explain yourself." He lifted his chin, glowering at me.

Just like that, sensing the height of his anger, my stubborn streak lit me up and took over. I crossed my arms. "Explain what?" I replied. Before he could show me more of how mad he was, I continued. "Why my dad would try to sell me to someone else? I have no fucking clue. He's a pathetic piece of shit who's only looking out for himself."

"The other part," he growled. "Explain why you thought it would be a smart choice to hide your pregnancy from me."

Well, that settled that. It wasn't a matter of him trying to figure out *if* I really was pregnant. He knew. One way or another, he did know now.

"Because."

He stepped forward as he pulled one hand out of his pocket. Pairing his menacing and thunderous expression with the lift of his arm, as though he wanted to grab me, he shook his head and muttered curses that sounded like Russian gibberish that I couldn't decipher.

"Try again," he warned in a serious growl.

"Because," I repeated, digging in to stand my ground despite how scared I was. My child would never have a weakling for a mother. I *would* survive this storm. "Because I figured you'd confront me just like this. Because I worried that you'd go berserk about this news, one way or another." Tightening my arms around me, I tried to use my defensive stance as a shield to hide behind before he'd lose his temper.

"I wouldn't be confronting you about this at all if you'd just told the fucking truth to begin with."

"You never asked me if I was pregnant," I retorted, regretting it the second I spoke. It sounded so childish, so stupid.

"You've lied by omission," he yelled. "You have been dishonest to hide such a huge thing from me at all!"

"And I would do it all over again." Hiding this pregnancy was only something I could've tried to pull off for so long. Sooner or later, I'd start showing and it would be obvious. Until then, I'd hoped to determine if it would be safer to do this parenthood thing solo or with him.

With how mad he was, I had my answer.

He was *not* pleased about this news. In the back of my mind, I had to consider that he might just be furious about how I'd kept it a secret, not that he was mad about my having his child. Time would tell, but I wasn't backing down now.

He could be miffed about my hiding it, but couldn't he also respect that I was limited in power here? That I'd be afraid and act accordingly?

"You would lie to me again?"

"I would keep this information to myself until I could know whether I could trust you with it."

"Trust *me*?" He ground his teeth, glaring at me with a seething fury. "How can you claim that you can't trust me? After all I've fucking done for you. After—"

"After you kidnapped me?" I screamed back, letting my anger cover my fear. I wouldn't retreat like a docile whore. "You took me. Remember? I had no say, no power, no control in my life. And now that I will be bringing a new life into this world, I'll be damned if you can assume you'll just take him or her too!"

"Don't even suggest getting rid of—"

"I wouldn't!" At least he could appease my concerns about that.

"And get it out of your head that you'll have any authority over my child."

I growled, fisting my hands and hating him with every fiber of my being. He was wrong. He was so goddamn wrong. He could tell me that he owned me, but he would not own my baby.

"I do," I bit out once I felt like I could speak, not screech. "I do have every fucking right to this baby. You will not beat submission into me with this. I *will* be in charge of my life to the extent that I will raise this baby. Me. Not your army."

"I'd like to see you try." He chuckled darkly, shaking his head. "Go on. See how far you can run if you try to be a moron and escape."

His goading me like this was so uncalled for. It was cruel of him to taunt me at all. No matter what he said, I would not be intimidated to give up this fight. "I'll be damned if my baby is used."

Lifting my chin high, I let him see that while I wouldn't argue with him point by point and be so cocky as to say I could escape if I really wanted to, I wouldn't back down at all.

"I won't stand for my baby to be sold. Like all you criminals want to barter with *my* life." I stabbed my finger at my chest.

He shook his head, looking angrier yet. "There is no bartering. The discussion with the Riveras isn't even a real concern. Your father gave you to me as a payment for his debt. And it is nonnegotiable for anyone to even think about taking you or calling the shots."

"Is that supposed to make me feel better? To know that you don't plan to discard me yet?"

"I don't particularly care about how you feel after hiding this news from me," he growled.

I shrugged, wishing I could feel an ounce of the bravado and indifference I projected. "Regardless, my stance won't change. I will not allow my child to be sold or trained to be a robotic killer."

"Oh. You mean like my other child? My son?" He sneered. "Like Emil? He's a robot now?"

I wasn't in the mood to discuss Emil. I still hadn't forgiven him for his part in my kidnapping. I'd be giving birth to his half-sibling, and I wasn't sure how I wanted to think about that connection. How could I raise a child to be a decent and loving person who'd want to give back to the world when he had an assassin for a brother?

"I'm not discussing Emil with you. I'm not talking about anything but the fact that you need to drill it into your head that I won't let you have this baby to do with as you want. This is *my* child. This is *my* baby that I am carrying in my body. I have wished my whole life for a family, and the second I can look forward to really having one, I will not let you think that you can step in and determine exactly how it will go."

He opened his mouth to argue, but I kept going.

"I lost my mother when I was still so young. I despise the idiot I'm supposed to consider my father." Protectively placing my hand on my stomach, I sighed and caught my breath. "This baby is the only family I have. And I will protect him or her with all my heart."

Getting in my face, Luka loomed over me closer yet. "Oh?" He scowled, looking me up and down. "I advise you to think again."

"Nothing you say will change my mind," I replied with heat. My survivalist instinct burned too hot to cool it now.

"Wrong. *I'm* your family now."

I rolled my eyes, too mad to speak.

He gripped my chin, forcing me to make eye contact, though. It was a small mercy that gazing into his blazing eyes, so full of loathing, didn't make me wilt or cower.

"Because you and I are getting married."

29

LUKA

Her plump lower lip hung open as she gawked at me. "Married?"

Fuck, it wasn't supposed to be so hot to see her mad like this. She wasn't supposed to turn me on when she was furious and brave enough to fight back with that fire and sass that had never died out while she learned to submit to me.

"No. Not a chance in hell is *that* happening." She shook her head, tossing her long, brown waves over her shoulder. "Oh, hell *no*. You're not going to kidnap me, mess with my head, and then order us to get married."

Want to bet?

Staring her down, I grew curious about when her willingness to argue with me would fade. And what would happen next.

Now that I could realize how scared she had to have been to realize she was expecting my child, I wondered what she thought could follow.

Her naïve views of this world were so obvious. She would assume that all men turned into killers and machines to do what I ordered. And after how those Rivera men talked about her when they ambushed us at the resort's parking garage, I couldn't fault her for guessing that all women were traded and sold. Arranged marriages were very much a thing, but in the Dubinin Family, I never meddled in those matters.

After my marriage ended with Maria's death, I didn't even take the time to think about anyone's marriages. Then when Alexsei's wife died, it reinforced my belief that life-long commitments would always fail in the end. I had yet to witness a union that could stand the test of time for good.

It didn't seem like Gabriella had much inspiration to believe in it either, because of how her mother died and how poorly Miguel had treated her as her father.

As I endured the heat of her glares, waiting her out about this topic of a marriage, I picked apart her argument in my mind.

She truly didn't understand the blessing and rare privilege it would be to fall under my protection. She was so sheltered and not from my world that she lacked the comprehension of how many others would kill to be in her position. That to be the mother of my child, she had acquired the protection detail of a ruthless army.

She'd never have to fear someone raping her in her pathetic apartment. She wouldn't have to be nervous about anyone successfully reaching her and shooting her.

My men would prevent that from happening.

I would stop that from occurring.

Protecting her was ingrained in my psyche now, and that would fall onto our child as well.

"I'm not marrying you," she repeated, not softening at all. "I don't need to feel *more* trapped and stuck here."

"It's funny that I haven't heard you complain much yet."

She glowered at me, sharpening the fierce anger in her eyes. As if she could bore me with the wrath of her laser-like stare.

"I hated to be trapped and stuck. I can't stand the worry that as long as I'm here, I have no choice in anything. You've kept me here without a break. And I've overheard enough of the horrors that happen outside these walls to convince me that there will never be any peace if I stay."

I shook my head slightly. I heard her, but it wasn't enough to convince me to think otherwise. I wouldn't budge. Maybe pushing the idea of marrying her was a rash and impulsive concept that could wait. Letting her stay as my mistress didn't quite cut it.

"You will have no say in this. No possible means to change my mind." I would lock down on this, on her, regardless of what she said. "And from this moment forward, I forbid you from even thinking about leaving."

"Just because you knocked me up?" she exclaimed. "I don't need you to help raise this baby. You've got Emil. You've got your army. Just let me have this child and enjoy having a real family for the first time in my life."

"No." *Fuck no.* "You will stay here. I will have Allen arrange for an appointment with a doctor to begin the checkups now."

Leaving her with that final, last word, I turned and exited her room.

Distance felt both right and wrong where she was concerned. It was hot to see her so furious and mad. She had never looked so alive and full of fight like that.

But I needed a step back. Again. With her keeping my life interesting and never the same, I had to temper my fight, too. If I used too much of a control on her, I just knew her spirit would diminish because I was in charge and I was the

Alpha. I didn't want to crush her soul. I didn't want to make her not fight back.

In the light of this pregnancy news, though, space was needed. We both would benefit from taking a breather.

I had to come to terms—on my own—about how I'd feel about being a father again.

She had to adjust to the reality that she would not be allowed to leave.

The first few days were the hardest.

She stuck to her room or the dance studio, and I steered clear.

The first couple of weeks were difficult.

I avoided initiating any contact with her, determined to wait her out and make her come crawling back to me. It was much like the beginning, when I gave her space until she gradually warmed up to me and couldn't deny how much she wanted me in the end.

After the first month had passed, I wondered if this was the proverbial hill she'd choose to die on. Her submission seemed like a thing of the past.

"Maybe you're giving her too much space?" Alexsei asked one night when I had dinner with him and Misha at their house.

I shook my head, rejecting that possibility. Pushing Gabriella to want to be near me again would do more harm than good. This was merely how to handle a headstrong and defiant woman. The wait would make her submission all the more sweeter.

"No, I'm not giving her too much space."

Alexsei sighed, shrugging as he offered Misha another serving of the chicken he loved so much. Chicken nuggets, that was. I recalled when Emil was a fearless five-year-old testing his independence to insist on only eating one or two.

"How is she handling the pregnancy?" he asked.

I wasn't giving her so much space that I was slacking in her care. Providing her with qualified and top-notch medical care, I was informed weekly of her vitals and how she was progressing.

"She's got to be what, five months now?" He raised his brows.

Even though everyone was aware of the rift between me and Gabriella, they were interested and concerned about her anyway. A new heir to the Dubinin name was something to rejoice. Yet, her stubbornness about not trusting the Mafia lifestyle kept it complicated.

You will submit to me, Gabriella.

I needed her too. These past couple of months without her present and in my bed felt long and hard. Missing her wasn't something I wanted to prolong. Allen claimed that I was acting more stubborn than she was, and I ignored him for a day. Emil seemed to be on her side as well, telling me this morning that maybe I was being too hard of an asshole with her, not bending on how she wasn't used to the family structure we operated with.

"The baby is healthy. So is she." That was the most clinical, emotionless way I could sum it up.

"Is she still dancing?"

I sighed, hating that I'd reverted to the old habit of watching her in the surveillance feed. Instead of approaching the studio and watching her in person like I'd enjoyed previously, I was reduced to watching her from afar. In that way, I wasn't actually avoiding her. I was still keeping an eye on her and involved as a spectator. It wasn't the same, but it was better than driving myself insane wanting to be with her like we were before.

"Yes. For now, she is." It was only a matter of time before

her belly would be too big for her to pull off most of her moves. She was nearing the end of her second semester, six months along, not five like Alexsei had guessed.

Viewing her on the surveillance feed from the dance studio was a paltry replacement for seeing her in person. But the remote view I had of her showed me how gorgeous she was with her belly swelling. It put another factor to how artistic she was as she danced and moved through the air. Art, but with the addition of the signs of pending mother-hood on her figure to give her more of a glow.

When she reached her seventh month, this cold treat-ment between us gnawed at me. I couldn't take it, but I was just as stubborn, giving her distance until she'd cave and come to me.

Thanks to Emil's interference one night, when he tricked us into being in the dining room at the same time, the impasse was over.

She furrowed her brow at the sight of me entering the room. Pausing in pulling out a chair to sit for dinner, she looked me up and down with derision.

I sighed, shooting my son a glare.

"And there you have it," Emil quipped sarcastically. He clapped his hands once and backed up. "I told Ivan I could pull it off. Enjoy dinner, you stubborn fools." As he exited, he tugged the double doors closed to keep me and her in here.

"Funny," she replied blandly.

"Hilarious," I stated.

"Did you put him up to that, getting me in the room to have to suffer your presence?"

I narrowed my eyes. "No. I wouldn't go to the bother," I lied.

Seeing her up close and actually speaking to her felt like

being born again. Like I was reliving the glorious thrill of her attention. Fuck, these past months were hard. I was desperate for her, but I was more desperate to hide how much I loved her.

"I see that the doctor has been updating you on the pregnancy." She rested her hands on her belly, clasping them so her arms bracketed her bump.

"Of course." I was in charge of everything in this house, in my world. She, and our child, were no exception.

"Which proves my point all along."

I arched one brow. "You have been too stubborn to enlighten me with your opinions or supposed points lately."

"Because you've demonstrated that what I want and my feelings don't matter."

What a spoiled, foolish woman. How could she not see that I gave her all this because I did care and because she mattered so much?

"This proves my point that you care only about this baby while not giving a damn about me."

That's not true. At all.

Yet, I couldn't be the first to cave. If this was the first fight we'd have as anything like a couple, I would not be the one to lose.

I didn't deny it. Instead, I flamed the fires of her hatred for me a little more. Maybe she needed to be angrier at me to snap and break at last. "Well, you have more worth now, giving me an heir."

She slitted her eyes, incensed as soon as I was finished speaking. Fury lit up her face, but with how tightly she clamped her lips together, she wasn't going to crack now.

I didn't mean a single word of what I'd said, but it was so much easier to fight with her than to give her the truth. The reality of this situation was that I was lost without her. I missed her and yearned for her. I was desperate to the marrow of my bones to be near her again, to kiss and hold and touch her once more.

But that was riskier to explain. Simply put, I didn't know how to love someone without destroying them. Maria had died because of her association with me and how I'd loosely trusted her to know how to defend herself as a born and raised Mafia woman, used to violence and threats. Emil had turned into a cold-hearted killer because he was my son and I'd encouraged him to work for the family.

No matter who it was, I would destroy them if I admitted affection and that I treasured them.

Feelings and sappy shit just didn't belong in my existence.

But when Gabriella shook her head before spinning on her heel to stride out of the room, I couldn't help but feel dejected. Despair claimed me as she walked away.

30

GABRIELLA

I left the dining room as fast as I could, too furious to see what was in front of me. Red-hot rage filled my vision.

"Whoa."

I collided with Emil. He caught me from falling, but once I was steady on my feet again, I pushed past him.

"Hey. Wait. What the fuck?" He hurried after me as I headed toward the studio.

It was the only place I could try to find some remnant of peace. Dance was still in my blood. It was still my passion. As this baby grew in my belly, though, the upcoming prospect of being a mother became a bigger passion and goal.

Just this morning, I gave up. I had to quit and call it a defeat. Being pregnant wasn't for the fainthearted. It wasn't for ballerinas, either. Between my swollen feet and the sciatic nerve pain that increased with lightning crotch as my belly got bigger and bigger, I just couldn't do it anymore.

I wasn't throwing the towel in forever. I couldn't. I would lose my mind if I never danced again. But for now, I was smart enough to know I was setting myself up for the risk of an injury to continue with my sport like this. The very last thing I ever wanted to do was harm this precious life inside me.

Although I couldn't dance in the studio where no one came to bother me, I could sit there and gaze out the windows at the cityscape below. Like a caged animal or a bird with clipped wings, I could look out at the freedom that would never be mine.

I wasn't stupid enough to try to run away. I wouldn't get free healthcare for my baby if I did. But deep down, I refused to budge from the conviction that this baby would *not* be a Mafia child.

"Hey!" Emil chased after me, following me all the way to the studio. "What the fuck, Gabby?"

He was the only one who had started to call me that on a routine basis. And I hated it. I figured that was precisely why he shortened my name like that, like a brother taunting a sister. But no, I was carrying *his* brother or sister even though I was younger than him.

"No." I whirled on him as I reached the studio. "That's what I should be asking you." I jabbed my finger at his chest. "What the fuck was *that* for, tricking us to get us in the same room?"

He rolled his eyes, unbothered by my attitude. "It's getting old, that's what the fuck it's about. We're sick of him acting like he's miserable missing you. We're all fed up with you acting like a quiet ticking bomb of wild pregnant woman hormones and emotions, like any little thing could make you lash out because *you* miss him." He flung his arms up. "You live together."

"No." I pointed at him. "I'm a guest. A thing. I'm trapped and locked up here."

He crossed his arms, smirking at me. "I don't see you suffering."

But I was. I was just good at masking it. It broke my heart a little more every day that Luka stayed away from me. Yes, we'd had an epic fight about my hiding the pregnancy. That was months ago, though. This baby would be here soon, and he hadn't done a single thing to alleviate my concerns.

"I'm not going to argue with you." I turned down the dial on my anger and gave him my back. Staring out at the cityscape didn't feel as soothing as I wished it would.

"Then don't," he replied coolly, coming to stand next to me, looking out the wall of windows. "But seriously, what the fuck, Gabby? You both were so good together, and now it's like you can't stand him."

I heaved in a deep breath. "I can't stand how he views me. He just told me that I have more worth since I gave him an heir."

"Well, that's true." He shrugged. "Another heir is an investment in the future of the family."

I hung my head briefly and groaned. "I'm having a *baby*, not a token of an investment." Before he could argue any further, I held my hand up, too numb to care about anything anymore. That didn't mean I'd give up with this fight, but I was just so tired of it all. My life was a huge mess, one that hadn't gotten messy from anything of my doing. Because I existed, because I was Miguel Lopez's daughter and he was stupid enough to be a traitor to Luka Dubinin, I was in this mess.

"I'm so sick of feeling trapped. I was used." And more than anything, I hated how I was starting to fully see that Luka had never cared about me. It was all lies.

"He didn't use you. For fuck's sake..." He shook his head. "My father was just saying that to piss you off. Trust me. It's his style. He respects how strong you are, how long it took for you to cave to him. He wanted to crack you for so long, and he admired your tenacity. If I know him, and I think I'm one of the few who can claim to really know him, he's goading you and saying shit like that to make you mad." He locked his bored and smug gaze on me. "To piss you off even more to make you snap."

"I'm not buying it."

"Hey, I'm just telling it like it is. I never thought I'd meet someone as stubborn as him, but here you are. He's determined to dig his feet in just as much as you are. He's keeping up this distance because he wants you to be the first to apologize. He's a proud man. A powerful leader. So don't assume he'll bow to *you*. Or anyone."

"No." I shook my head, sad that what he was saying couldn't be true. "You're wrong. He sees me as a possession to set aside while I carry his child. A person he's determined to view only as a thing to use."

"Like me?"

I stopped short, staring ahead.

"You realize that all your bullshit excuses about being scared—"

"I'm not making excuses! And if I did, they wouldn't be bullshit."

"Fine. Your stupid-as-fuck reasons to be scared about this situation." He scoffed. "You've got it all wrong. What, you're afraid that if you have a son, he'll turn into a killing machine like me?"

He had me there. I watched him, unafraid now. He was still on my shit list, but it wasn't like he could re-kidnap me for his father.

"You worry about having a boy because what, he'll turn

into a robotic monster? Like me? Every concern you have is basically an insult against me."

"So?" I shrugged one shoulder. "I don't like you."

"And I'm not nuts about putting up with you, either." He stepped into my view, blocking the cityscape as the nightlife kicked in down below. "But I see how much my father enjoys you in his life. For that matter, I'll tolerate you. That's how I can call your bluff about your worries. *I* am also Luka's son. I'm his heir. And look, I've turned out all right."

I gave him a droll stare. "That depends on who you're asking."

"Oh, get over it."

"Get over your kidnapping me?"

"Hey, you wouldn't have met my father if I hadn't. You wouldn't have this baby in you."

I refused to admit he had good points. But the end wasn't justifying the means in my book.

"I kill. I hunt down targets. No, I haven't been a fucking angel, but you know what else? I love my family. I fight for my family. In doing that, I *am* working for the greater good —just one that's not ordained and acceptable per the commoners in society."

I looked away before facing him again. I wasn't going to spend the night rethinking my opinions about good versus bad. I had opened my eyes—a lot—since being here.

"And if she's a daughter? She'll be sent to some man like a thing to possess?"

He shook his head. "If this is a baby girl, he'll be over the fucking moon to have a princess in his life. Like the sister I never met when my mother was killed." He sighed, frowning at me. "But you are supposed to be his queen. In case you can't get it through your thick skull, he wants *you* at his side again. Not as a thing, but as his partner."

"I'll believe it when I see it," I replied, giving up on this conversation to walk away.

Lingering to talk to him wasn't happening. He was poking and prying too close to the truth.

That maybe, just maybe, I had it all right.

That Luka might have room in his heart for me after all.

I'll be damned if I have to ask.

He can show me if I matter.

I refused to seek him out and be the one to grovel for even a single second.

31

LUKA

My moodiness worsened.

My patience was shot.

No matter what I tried, I couldn't sleep well anymore.

The longer Gabriella didn't come to me and apologize for hiding this pregnancy, the more strained things got in the house.

She was still there, always there, but more like a captive than the sensual lover I'd grown close to. I hated the reminders of how this resembled the beginning, when she first came here.

Yet, I wouldn't bend.

I would not be the first to break.

Caving to her would prove that she held the power over me. It would make me too soft, too weak.

Besides, her reluctance to bridge things between just proved that love really was a joke at this rate.

No woman could be that damn stubborn. The only alternative was that she was a fake. That she'd never cared for me like she'd suggested. She couldn't hold out this long to resist me if I had gotten under her skin like she had mine.

Most days, I felt like my flesh was too tight, like I couldn't breathe right.

Other times, I experienced this rabid delusional streak where the craziest fantasies taunted me to just go after her already and show her that her temper wasn't okay.

Love was such a fucking joke.

It was cruel and senseless.

The only thing that made sense anymore was my work.

Only knowledgeable on how to kill, to own, and to demand, I excelled in those darker ideals.

But the more I focused only on the family, I fell right back into the same old.

Now, that feeling of the same old shit consisted of the constant ache of missing her and needing her.

One night as I watched the surveillance in my office, Ivan entered, papers in his hand.

Even though Gabriella and I were at odds, with her pregnant, I'd only worked from my home office now, to be near her. Just in case.

"What is that?" We both asked the same question of each other at the same time.

He pointed at the computer monitor and I gestured at the papers in his hand.

"Oh." He raised his brows at the vision of Gabriella on the screen. "Still watching her from afar, huh?"

I sighed, taking the papers he offered me. "I can't help it."

"You know, it's not often that I agree with Emil, but he's right. You and Gabriella just need to get over yourselves and go back to the way you were."

Rolling my eyes, I ignored his unsolicited advice. I

wouldn't go backward with her. There should only be movement to the forefront. Progress. Change. Not returning to the illusion of what worked before.

"What do you have here?" I asked as I flipped through the pages. "Oh." I didn't need him to explain. These documents provided the transcripts of what our spies were able to get from the men who'd been close enough to Miguel to catch some of his plans.

It seemed that he hadn't learned his lesson at all. He was still at it, two-timing whoever he could. While he was no longer an affiliate or associate with the Dubinin name, he was trying to pit the Viper Cartel against the Italian Mafia. And both of them against us.

The change was that he now seemed to view his daughter as a prime asset to bargain with. I couldn't begin to guess if he'd done so many drugs that he lacked any brain cells anymore or if he was just naturally that fucking dumb, but he couldn't grasp the fact that Gabriella wasn't a limited-time offer. She was mine. She would be mine until I decided otherwise. And she wasn't going anywhere anytime soon.

Miguel lacked that understanding. He seemed to consider her his, if only because he was her father and that would never change. That bond no longer mattered—at all. The second I ordered her to be picked up and brought to my home, she was irrevocably mine.

"Where is that stupid fucker now?" I tossed the papers to my desk and rubbed my brow.

He shook his head. "Undetermined. He's staying on the move."

"He can't hide anywhere we won't find him." It didn't matter if Gabriella and I were at odds with each other. I would never stop protecting her.

"Agreed. I can put more men on it. We'll find him."

"And kill him." I almost regretted not taking his life when I'd had him captured and caught before. Emil had tortured him and beaten him to within an inch of his life, but the fucker survived.

No. I can't regret it.

If I hadn't chosen the backup idea of a punishment for Miguel Lopez, I never would've had Gabriella in my life. I never would've discovered this second lease on life that I had now, anticipating the arrival of another child.

"You want to have Miguel killed?" Ivan questioned, seeming surprised.

I nodded, curious why that wouldn't be obvious. The man would continue to be a threat to the mother of my child. Of course, I'd want him six feet under.

"Oh." He nodded slowly. "So you can release Gabriella and let her go after the baby is born?"

I grunted something like a laugh. "What the fuck are you talking about?"

"Well..." He shrugged again as he sat on the edge of my desk. Bothered that he'd even ask me that, I grabbed the papers to feed them in the shredder to destroy the evidence. I'd seen what I wanted to.

"Well, what?" I prompted.

"She hasn't exactly adjusted well to being a Mafia woman."

Then I'll continue to teach her. "She hasn't," I agreed, "but there is time for that."

"And you're not sure about committing to her. Officially."

It would shock you to know I intend to.

I hadn't forgotten about how I decreed to her that we'd marry.

I meant it.

But with this cooling span of distance between us after

our fight, I wondered if she'd dismissed what I said as nothing.

"With all this news about Miguel treating her like a prize he can sell to the highest bidder, as if he can't realize you have her, I imagined you were just keeping her here and safe until she can give you the baby."

I laughed, shaking my head. "Come on, Ivan. Stop joking. You're not that stupid."

He watched me, curious.

"She's never giving up that baby. She says it's the only family she's ever had."

"Okay. Then she's staying?"

I nodded. "Obviously."

"Not just to keep her safe from Miguel?"

I shook my head. "Correct."

"And you *still* can't just get over yourself and make up with her... why, again?"

I grimaced, uneasy to talk further about this. I wasn't in the mood to reveal how vulnerable she made me feel. How much the thought of losing her would destroy me.

"Never mind that," I told him as the papers finished shredding. "She's staying. And things will..." I blew out a big breath, wondering if my damn pride was the only thing standing in my way. "I'm confident things will work out fine."

Hopefully, before this baby comes.

Protecting her from Miguel was a no-brainer. But if he wasn't caught, my second-born could be taken from me as well. It wasn't only a risk of losing the woman I dared to love, but also this second take on growing a real family.

Just like she'd always dreamed of.

It would just have to merge with *my* dreams, too.

32

GABRIELLA

I grew bigger and clumsier every day, almost startled by how my skin would stretch to accommodate this little one. This marvel of meeting my son or daughter was the only saving grace from the turmoil of being mad at Luka.

No matter what, I would do my best to protect this baby. Even if it meant running. Even if it meant fighting Luka and his family for the rest of my life.

While it would've been nice to share this experience with Luka, I'd be damned if I'd heel to his desire that I apologize and make amends first.

It didn't help that the house staff treated me even worse. When it started, well before I even knew I was pregnant, it was just those side eyes and mean stares. Or they'd whisper about me as they dusted, belittling me as a cheap whore who'd never be a suitable partner for their leader.

In the beginning, I let it in one ear and out the other. As my pregnancy progressed, though, they only increased their wrath.

Still, it made no difference. With all these months I was

stuck here and ignored by Luka, my desire to stand up to anyone—except him—and fight back waned.

Until I wasn't the only one to realize how catty they'd become.

As I got up from reading a book that didn't even hold my interest in the study, I was immediately cornered by a maid.

Older than me and bearing the signs of a hard, weathered life, she scowled and pointed at me. "It's all your fault, bitch."

I raised my brows, surprised she'd put so much energy into criticizing me or accusing me of something. I was a nobody here. It was almost like a full circle. A nobody before I was kidnapped and relegated to a nobody as a breeding vessel for a Mafia boss.

"You got Susanna killed."

I shook my head, not necessarily to correct her but also to reject it. I hadn't done anything. Ever. That was the story of my life. I never did anything to warrant hardships and headaches to this degree. Calling myself the victim got old, but it was true.

"You did!" she snarled. "You got her killed. I heard the guards talking. Mr. Dubinin had her killed because she saw your pregnancy test."

"Ha!" I crossed my arms. A flare of a fight lit me up. "She did not. She went snooping for it. I hid that test in the trash. It wasn't lying out."

"Whatever. It's all your fault she's dead!"

I almost wanted to roll my eyes. I wasn't soulless, but they'd get no compassion out of me. Fuck around and find out. That was the name of this game. "It's her own damn fault. She had no right to snoop. And she had no right to sell that intel to the man who calls himself my dad."

Because of that maid, I'd almost been taken by the

Rivera Family. All due to Miguel Lopez's greed and loathing for me.

"You bitch!" The maid lunged at me.

I covered my belly, nervous that she'd escalate to trying to harm me.

But she didn't reach me. Alexsei and a boy were walking down the hallway and happened to see me in the study.

"Hey! Don't hurt that lady!" The young boy darted out, smacking the maid's hand away from reaching me.

"Misha!" Alexsei rushed in too, taking over the incident. He grabbed the woman and pulled her back as he called out for the guards.

I breathed hard, stunned, but deep inside, I was still so numb.

Heartache could do that to a person.

Grateful for the save, I watched the young boy. In the almost year that I'd been here, I'd never encountered a child. I was under the impression mine would be the only infant or youthful person here.

Alexsei handed the quarreling maid off to the guards and returned to me. "Misha. That's not what I've taught you," he scolded lightly.

"Thanks, Misha," I said, countering Alexsei. He shot me a wry look.

"I am thankful that he was eager to be a hero too, but my son needs to think before acting on an impulse."

"Son?" I furrowed my brow. "This is your *son*?"

He nodded as Allen came into the study. "Allen, could you watch Misha for a moment?"

"Sure. Misha, have you had a cookie yet today?" Allen steered him away, clearly satisfied that nothing untoward was happening now that the maid was gone.

"You have a son?"

"I do," Alexsei said. "He's five and full of energy." Likely guessing that I'd ask, he added, "My wife was killed a few years ago. I've raised him on my own."

"Oh. Wow." I blinked, surprised. Not only that this Mafia man seemed so normal about being a single father, but that he could claim to be alone in raising Misha. Alexsei was always with the others. I was sure Ivan and Emil helped with the boy, too.

"Puts a different perspective on our 'family' now, doesn't it?" He smiled slightly.

"Um." I wasn't sure what to say. That boy looked so normal. Like any other five-year-old. Not a robotic slave or trained soldier. "I'm sorry for your loss. About your wife, I mean." I was aware that Luka had lost his first wife decades ago, but he didn't seem eager to ever bring her up. Emil had told me about her when I'd asked once, merely curious.

"Thanks. Time heals all wounds, but it's taking a while to move past the grief."

I winced, immediately thinking that his wife had to have died because of his association in the family. This wife would've been a target. Like I will be if I stay for good.

Wait.

No.

That bias wasn't adding up.

My mother had been killed in a drive-by, and that drive-by likely happened near home because of my dad's connection to criminals.

I was damned if I did and damned if I didn't.

Sobered by the realization that I was a target in my "former" life before I'd been kidnapped as much as I was currently a target to be in the Dubinin Family, I had to admit my odds of survival were a hell of a lot higher here.

"We're still a family," Alexsei said gently. "Not just lawless heathens."

"Heathens?" I laughed lightly at his choice of words.

"I've noticed how scared you are to bring someone into the Dubinin Family, but if it would help you to see how balanced and loved and protected *my* son is, you only have to ask."

It really did change my views. A lot. Just knowing a normal-looking and sweet boy was here at all morphed me from worrying my baby would be conditioned into a monster.

But it still seemed too late.

The danger would always lurk too close.

"Anyway," I said, unwilling to admit my fears were magically erased, just like that, "I appreciate your, um, standing up to that maid."

"I guess I was in the right place at the right time, huh?"

I nodded.

"If you ever need help keeping the house staff in line and don't want to tell Luka, then you can always count on Allen. Or me." He smiled slowly. "Even Misha when he visits here."

"Thanks."

"You doing okay?" he asked, seeming reluctant to leave me.

I shrugged. "More or less." It was less. I was less than okay, actually, but he was one of the few to ask me that.

Alexsei seemed as intense as the others I wanted to call my found family. He was nice. Obedient, though.

"What's on your mind, Gabriella?" He wasn't prying. I doubted he was spying for Luka.

I shrugged. "Too many things."

"Like what? Ask me anything."

That seemed like a generous offer. "Okay. Um." I recalled how he'd surprised me, taking my side against that maid. Like it was automatic to stand up for me, for family. "Have you ever considered a different life? Not being mandated to serve your uncle?"

He shook his head. "I was never mandated. Family is family. Loyalty to family is everything."

I frowned.

"Is that bad?"

"It's just that I don't have any family anymore. Or ever. My mom died. My dad is trying to pawn me for the highest profit. And I'm stuck here, unable to escape to raise my child on my own—with love, not a demand for loyalty and service."

Furrowing his brow, he regarded me closely. "Are you telling me that you really don't see how Luka cares about you?"

I sighed, having no spark of my former sass anymore. No sarcastic quip was ready for him.

Shrugging and hating how low my morale and mood had sunk, I shook my head. "Luka doesn't care. I'm just his thing to treat as he pleases. And if actions speak louder than words, he's made it clear he doesn't truly want or need me in his life." Owning up to that hard truth hurt, but this dejection and dismay weren't letting up anytime soon.

33

LUKA

I leaned against the wall. Further down the hallway from the study, I couldn't help but overhear Alexsei talking to Gabriella.

I'd planned to go to the study to drink and mull over how I was handling her being here. This distance was going on too long.

But when I caught word of Alexsei calling for guards, I stayed pressed against the wall, slightly out of obvious sight. Two men hurried to haul away that maid who'd dared to talk so horribly to Gabriella.

Then Allen strode by, taking Misha to the kitchen.

Still, I stayed put. Since she'd stopped dancing in her studio this late into her pregnancy, I had no means to watch her from afar, in hiding.

Like this, I heard her voice. I felt her presence so near, but seeming so distant in the study while I lurked out here.

I was doing this to myself. I was punishing myself to keep away from her. Part of it was to punish her, too. I was still bitter about how she'd ever thought to hide her pregnancy from me, to decide to be deceptive like that.

I supposed in that regard, we really were well-matched. She would never forgive me for how she'd been kidnapped and taken. And I'd never get past how she'd lied by omission for so long.

She sounded down, low in spirits, and that tugged at whatever heartstring I still had.

As she talked a bit with Alexsei, I felt the sadness that gripped her.

Well, you've fucking done it now.

I'd broken her.

I "won".

I'd kept away to teach her a lesson about what it was like to fight me, and she was no longer the woman I'd desired so much.

She was a shell of her former self.

Hearing her assume that I didn't care about her chipped at my pride.

I'd done this.

I'd pushed for her to sink this low. And I hated myself for it. I missed her fire, her willingness to challenge me. With her admission to my nephew, I realized that I'd dimmed her fight, her drive.

She could only take so much, and the gap between us had yawned and stretched for too long.

She could've fucking come to me.

She could've submitted—again.

But as I clung to that belief, I knew I was wrong. She shouldn't have had to. She'd already done that. She was the one who had to admit how badly she craved me in the beginning. It was nothing but a cruel trick to expect her to submit and bow again like this.

Especially when she was pregnant and protective in that regard.

Particularly when she was vulnerable with the repeated attempts on her life or the capture of her body to give to another.

Alexsei exited the room after she did. Grateful that she turned to walk the other way down the hall, I braced myself for facing my nephew. I pressed the side of my head against the wall, unable to stand straight as I accepted the full hit of guilt that I'd caused her to feel like this.

He frowned, spotting me, and didn't waste a second to approach me.

"She's—"

"Save it." I let out a long breath as I pushed off the wall and shook my head. Lifting my hand to indicate that he didn't need to go on or elaborate, I walked toward the study where she'd just been.

"I heard. I heard her."

"Then you realize that this... fight has to stop." He didn't stop frowning, assuming he could have the right to scold me.

I was the boss. He answered to me. But in this case, he could get away with calling me out on this bullshit.

"I heard. And I do realize that." Passing him, I continued to the study.

Fortunately, he had the wisdom to hear the defeat in my tone. He didn't follow me to press his case. Alexsei was a kind man with a good heart. He was also smart, aware that he didn't need to nag like Emil could sometimes.

Alone in the study, I drew a deep breath and tried to catch a lingering note of Gabriella's scent. Of her sweetness. Of her lovely allure, a tangible presence I once was so blessed to enjoy whenever I wanted.

She was gone.

She wasn't in the room anymore.

And if I wasn't careful, the soul of the woman I wanted to love would vanish too.

See? This is what always fucking happens.

To love was to lose.

In my life, to love was to destroy.

I poured myself a drink and downed it, wishing the burn of the alcohol would dull my senses so this heartache of missing her would sting less.

It didn't work.

So, I poured another. And another.

Slumping into the leather chair, I wondered how long it would take to fall asleep. Maybe fate would be kind to me and spare me from having to dream of her. Again. It was one thing to avoid her by day, but in the clutches of sleep at night, I had no escape from her.

Erotic dreams twisted into nightmares of watching her die.

Weird illusions of her running from me shifted into her being Maria, then herself again.

She was messing me up in the worst of ways, but I couldn't see how I could even go about fixing it now.

What, was I supposed to just go and apologize? I never told anyone I was sorry. I wasn't that smug, but everything I did in my life was a deliberate choice I would stand by. That coldhearted ruthlessness was how I'd become the boss and ruler that I was in this city. That was how I was the master, the leader, never the loser.

With her, though, I *was* sorry. I hated that I had been so stuck in my head and in my thoughts that I couldn't realize that we were pushing each other too far away all this time.

How could I start? Approaching her would be a challenge when she was still too aloof.

Would it even matter now? From how sad and numb

she'd sounded when talking to Alexsei, I had to face the very real possibility that there was no way to reclaim her and get us back to where we were.

Vodka warmed me inside and out, but it was her heat and her affection I wanted to course through my veins. Getting drunker by the second as I tried to drown my sorrows and regrets, I knew it was her sway over me that I wished for. I wanted to be intoxicated by her again, nothing else.

Fuck it.

I can't do this.

I can't stand by and watch her become any more of a shell.

When I lost Maria, it changed me.

If I were to screw up with Gabriella, a second chance the universe never should have teased me with, I wouldn't recover. Ever.

Leaving the study, I resolved to just see her. To check on her. To bask in her presence, even if she was already asleep.

The night wasn't so young anymore. Striding down the hallways and climbing the stairs to my personal wing, I hated that she'd been toughing out this pregnancy all on her own. She never asked for help. She never requested a spa day or massage. She had to be so damn tired, physically as she carried our child and also to put up with my bullshit.

Because that was what it was.

I was a fucking dumbass to resist her in this game of pride.

I didn't fight kindly. Life wasn't fair. But this was all on me. I'd own it.

Stepping into her room, I stayed as quiet as I could so as not to startle her. I didn't want to risk pissing her off like this, showing up uninvited when she really did need her rest.

The moment I closed the door behind me, I closed my eyes at the smell of her in this room. Her lotion. That shampoo she favored. Even the scent of her skin, somehow unique and even tastier when I could kiss and lick her anywhere I pleased.

She was asleep. The lump of her on the bed proved that she hadn't stayed up for any reason. Just the sight of her gave me such a poignant pang of longing that I stifled the grunt that almost left my lips. Seeing her was a sucker punch to the gut. That was how much I'd been missing her like an idiot.

Alexsei was right.

Our fight had gone on too long.

If this was the time for forgiveness, then so be it.

As soon as I was sober in the morning—

A sniffle.

Then another.

I froze, squinting to see her in the darkness.

I was wrong. She wasn't asleep. She was faking it. Apparently, she was masking the fact that she was crying as she lay with her head on the pillows.

The sound of her so sad ripped at my soul. I had to stop this. I couldn't stand by and witness the results of my cruelty. Stumbling forward, I stubbed my toe against a table.

That was all it took for her to jackknife. She sat up as she slapped her hand at the nightstand, turning on a low light. As she met my gaze, she wiped at her cheeks. Like that could erase the evidence of her tears.

"Gabriella..."

No words were ready for her. I hadn't rehearsed anything. A speech wouldn't be happening, but I had to utter something more than her damn name.

Her lips curled down in a pout. Even like that, she was

irresistible. Yet as she continued to wipe her eyes, reminding me that I'd walked in to witness her so sad, so numb and at a loss for how to carry on, I was instantly annoyed.

Not at her.

At myself.

Anger took root as I walked toward her sitting up in bed. I'd never forgive *myself* for taking this so far with her. I really had treated her like a thing, not a person to love. I'd thought that it was implied, that it was obvious. After all, how could she have ever doubted that I gave a damn about her and our child when I provided for her?

Letting her watch me as I trespassed further into her room until I stood at the side of her bed, I let her words wash over me again.

"And if actions speak louder than words, he's made it clear he doesn't truly want or need me in his life."

She was fucking wrong. All this absence made me yearn for her more. I wanted her. I needed her. I'd be lost without her. But she needed to hear it, not see the proof of all I gave her. Material things and even medical care and armed security weren't parts of her language. She wanted to hear it.

"Gabriella." I repeated her name in a hushed whisper as I took in the sight of her like this. Quiet but observant. Wary but defensive. She wasn't as numb as she thought she was. With another drag of her careful gaze over me, she proved that she wasn't impervious to noticing me.

To tolerating my presence.

As she looked her fill, participating gamely in this spontaneous staring contest as if we hadn't seen each other in years, I admired how beautiful she'd become.

The swell of our child in her belly turned me on. That was *my* heir. I'd done that. I'd fucked her and made my cum take root so we'd create a new life.

Her breasts were fuller, straining against the silky fabric of her nightgown. As I stared, unable to hide my raging desire, her nipples hardened enough that the points poked at the material trying to hide them.

And the heat in her dark eyes, those fathomless pools that always captivated me...

Fuck me. I couldn't walk away this time.

I'd come in here just to see her. To be near her and feel her presence.

Tomorrow would make more sense to apologize, but like this, I was unable to rein back this feral, physical lust.

She frowned, lowering her gaze to the erection I couldn't hide beneath my pants. It was tented, with no room for my dick to move.

"That's what you've come here for?" she asked. Her tone was cool, but curious. It was obvious she still hated me, but she wasn't any better at hiding how much she lusted for me, too.

Needing her so badly, even like this, I leaned down to cup her face and force her to tip her chin up higher. I met her gaze head-on as she licked her lips.

"No. I didn't come here to fuck you."

I want to make love.

"But now that I'm here..."

She furrowed her brow, setting her hand on top of mine, as if she despised that she wanted to keep me here. Like she wanted me to stay.

34

GABRIELLA

He wasn't here to apologize. With the smell of liquor radiating from him, it didn't seem like he was all that cognizant of planning to come in here at all. Like he wasn't even thinking, just following the pull to me.

He wasn't here to gloat over my tears, either. I only allowed them at night, when I was so lonely and missing that soul-deep closeness I'd felt with him, like when he'd held me all the twilight hours in bed with me.

And he wasn't here to make demands and rehash another round of any of our arguments. The sadness mixing with desire in his eyes gave the suggestion that he was only staying to reconnect with me.

Even if it was for sex.

Despite how mad I wanted to stay at him, feeling his callused, hot hand on my cheek rejuvenated me.

It sparked the memory of what it had felt like when I dreamed I was his whole world. When he acted like I was the treasure he never wanted to let go of. When he worshiped my body without any pause, taking at the same time he'd give so much.

It wasn't love.

Yet, as I stared right back at him, I just couldn't keep up this fight anymore.

I wanted him. I needed to feel again.

"I don't want to miss you anymore," I admitted.

It wasn't an apology either, but I was too powerless to stop myself from telling him that truth. I was caving first. I was throwing in the towel and giving up resisting him. Perhaps we were both too damn prideful for our own good.

I just couldn't hold out any longer.

"I never wanted to miss you in the first place." His tender words matched mine, but he sealed it by leaning over to kiss me.

Both of his strong hands were on my face. Delicately framing my cheeks, holding me in place as he slanted and dipped down to kiss me soundly, he gave me the hunch that he was trying to pace himself and savor every single second of reconnecting with me like this.

Because we were. We had to. I never wanted to go back to feeling like a nobody, a reject and unworthy of affection. I couldn't do that to myself, and I couldn't stand for that kind of an environment to bring this baby into.

I owed him or her better. I owed both me and Luka more than stubborn fighting.

"I will never miss you again," he promised after he parted from my mouth. Rubbing his thumb along my lower lip, he watched me closely. His words weren't slurred, and I bet he wasn't making this up just to get me naked and willing to help him with that erection pushing up his pants.

"Because I will never let us grow this distant again."

Music to my ears. It was as close to a sorry as I could count on, and I'd take it.

"Me neither," I replied, climbing to my knees to kiss him again.

He wrapped his arms around me, clutching me close. The hint of vodka changed his taste, but the possessive hunger he demonstrated was all the same. He was desperate for me, as much as I was for him as I rubbed against him. He was impatient to hold me, as greedy as I wanted to show him as I lowered my hands to unbutton his shirt.

We'd been apart for too long. Within reach but stubborn to fight, he'd been there as a temptation I couldn't allow myself. I was feral for him. This wouldn't be the time to take it slow and explore. Our reunion would be frantic and hurried, but that was all I was capable of. I would take faith in his commitment. We were making up, and we could take it slow next time.

I wasn't going to torture myself with proving a point. Forgiveness was due.

I was also due. In four short weeks, this baby would be here, and it was with happiness that another tear leaked from my eyes. Reconciling with this mighty Mafia boss before the baby came was the miracle I'd been waiting for.

"I will never stay away again," he vowed, leaning back to help me get his clothes off.

"I dare you to try," I whispered in a rush, lifting my arms as he dragged my nightgown up over my head before tossing it aside.

"Oh, fuck..." He growled it, low and gritty as he cupped my breasts and gently played with my nipples.

It was too much. I needed him too badly.

"Ah!" I hissed, cringing at the sharp bite of something almost like pain.

"Tender?" he guessed playfully as he lowered to kiss over my breasts.

Moans replaced my hiss, and as he sucked and teased me, giving both of my nipples attention, I held his head close and nearly swayed with need. "I won't last," I warned him gently, not really caring how he wanted to direct this make-up sex. Because it would be his call. I'd missed his dominance because of how secure it made me feel.

"I won't either."

"Fuck me, Luka."

He stood up all the way as he moved his hand to rub my pussy. Back and forth, he slid his fingers to collect and smear my arousal that leaked so quickly for him.

"No." He kissed me, drugging me with the hungrier and more brutal press of his mouth on mine. "I'm not going to fuck you."

I frowned, trying to keep up with this wild ride. I'd gone from that numbness mixed with sadness to surprise. Then the euphoric elation of his wanting to make up. Now this desire. I was a mess of too many emotions and so damn confused. His words suggested that he was rejecting me, but as he worked on lowering his pants while using his free hand to keep me pressed flush to him as he kissed me again, his actions said he was all for it.

That hard dick that sprang out proved he was in the mood to get busy and deep inside me, too.

"I'm going to make love to you," he amended.

"Oh... Luka." I sniffled, framing his face as he guided me to stand. Leaning into him, I let him practically pick me up.

"No more tears."

"These are happy ones."

"Hmm." He turned me, guiding me to crawl up on the bed with him behind me. "No more tears," he repeated.

"Because I don't want to worry and assume something else."

Feeling his dick poke and prod at the backs of my thighs was all I needed to shut up and not even think anymore. The touch of his big cock was plenty for me to focus on. As he situated us, with him kneeling and on his haunches as he held me close to him, my back to his front, he explained further.

"I want to fucking make love to you." He smoothed his hands over my baby bump, his caress reverent and careful. Possessive.

"And I never want to stop."

I smiled, reaching up to smooth my hand over his face as he nuzzled my neck and kissed me with the perfect hint of suction.

"You might need to give me a few weeks off after the baby comes."

"Hmm." He kept thrusting, rubbing his dick between my legs. Lowering his hand toward my pussy, he stopped to tease my clit with torturously good circles of his thumb around that nerve center. "Only four weeks and one day left to wait."

My lips stretched in a wider smile. He had been counting down to the arrival of our baby. He hadn't been that distant, still concerned and involved. Just stubborn, like me, to keep up his grudge.

"Does this mean that you've changed your mind about marrying me?" I asked.

Holding my breath as he lined his dick up to my entrance, I relished the security of him bracing me like this. Having sex with a big baby bump took some posturing, but he proved to be ready to see to my comfort *and* pleasure.

"Oh, fuck..." He growled as I slowly sat back down on him. Not until he was seated all the way in did I let myself moan. The long groan was ripped from my lips as I closed my eyes.

"Wait." He didn't move.

"Oh, my God. No. Please don't tease me like this." I whimpered. "You've neglected me for months and now—"

"No, no." He turned my head to kiss me. Then he eased back, intending to slide into me again. "But can't sex cause labor?"

I laughed lightly. "No? Maybe? I don't know."

He kissed me again, chuckling. "Never mind." Another hard kiss nearly pushed me over. That was how on edge I was to reconnect with him, to *make love* with my one and only. "Just don't come hard."

I shook my head, pushing my ass back to him. "No promises."

"Then I'll promise," he whispered as he drove into me steadily. Keeping one hand on my clit, teasing me, and his other cupping my breast as he thumbed my nipple, he seemed to be challenged to talk at the same time he filled me.

"I promise to apologize as many times as you need me to. For anything I've done wrong."

My heart swelled. But I couldn't manage it racing any faster than it already was. His words were too sweet, too tender. All my fantasies were coming true.

"I'm sorry, Gabriella, for ever making you feel sad enough to cry yourself to sleep."

"Luka." I told him I wouldn't cry, and I was determined not to. Framing his face as he pounded into me, I focused on how good he made me feel to stave off the tears of joy.

"I promise to never be at odds with you this long again." He pumped faster. "We will fight. But never like this again."

I might have nodded.

"And I promise I'm going to marry you. Or I promise to convince you to marry me."

I smiled, biting my lip. All these months he'd stayed away from me and avoided me while keeping me trapped in his house, I wondered if he even remembered that he'd told me that. His highhandedness didn't expire. But with him being so mad at me, and me furious with him, I figured he'd taken back that comment.

"We're going to get married as soon as we can."

He *was* drunk. But I only heard genuine vows as we made love.

"You'll be my wife. And I'm going to keep you pregnant. I'll knock you up until we have as big of a family as you want. A real one. Because I'll do whatever it takes for you to understand that I love you."

There it was. He was really putting it all out there. "I love you, Luka." My breath hitched as my orgasm came closer to overwhelming me.

"And I'll never stop loving you. I will love you so fucking much that you'll never want to think about leaving again."

I had already given up on that idea. Escaping wasn't happening. But now, my goal to stay was a decision backed by love.

As I came, crying out loudly and breaking my word about no tears, he held me close and thrust faster until he joined me. I leaned and sagged against him, so spent and fatigued in the efforts we'd put into making up at last.

He had me.

I didn't suspect he'd ever let me go now.

But as he pulled out, letting the suctioning sounds of our cum be so audible, he chuckled.

"I *told* you not to come so hard..."

I laughed lightly, seeking out his warmth as he stood and then bent to pick me up. Carrying me to the shower, he kissed my brow, and I tried my best to stay awake. Even if I did fall asleep, it'd be with a lazy smile on my face.

35

LUKA

Gabriella was sluggish in the shower, barely able to stand fully. Curling against me, she seemed too tired to care about cleaning up. Her peaceful smiles suggested she felt too damn good within my embrace to even think.

It didn't matter. I held her up. I kept her close. Sobering by the minute because I knew she was relying on me to clean us up and make sure she didn't slip or fall, I concentrated. It was a reward for me to feel her, to have this contact between our bodies again. And it was a break for her, letting her have the chance to do absolutely nothing but be pampered.

Once I got us rinsed off, I steadied her to grab a couple of towels. She was sleepy and clumsy, so I gave up on wrapping her in the terry bath sheets. Instead, I picked her up naked and walked her to my room.

The second I laid her on the mattress where she'd belonged all this time, next to me, she was out. Literally, she was *out*. Sleeping with her head not even fully on the pillow, she smiled in her sleep.

"Sweet dreams," I whispered, leaning over to kiss her before I climbed in around her.

Tucking her against me was the best feeling in the world. She stayed on her side, as she had to this late in her pregnancy, but it didn't change how perfectly she slotted against me. Spooning her like this, I could finally admit that all was right in my world.

I had her back, or rather, she had *me* back. We'd moved past the fight that made me so stupid and prideful as to miss all this time of her being pregnant.

Don't worry.

I closed my eyes, breathing in her scent.

I won't miss a second of the next one.

Early in the morning, she woke up to go to the bathroom. Despite drinking last night and no matter how tired I was from staying up late to make love to her, I woke up too.

"What's wrong?" I asked, tossing the blanket off to follow her to the bathroom. It couldn't be morning sickness. The doctor reports never mentioned that she had it.

"Bladder pushed on by a baby," she whined comically, hurrying toward the other room.

I smiled, sitting on the edge of the bed to wait for her to come back. Yawning, I checked the time and dreaded that I'd have a full day to expect to get through.

She waddled back into the room, also yawning, so I extended my arms to welcome her back under the covers.

"Now I won't fall asleep again," she mumbled.

I spooned her, resting my hand on her belly where I felt the proof for why she'd said that. "Active, huh?"

"As soon as I lie down," she admitted.

"Not long to wait now. Then I can handle the active hours while you rest."

"Oh?" She peered back at me. "You're a hands-on kind of dad?"

I sighed, kissing her and encouraging her to snuggle and relax with me again. "No. I wasn't before. When Emil was born, Maria insisted on handling his care because I was so busy."

"Oh."

We'd never talked about Maria, but as I kissed the top of Gabriella's head, I planned to discuss her more so as not to lose the memory of her, but also to prove to my new love that I wasn't pining for the ghost of my first wife.

"And I was busy. Too busy with being the boss and not yet reaching the degree of being able to delegate and trust those in the organization. Coming into power included a phase of weeding out dissenters."

She yawned, and I reflexively did as well.

"Now, I know how to be the boss. You won't be stuck raising him or her on your own. I will be there. So will Emil and my nephews." I yawned again, tiring myself from speaking. "Allen's sister was Emil's nanny. She passed away already, but I can think of more staff to hire for us."

She sighed. But the longer I waited for her to reply, I realized she was already asleep again.

"You let her rest," I whispered to the baby in her belly as I kept my hand pressed on the swollen girth there.

Later, when we woke, I grumbled at all that would keep me from her today.

We showered and ate breakfast together, meeting everyone with smiles as the others came in and out of the house.

"Fucking finally," Emil said dryly as he came to the dining room.

I held Gabriella's hand and lifted it to kiss the back of it.

"What final—oh." Ivan filed in, stirring a coffee cup. He smiled. "Just in time to make up, huh?" He shook his head as he sat next to Emil.

"That's enough," I said, mildly annoyed. I still wasn't going to talk about emotions and sappy shit. With her, I would open up my heart as much as she wanted me to. It'd take me time. I'd approach it with baby steps, but I was ready to be whatever Gabriella needed me to be.

"Speaking of time," she said, "will you be able to come to my appointment?"

I sighed heavily, wishing I could swear I'd be there. Most of her checkups had been done here. All but one were completed in the privacy and comfort of her room. At the last checkup, the monitoring equipment got damaged on the drive. For this reason, she was being taken to the medical facility.

It was the first time she'd be out of the house since the resort I'd taken her to. That fated day that kicked us into turmoil, when I discovered she was carrying my child.

"We've got a thorough security detail arranged," Ivan said, glancing at me, then her.

"I figured that," she said calmly. Still, she looked at me.

"I want to be there," I replied honestly. "It just depends on how my meeting goes this morning."

She nodded. "Okay. I just wanted to know. I bet they'll do another ultrasound and you could hear the baby's heartbeat."

I leaned over to kiss her, fucking smitten with how happy she was now. Hell, I was pretty damned happy, too.

"But you'll be there for the big day, right?" she asked, raising her brows.

"Nothing would keep me away," I promised.

"Well, there are still a few more weeks for that." She

groaned, rubbing her stomach. "I don't know how I can get any bigger. I'm already a beached whale."

"Nonsense," I replied.

"And you still don't know the gender?" Ivan asked.

She shook her head. "No. I want to be surprised."

I just shrugged, going with what she wanted.

Emil and Ivan spoke a little more about the meeting I had to attend. It was something to do with a wealthy philanthropist who'd needed a favor—the kind of favor Emil specialized in. Since it was a big deal and an important transaction, it was requested that I attend as well.

"I will try to come to the appointment," I told Gabriella before I left, hating to be apart from her now that we'd found our way back together.

"Okay. Don't stress about it. I'll be safe."

I arched a brow. "Without me?"

She smirked. "Oh, stop. You know I feel safest *with* you." And she meant it. I knew she did. I'd killed to protect her.

"But I also know that your guards and everyone will do their jobs to protect me and this little one as well."

That vote of confidence was something I never thought I'd hear from her lips. She wasn't bluffing or mocking anything. In this year she'd been here, she really had grown into accepting how my family worked. She didn't flinch at the concept of having a small army go with her to an appointment. Likewise, I trusted that she'd stick with them and not try to flee.

How could she when her future is with me?

Hours later, I grinned with the satisfaction that my meeting had wrapped up sooner than I expected. With this timing, I could surprise her at the medical facility, arriving right when she would.

Riding in the Rolls Royce, *my* car, I sighed and watched the scenery pass by.

Allen was on speaker, hurrying to assist with a project Gabriella hadn't put any effort into handling.

The nursery.

In the back of my mind, I knew she'd put off talking about the nursery at first because she was adamant that she'd be better off on her own to raise our child, away from danger. She'd at last come to realize she would be more secure *with* me than away from me, and I appreciated that she'd had that epiphany.

"Ask her," I told him as he debated between furniture ideas. "After the appointment, ask her." I didn't care. Whatever she wanted, I'd make it happen.

He scoffed at my unhelpful nonanswer. After we disconnected the call, I mused on how anxious I was to surprise her. It wasn't just that I was eager to hear the heartbeat and be there to see our child on the ultrasound. This wasn't my first time with this. I still remembered when I was waiting for Emil to be born. The daughter I was supposed to welcome into the world with Maria had been my second experience of doctor visits and obstetrician offices.

But this was Gabriella's first time. I hated to have punked out and failed her by not being with her when she had her checkups all along, but I was here now. And I would be there for all other pregnancies she'd be blessed with.

Coming to meet her at her appointment was a sign of deeper commitment. That mattered to me. Now that I'd gotten my head out of my ass and I could see my future complete only with her in it as my partner, not a thing I'd acquired from a rat, I wanted her to know how deeply I was in this thing called life with her.

On the ride, I rehearsed my ideas of how I could soften

my dominance where she was concerned. I never wanted to witness her fire and spirit be so diminished again. She would submit to me. I knew that now. It was only a matter of explaining that I loved her so she'd feel powerful alongside me.

Not as something I'd taken.

But after our fight, something I'd earned back.

The car slowed to a stop, braking at the entrance of the parking garage. Before the driver continued on, a couple of vans sped by. They zoomed too fast so erratically that they clipped the bumpers of parked cars. Just like that, they were there.

"What the fuck—"

I watched, panicking as the vans rocked to a stilted stop at the doors that led to the medical facility where Gabriella was in the waiting room for her appointment.

Men filed out. All armed.

"The fucking Vipers," I growled, grabbing my gun and hurrying out of the car to chase after the men.

It was another ambush.

Another attack on Gabriella.

On our child's life.

Sprinting to get there in time, I shouted into my phone, ordering more men to surround the facility and protect the love of my life at all costs.

I wouldn't lose her.

I just couldn't, not after all we'd been through to be at this tentative potential for peace and love.

36

GABRIELLA

It was different to sit here in a real waiting room to be seen. All my other checkups were done in the privacy of my bedroom. Luka hadn't hesitated to start medical care and supervision, going to the extreme of hiring private doctors as soon as he discovered I was pregnant.

Seated in an uncomfortable chair in this medical office that was an auxiliary building on the hospital's campus, I almost felt like a normal person again. Not a lover of a Mafia boss who got special treatment, but an ordinary, standard citizen, expected to wait like anyone else.

No other patients were in here at the time. Luka had requested that I not be waiting for long. Still, he'd shown how much he wanted me to feel pampered like that.

Maybe I should get used to feeling like a queen.

I rubbed my hand over my stomach, wondering how much longer it would be until I could get this over with. This large, I was just plain uncomfortable. This far along, I was simply unable to find a good spot to breathe fully, not feel the urge to pee, avoid heartburn, and also spare myself from that sciatica pain.

"Impatient?" Alexsei guessed.

He sat next to me while another Dubinin guard stood near the door. It seemed like overkill. No other people were in here since Luka ordered the doctors to clear their schedule for me. But with how my last two times of leaving the Dubinin mansion had gone—my audition and that time Luka took me out to brunch at that resort—it wasn't a bad idea to ramp up security.

If it stayed like this, where I'd be a target anytime I reentered society, I'd never want to think about "freedom" again.

So far, so good, right?

No one was bursting in here to shoot at me.

Yet.

I shook my head to dispel the thoughts.

Have faith.

Luka loved me. He wanted to marry me. It was sufficient to convince me he would protect me no matter what. His nephew was the security expert, and he was right next to me.

"You're not impatient?" he asked, interpreting the shake of my head as a negative reply. He chuckled. "Because if I remember those last weeks before Misha was born, my wife had been miserable."

I smiled slightly. Now that I knew he'd had a wife and fathered a son, I was excited to learn more about them. About all of them. My views of the Dubinins being a family, not *the* family, were changing my opinions so quickly.

I hated that I'd assumed too much for so long.

"Oh, I'm impatient." I sighed, then winced as more tension kicked in.

"Are you okay?" He watched me closely, worried.

"Yeah. I mean, no. I'm huge."

"Are you having contractions?" He glanced at how tightly I gripped the armrest as I rode through them.

Ever since I woke up this morning, I'd felt off. "No. Not real ones. Based on what I've read and what the doctors told me, this is when I'll have Braxton Hicks."

He furrowed his brow. "They look intense."

Fuck, I can't even breathe. I forced a smile. "Just practice." I stifled a groan.

The universe couldn't be that much of a jokester. This couldn't be early labor because I'd come so hard last night. If that were the case, and Luka missed this delivery, I'd never let him hear the end of it. He'd also never let me hear the end of it that he'd basically fucked me into childbirth.

"You know, when my wife was pregnant and claimed to have those Braxton Hicks, it was the real thing."

Please, don't tell me that. I wasn't ready. I needed Luka to be here when the time came. His comfort would ground me and make it more bearable.

"She was just dehydrated and they managed to hold off on her having Misha for a couple more weeks."

I grabbed my water bottle and chugged it. He laughed, but when the heartburn came even from the plain water, I cringed. My stomach was pushed up too high and squished.

"Gabriella?" A tech entered the waiting room and escorted me back to a small room. Alexsei stuck with me, and the guard trailed after us. Even though the ultrasound technician raised her brows, not used to the security like this, she didn't comment until I was on the bed and a nurse popped in to get my vitals.

"Feeling okay?" she asked.

I nodded, but that felt like a lie. If these were Braxton Hicks contractions, I wasn't sure I'd be strong enough for the real thing.

"So... is Daddy staying for the scan?" The tech glanced at Alexsei, then the guard, as she readied the gel for the ultrasound while the nurse exited.

"No. They're not the father," I replied.

Alexsei nodded at the guard, excusing him. Perhaps he thought I needed more privacy, but the room did feel less cluttered when the Dubinin soldier left.

The technician began scanning, but the look of alarm on her face scared me. "What is it?"

"Are you *sure* you feel okay?" she checked.

"As okay as I think I can—ow." Another sharp strike of pain hit me.

"That," she said, moving the wand over my bump, "doesn't fall under the realm of *okay*."

"It's just Braxton Hicks."

"No, that's just a really intense contraction." She moved quickly, grabbing a heart monitor to strap to my belly to track the baby's pulse. "And you are about to have this baby."

"What?" I tried to sit up, shocked.

"This isn't a rehearsal," she said glibly, smiling as she hooked me up.

"I told you," Alexsei said, chuckling as he got his phone out.

"No. It's just—"

"It's *just* contractions," the tech said. As she continued to secure the monitors to me, she picked up a radio-like piece hanging off the wall, calling for a nurse to come and to page the doctor.

I turned to stare at Alexsei. "But Luka—"

He held his hand up then rested it on my shoulder. "He's coming. He was already on his way, done with his meeting early. He should be here any minute."

"Oh, thank God. Thank—" I cringed, buckling down to bear through another wave of agony. "Fuck!"

"Whoa. Easy, easy. Deep breath in." Alexsei was a surprising source of comfort, having gone through the birth of his son. I was so damn glad I wasn't alone, that he was here instead of the others. But it was Luka I wanted to see. I wanted him to be holding my hand.

"Don't move," the tech said as she retreated.

"Very funny!" I bit out through clenched teeth as the contraction claimed me.

The tech winked, stepping aside as a nurse opened the door.

While the panel was ajar, someone else showed up and entered too. It wasn't the doctor.

But a man wearing a mask, toting a gun. He shot the nurse in the back of the head. She fell, blood and body matter spraying out. The guard attacked the next man trying to sneak in.

I screamed. Through the pain of the contraction. The fear of violence. The gruesome sight of that nurse shot dead right before my eyes.

This couldn't be happening. Not now. Not here. I was so fucking determined to bring this baby into a world where he or she would meet love, not death and danger.

Alexsei moved like a blur. He had his gun out, firing at the men as they tried to enter. One after the other, he shot them dead. Past this door, now held open with the dead nurse's body preventing it from closing, more gunfire erupted. The guard at the door was hit, but he added to Alexsei's shots.

"Don't move!" he yelled at me as he hurried to secure the door.

I was too traumatized to roll my eyes. Where else *could* I go?

My stomach was clenching in pain. Air couldn't fill my lungs. My heart raced. And why was I so sweaty?

I was having a baby. I couldn't hide and protect myself. As the medical facility turned into a warzone, I fought through the contractions to sit up. Alexsei and the other Dubinins were guarding me, not letting anyone enter the room. But that wasn't good enough. If this baby was coming now, I would not be defenseless.

Where is Luka?

Why is this happening?

When will it ever end?

Dropping to my hands and knees, I cried out at the pain of another contraction. It ripped at me, nearly making me fall and pass out, but I didn't stop crawling. Ignoring the blood and fighting the urge to puke from the labor and the grisly scene of death, I kept going.

My fingers shook and trembled, but I didn't stop until I pried a gun from a dead man's hands near the open doorway.

I'd never used a gun. Never fired one. But for fuck's sake, how hard could it be?

The energy of crawling, of moving at all, worsened the pain. Once I held the weapon in my hand, I slumped to the side. Lying on a clear spot on the floor, I gritted my teeth and breathed through the contractions that came so quickly, one after the other.

Screams filled the air, broken up only by the gunfire and shouts. Even though I was the only patient in the waiting room, other expectant mothers were in other rooms. More medical personnel were out there. So many innocent lives were taken, cruelly and horribly, in this place where new lives were supposed to come into the world.

I didn't need to focus on what the gunmen were saying.

I knew they were here to get me.

Miguel had told them to get my child, all to pawn him or her off to the Italians. That was what two men said in the hallway. It sounded like it was Pyotr, the one guard who'd once scared me. He was punching and fighting someone trying to get into my room, and that was how I caught word of the confession.

"No." I shook my head, delirious with this shock.

"It can't be like this."

The Cartel wanted me dead to wound Luka.

The Riveras wanted to take my child to hurt him too.

I was a target. I'd become collateral damage because he dared to love me.

"Gabriella!"

I tensed, opening my eyes as someone neared my room. On instinct, I lifted the gun and aimed it shakily.

A guard's arm reached out to stop a nurse, but she pushed at him. "No. Let me in. She's in labor!"

The brave woman ducked, rushing into the room. "Fuck." Her eyes opened wide, but she stayed clear-headed. "Fuck."

I nodded, agreeing with her assessment as she dropped to her knees and tugged on gloves. "I'm scared."

"You and me both." She didn't stop moving, removing my panties and pushing my skirt up as she helped me get into position. "You're crowning."

"What?" I cringed, shaking from more gunfire. "I'm what?"

"Crowning. This baby isn't going to wait."

"No. Not like this. I can't—" I shook my head, nervous

about how I could defend my baby when they were out of me. "It's too soon and it's too dangerous."

"It's happening. This baby's coming now. Stay with me and push when I say."

I cried, so terrified by this traumatic birth and the danger of so many strangers who wanted to get to me and my baby.

"One, two, three, and push."

I ground my teeth and pushed, ending up screaming from the agony. I was being split in two.

"Gabriella!"

My eyes popped open.

That was Luka!

I swallowed hard, amazed he'd made it. He was here, joining his men out there. He was fighting to protect me, like always.

"Okay, again. And one, two, three, push." The nurse shifted, helping to get this baby out of me.

I cried again, giving it my all and feeling like I had not a single ounce of energy left to move at all.

The urge to call out for Luka taunted me, but I feared that saying anything would only alert these intruders to my location and put me and my baby at more risk.

"Almost there," the nurse coaxed. "Stay with me. Almost there. Your baby is almost here."

"I'll be taking that bastard," a man snarled as he rushed into the room. He aimed his gun at my head, but he was the one who took a bullet.

Luka was there. He came up behind him and shot him dead with one clean shot to the back of his head.

The second the man dropped down, he staggered into the room. Blood covered his face. Injuries had to pain him all over his body. But nothing would stop him from positioning himself between me and the danger surrounding us.

He saved me.

"Push, Gabriella. Push!" The nurse furrowed her brow, coaching me sternly. "The baby is stuck and you need to listen. One, two, three, *push*."

I fisted my hands as Luka turned. He tucked to the side, taking a hit, but he didn't stop firing at the men trying to get to me.

If my baby was in danger, I had to do all I could not to lose him or her. If Luka was being shot at because I was here, I had to do all I could not to lose him, either. We needed to get somewhere safe, all of us, because I vowed with all I was not to lose my family.

37

LUKA

"Gabriella, stay with me." The nurse didn't move away from her, staying between her legs as she singlehandedly worked to deliver this baby. "I need you to push."

I blinked, leaning against the door as more Cartel fuckers rushed in.

They'd surrounded the facility with too much practiced ease. I couldn't be sure it was only the Vipers here, or if they'd brought along professional help. More hitmen. Maybe the Riveras.

It didn't matter. So long as I was here and could breathe, they were not getting to the woman I loved.

"I can't," Gabriella said, her voice weak and trailing off. "I just can't."

"One more push," the nurse said. "You can do this. You can."

The sound of her in agony broke my heart. But I couldn't take this from her. I couldn't spare her this pain.

More men came, and Alexsei joined me in shooting them back.

"One, two, three," the nurse counted sternly, a no-nonsense woman who would be rewarded for her bravery not to flee like all the others had with this ambush and attack. "Now, push!"

Gabriella growled, straining, but I couldn't turn back and hold her. I couldn't be there to take her hand and let her squeeze it as she bore down.

That last hit I'd taken was bleeding too damn quickly. My energy waned. Staggering to stay standing, I blinked again and warded off this lightheadedness.

I'd come in here in such a rush, fueled by adrenaline and the bloodlust to kill anyone who targeted Gabriella, that I was running on fumes now.

Still, these assholes tried to get to her. Too many Dubinins blocked the way now. Casualties lined the floor, both theirs and ours, but the tide was turning. More of my loyal men were holding back the gunmen. As the screams, shouts, and rapports of gunfire ceased, my soldiers chased the Cartel members out of the building.

But then another sound reached my ears.

A beautiful cry.

The result of tiny lungs wailing loudly.

Again and again, the baby cried.

Perhaps he or she wasn't too happy about the chaos that heralded this moment.

Turning slowly, knowing the men would have my back, I lowered my gun and sought out my love on the floor.

It was too much of a spin, too fast. I blinked again, unable to stand. Dropping to one knee, I gave up the fight to be upright.

"Gabriella..."

Tears streaked her face. Sweat matted her hair down.

As she smiled and cradled our child against her chest, I

swore my heart swelled so much and burst from the deepest love I never could've imagined feeling.

Love wasn't a joke.

While I crawled toward her, damning my injuries for threatening me to pass out, I knew that love was a miracle. A salvation.

"Gabriella..." I whispered it again, in awe. I couldn't tear my stare away from them. Mother and child. The mother of *my* child. The woman I would love until I no longer breathed.

"You..." I huffed a weak laugh, working on reaching them. "You did it."

"*We* did it," Gabriella corrected, giving me a weak smile.

The nurse kept working on cleaning up and tending to the afterbirth, not getting in my way. But she was watchful of me, too. "Easy, sir. You're bleeding."

"Fuck that." Ten seconds ago, I'd been in a fight to the end, not caring if I died to protect Gabriella and this baby.

Hearing Gabriella call us a team, partners, made me damn near ready to cry myself.

So grateful she'd come into my life, and so proud of her to stay strong no matter what happened, I reached her and the baby.

"A son," she said, her voice heavy with emotion, too.

"I love you," I told her, holding her close. My arm was on fire. Pain radiated from the gunshot wounds I'd acquired to save her. But nothing would stop me from telling her that and touching her. "I love you so fucking much, Gabriella."

She sniffled, crying happy tears as she leaned over. I kissed the top of her head, watching our son pout in her arms.

"I love you, too, Luka." She rested against me, holding our son close.

"Don't hate me for ruining the moment, but you're both losing too much blood." The nurse shook her head, eyeing us both.

I wasn't in the mood to argue with her. I wouldn't protest medical advice to keep Gabriella and our son safe. I was a tough old guy, though. They came first.

As the building was cleared out and law enforcement arrived, my men handled the situation. Emil showed up, dealing with the cops who tried to interfere on the scene. It was a mess out there, but with the help of a few nurses and doctors, my family was taken to the hospital next door where we were checked over.

I didn't make it easy. Insisting on keeping Gabriella in my room, within my sight, I ensured that she was stabilized where I could see her and keep her safe.

She was traumatized from the birthing process happening like it had, delivering our son amid the violence, but physically, she was fine.

Our son was healthy, too.

It turned out that the doctors had tried to guess at the gestation timing all along. Gabriella hadn't been having cycles before she was kidnapped. With an athlete's physique from dancing and malnourished from scarce food at home with Miguel there, she'd missed her periods so often that it wasn't easy to determine how far along she was. Based on the baby's measurements, an older, more experienced doctor said the baby was more like thirty-seven and a half weeks.

What mattered was that no time in the NICU would be needed. The baby was healthy, showing no signs of distress or concerns, but we would keep him overnight for all the necessary precautions and checks.

I was checked over as well. Emil and the others would

continue to handle the technical matters of reports for the pesky cops who'd get in the way. But while they took care of those details, I was free to relax in the room I shared with Gabriella and our son.

Stitched up, X-rayed, and checked over, I was on my road to recovery. The gunshot wounds I'd obtained weren't life-threatening in the end. I would survive. Just like Gabriella and our son, I was a survivor.

Surgery wasn't necessary, but it seemed like it took hours to be sewn up and cleaned up from the injuries I'd collected in my pursuit of protecting my love.

When night fell and the sky turned dark out the windows of our private suite, I got out of bed.

"Luka, what are you doing?"

I tugged off the straps that connected the monitors to me for the vital checks. "Coming to you."

She smirked, watching me pull out the connector to the IV they'd insisted on giving me.

"Stubborn man," she teased as I crawled into bed next to her.

"Stubborn woman," I replied, tucking her against me. "I told you not to come too hard."

She laughed lightly, resting her head against me as she sighed.

"I can't believe it's taken me this long to see you like this."

I threaded my fingers with hers. "I can't believe you picked up a gun off a dead man."

"I knew you'd come and save me, but still..."

I kissed the top of her head, at peace. "But still, you're such a badass you would step up and handle it yourself, too."

She smiled up at me.

"What do you mean, it's taken you this long to see me like this?" I recalled when I'd come home bloodied and wounded before. The last thing I wanted was for her to be scared she'd lose me.

"Like this." She lifted our hands and kissed the back of mine. "Not as my captor, but as the brave, strong man who loves me."

I tipped her chin up so I could claim her lips in a tender kiss.

"Not as my captor, but as the fearsome boss who would risk his life to save me."

Again, I kissed her, savoring the sweet serenity of her gentle smile.

"Not as my captor, but as the powerful leader and lover who'd be willing to die for me and our son."

I sank my fingers into her hair, reveling in the love she gave me. The allure of keeping her in my life had paved the way for us to get together, but it was this intrigue, this thrill of adventure and how much her love made me a better man, that excited me for the future.

"You're the captor," I told her as a nurse came into the room to do the routine check on our son's vitals. He slept in the bassinet at the foot of Gabriella's bed.

She gazed up at me, mesmerizing me with the adoration in her eyes.

"You've captured me. Heart, mind, and soul."

This time, she leaned up to drug me with a deep kiss.

I can't wait to make you mine for good.

38

GABRIELLA

ne month later...

FOUR WEEKS SHOULD HAVE FELT like a long time, but they blurred by so quickly. One minute, I was being discharged from the hospital with Luka and our son, Andre, and the next, I was trying to adjust to being the supposed woman of the house.

"I'm not joking," Luka said as he rocked Andre.

I sighed, putting my hands on my hips. "It's too many changes to handle at once."

I was blessed to have such a smooth post-partum experience. Despite the dangerous situation where I'd given birth, too early and among violence, I was doing fine. My years of dancing had likely set me up for having a good birthing experience—physically. In just a couple of weeks, I would go back for one final checkup. I couldn't tell if I was more excited for it or Luka was. Having the all-clear to have sex again was something we were both anticipating. We were so stubborn for so long, keeping our distance all through my pregnancy, that we agreed we had so much lost time to make up for now.

Recovering from having a baby was one part of it all. Adjusting to being a new mother was something else.

And per the massive ring on my finger that Luka had given me in the hospital before we left, when he proposed with such a romantic speech, I was expected to embrace the role of a bride-to-be.

"I'll help," Emil said, getting up to take over holding his half-brother. He was still an arrogant, cocky man, but it was too sweet to see him hands-on with this new Dubinin in the family.

"You'll help her pick out new house staff?" Luka asked, huffing with a dry laugh.

"Sure." Emil grinned, looking up from Andre to wink at me.

"That means he'll chose the ones he'd want to fuck," Luka said.

I shook my head, rolling my eyes.

When we brought Andre home, Luka ordered Allen to round up all the members of the house staff. They were subjected to a loyalty test, questioned and interrogated. I suspected they were tortured to talk. And I really couldn't feel guilty about that.

Because of someone in the house, Miguel was informed about my appointment at the medical facility. I was getting more on board with the idea of killing anyone who threatened me or my son.

But it was a lot of work. In the end, Luka decided to fire them all unless they were old loyalists who'd been working for the family since before he was even in power.

"I don't have a clue how to hire maids or cooks," I said.

"You just pick whoever seems best," Emil replied.

I sighed. "Sure. That makes sense."

Luka approached me with a smug smile. "You trust your judgment."

"I have no judgment."

"You do. You have sharp instincts to survive. If it comes down to choosing people you'd trust in our home and near our son, you'll choose according to that survivalist instinct."

That was a macabre take on it, but I supposed he was right.

"Still, it's a lot to handle right now," I protested. I leaned against him, setting my hands on his chest to better reach up and kiss him. "On our wedding day."

He smiled, kissing me deeper. "Then wait until tomorrow."

We had enough staff to get by. Yet, I wanted to start my life as an officially married woman not having to deal with anything that felt like work.

Right then, Andre cried to be fed, and I laughed to myself.

Who am I kidding?

I most definitely had a job now. I was working to be the best mother possible, learning my way as I went. It was undoubtedly the most important job I'd ever have, and I relished the freedom to experience it with Luka. With all these Dubinin men who'd protect us.

After tonight, I'd also work to be the best wife to the one and only Dubinin boss, too. It might have seemed cruel to say he was a job, but it was true. Every relationship required work. With how we'd fought before and stayed apart in the house for so long, I now knew that being together meant compromising and setting aside pride. We'd both work on it.

Later that evening, despite having cleared out most of the staff in the mansion, Luka and I prepared to get married. Because of the drama and danger that seemed to cling to me whenever I dared to set foot outside the house, I didn't want to go big. I didn't want to deal with a ceremony at all, actually. The smaller, the better. The more intimate, the better.

I wasn't in the mood for some huge wedding. Andre was only a month old and with him entering the throes of cluster feeding as he grew so quickly, I wasn't in any state of mind to leave him with a nanny. Breastfeeding had come naturally to me, and for him, so it wasn't like I'd have any milk to leave with a sitter.

Luka was insistent that we marry sooner than later, though. It saddened me that even like this, it was a legal matter or a transaction. To marry me so the whole world would know not to mess with me. As Mrs. Dubinin, I would be granted the utmost security.

But I already was. I was safe in his home, behind his doors and with his men around us.

I understood the image of it, the symbolism, and for that reason, I was fine with hurrying to marry.

In a dream world, we could've spent time to plan and make it more of a celebration than covering the bases for a technicality.

He was my dream, though. I'd wanted for so long to count on someone to support me and love me, and he handled both of those tasks expertly.

Andre was my dream too. Having a child was a blessing I would never take for granted. Every morning—or, truly, all through the night when he woke me—I got up with the gratitude that I was lucky enough to be able to call him my son. Each night, I fell asleep with the love and warmth of knowing I would always do my best by him.

No drive-by shooting would snatch my life and make him grow up without a mother.

No spineless, greedy person like Miguel would call himself a father and pawn him off.

Luka and I would always be there for Andre—and for any other children we could be so fortunate to have.

But tonight, it was about *us*. About me and him and our love.

"Ready?" Allen asked as he entered the room after a knock.

Emil stepped in with him, smiling as he looked at me in the bridal gown. "Damn."

I was just happy it fit. Losing the baby weight was a weird process so far. Breastfeeding had me slimmer than I thought I'd be, from burning so many calories like that.

I smiled wryly. I couldn't help but be amused that he and I were getting along this far. I trusted him. But still, the memory of how he'd helped to kidnap me lingered.

"Thanks," I replied, knowing he was praising me. He would never be a man of many words, but I was fine with calling him my family now too.

"I'm still not going to call you my stepmom," he said as he escorted me out of my room to meet Luka in the ballroom downstairs.

"I'm not calling you my stepson either," I quipped.

"It wouldn't make sense," he added.

"No, it wouldn't." I was younger than him, so that alone made it weird.

"You sure you want to shackle yourself to my father, though?" he teased.

I rolled my eyes and smiled. The age gap between me

and Luka was never an issue. If anything, I was glad to have an older, more experienced man to be my lover.

No. Not just a lover.

I smiled wider.

In an hour, Luka would be my husband.

He was already the father of my son. As we readied to be a true couple, I knew my misgivings and worries from the past would never matter again.

I wasn't a thing.

I wasn't a possession to lock up.

We would be partners. Equals. Spouses.

"He's already shackled to *me*," I replied as Emil brought me to the ballroom.

At my request, decorations were minimal. I wanted no fuss, no frills.

I'd exchanged my dream of being on stage as a ballerina with being the wife of the sexy Mafia boss waiting for me at the end of the long red carpet someone had unfurled for me to walk down.

I couldn't wait to reach him.

I couldn't wait to make love to him again, too.

Two more weeks. Only two more weeks...

I sighed, ready to go as the music played. Only a dozen or so people were in here, the closest family members Luka wanted to witness this.

Emil hesitated, though, waiting to walk me down the aisle. It seemed like a silly full circle, that he'd been instrumental in taking me from my former apartment to be walking me down the aisle now.

"Do you regret that it's like this?" he asked when I urged him to go already.

"Regret?" I smirked at him. "I have none."

"Not even that *I'm* walking you to marry him?"

I sighed. "Look, I might forgive you someday, but—"

"No. That I'm walking you. Not your dad."

I pursed my lips. "No." I didn't want *him* in my thoughts at all right now.

"I have no dad." Miguel was just a bastard determined to ruin my life. I ceased seeing him as a parent after what happened when Andre was born.

"You're really sure about that? You've got no love for him at all?"

"None." I frowned, glancing at him before whispering, "Why are you bringing this up now?"

"Because traditionally, a father walks his daughter down the aisle to be married."

"Okay." I shrugged one shoulder. "Nothing about me and Luka has been traditional. And I'm fine with that." It took me a while, but I got over the sting of how we'd met and connected. I was only glad we had.

"Good."

Still, I knew he was up to something. Emil didn't talk much, but most of what seemed to go through his head was strategy.

"Why are you bringing him up?" I asked.

"Because he's been demanding all of us to hunt him down." He inclined his chin at Luka, who watched me approach with heat and love in his eyes.

"Good," I repeated, meaning it.

If there were ever a sign that I was becoming a Mafia woman, this was it. I wouldn't cry at the idea of my dad being killed.

He deserved it for ever endangering my life. Not necessarily for giving me to Luka. That ended up being my blessing in disguise. But it was all the crap of his trying to give me away. To sell me. To target my son.

I would breathe easier knowing Miguel Lopez was gone.

Right now, though, it was time to shove all those dark thoughts aside.

Luka arched a brow at me as Emil handed me over to him. "Serious chat you had there."

I smiled. "No. Nothing as serious as my chaining you to my side forever."

He growled, pulling me in for a hard kiss.

"Hey, that comes later, Boss," a soldier said, one who was ordained to be the officiant.

"Later? How about right now?" Luka grinned, retreating and gesturing for the vows to begin.

I smiled, falling that much more in love with this rugged crime boss.

Now.

I still thought that junk about being present and living in the moment was lame, but as I spoke my vows and promised to love this man for the rest of our lives, I embraced the beauty of it anyway. This moment, and every one that would follow with Mr. Luka Dubinin, my husband.

39

LUKA

After Gabriella and I said our vows, we received congratulations from the small audience we'd invited. A simple dinner followed. *Simple* was the understatement of the year for the gourmet feast, but it was a toned-down affair.

This was how I wanted it—with her comfortable and owning her position as my wife.

As she fed Andre, covering up our son as she talked to Allen at the table, I stood back and sipped my drink.

She was already settling into her new roles.

As a mother.

As my wife.

As the head of the household, too. I knew that firing the house staff shocked her, but it proved, again, that I would take no risks with her safety. She was overwhelmed with the idea of hiring new staff, but she'd do it. She was scrappy. She was smart. And she had my trust. Just like I knew to count on everyone else who called themselves a member of the Dubinin Family, I could rely on her as well.

Emil approached the bar where I sipped my drink. Ivan

was there as well, nursing more vodka than was typical for him.

I hated the possibility of his being sad at my wedding, but I could understand it. He'd lost his one true love, and if there were ever a time for him to be lovesick, this would be it.

"What the fuck were you talking about with Gabriella earlier?" I asked my son.

He shrugged. "I was testing the waters. Seeing how she'd feel about Miguel being killed."

I scoffed. "She can't wait."

"I bet she's eager for that fucker to be dead," Ivan said. "He's threatened her every time she leaves the house."

"I know." Emil shoved his hands in his pockets, watching as she gently burped Andre. "But she's still a stranger to so much of our world."

"True," I admitted. "But she's adapting well."

Leaving them to join her for a dance, I appreciated how Alexsei offered to hold the baby.

"May I have this dance, Wife?" I asked, extending my hand to her.

She gave me such a dazzling smile that I wondered if going down on her would be breaking the rule of no sex until after her checkup.

In this wedding gown, she was stunning. Ravishing. Gorgeous. And I'd spend the rest of my life reminding her of that.

"You sure can, Husband." She stood, moving into the open area of the ballroom to dance with me. No other couples were out here. It was only my closest men joining us for this ceremony and dinner. But that didn't matter.

I kissed her, committing this memory to my heart. With just the two of us moving to the soft music, it was as if we were in a bubble of our own. Where all that mattered was that we were together and in love.

"You're not overdoing it, are you?" I asked as we moved as one. Feeling her slender, still-athletic body swaying with mine teased me.

"No. I'm fine. Remember, I've been dancing for most of my life." She kissed my cheek. "Taking a few months off won't set me back that far."

"When do you think you'll return to the studio and dance again?" I asked. I wanted her to keep her passion, to never stop pursuing her dreams.

"Soon." She shrugged. "That's a question you should ask our son."

I smiled, amused but also aware of what she meant. Breastfeeding him took a toll on her sleep schedule, to say the least. I was always up, helping her, but she was the one with the milk.

"I doubt I'll try to perform again," she admitted.

"Because of how the audition ended?" I asked, hating that it had been interrupted.

"Not only that. It's just how my life has changed. I'm a mother now. A wife. I have a family." She beamed at me, making me feel like a god. "You can't understand how over the moon I am about how everything is falling into place. I've never been happier, Luka. I have a family now. A real one." She sighed and shook her head. "A real family, unlike the waste of space who was supposed to be my father, the fool who went on the run."

I kissed her. Not only to quiet her but to distract her. Damn Emil for mentioning Miguel today.

"Don't worry about him."

She smiled slightly. "I'm not."

"I mean it, Gabriella. Don't worry about him." It seemed

so flimsy of a command to give her. We were having a fraction of a wedding here in our home because she was rightly nervous to exit the security I had here.

"I'm not worried. I know you'll get him. You'll find him and kill him and I'll never have to worry about him again." She licked her lips. "I know other threats will come, but I have faith in you, husband of mine, that you'll handle him and dispose of him."

I nodded then rested my brow against hers. "I swear on my life that no one will ever hurt you again. No one will ever get close enough to hurt you on my watch."

She lifted her hand to caress my cheek. "I believe you. And even if something were to happen, I'll start taking self-defense classes and learn how to handle a gun once Andre isn't nursing as often."

I kissed her, so damn proud of her. To trust me but also to be interested in participating in her safety as well...

Three days later, I delivered on my promise.

Emil and Ivan asked to talk to me in my office, and I nodded.

"Here, I can take him." Gabriella extended her arms toward me, suggesting I hand her Andre.

"No, no." He'd just fallen asleep. I doubted either of us got an hour of rest last night with how he'd cried to be fed. Cluster feeding was *hell*.

"You sure?" She glanced at my son and nephew. "If you need to handle business..."

"Chill, Gabby," Emil told her.

I shot him a stern look since everyone knew she disliked that nickname.

"Andre's too young to understand what we'll be discussing." He huffed. "You look like crap." At my scowl, he winced. "I mean, you look like you could use a break."

She yawned, taking his critique without a bother. "I could use a week of sleep," she replied dryly, giving up on her breakfast.

As I left the room, I stopped Allen. "You're on baby duty for the rest of the day."

He nodded once.

In the office, I rocked Andre with that weird swaying, bouncing stride that seemed to calm him.

"I bet he's only relaxed when you move and don't sit because she danced so much during her pregnancy," Ivan said. "He's used to the movement."

"That's what you wanted to talk to me about?" I asked, eager to get back to my wife and let her rest.

"No. We've got Miguel Lopez," Emil answered. "He's in a holding cell at the warehouse near the docks."

I gave up on the plans to relax with Gabriella. A slow, wicked smile lifted my lips instead. "About fucking time."

We made quick plans to head out as soon as possible.

It seemed like an oxymoron to express impatience to end Miguel Lopez's life.

We'd captured him before. When I suspected he was lying or up to something, we'd set that trap and gotten him. We'd held him and tortured him until I had the idea to exact a different payment from him. Instead of taking his life, I'd taken his daughter.

His loss was my gain.

But now, it was time to return to the original idea of killing him.

Perhaps he'd paid for his sins of two-timing us. I'd taken Gabriella because he'd sold intel to the Vipers and the Riveras. For his even graver sins of trying to hurt Gabriella and have her removed from my life, he'd pay with his.

It was past time to kill him.

After handing Andre to Allen and checking in with Gabriella, I prepared to leave.

"Important business to handle?" she asked as she came out of the bathroom from showering.

"Very," I replied. I got the impression that she wanted to ask if it was about Miguel, but at the same time, she didn't want to know.

Sparing her the indecision about asking or not, I kissed her. "I love you."

"I love you, too. Please be safe."

"Always." I would always be safe for her and Andre. As the boss, I had to be careful that I came home safe and sound. Too many counted on me and relied on my guidance. But it was the love for her that propelled me to hurry back.

The ride to the warehouse was a quiet one. Emil didn't ask me questions. Ivan didn't comment about other business. All of us were looking forward to having this matter over with.

Ten minutes later, I strode into the nondescript building with my men. Every step that brought me closer to the cell where Gabriella's father was held felt a march to salvation. The scales of justice had yet to be righted.

Then as I shoved my hands into my pockets and peered at the broken mess of the man who'd dared to fuck with me, I smiled.

"Mr. Lopez. We meet again."

Bloody and shaking, he was nothing more than a lump on the floor. Gabriella was right. He truly was a waste of space.

"Fuck you. Fuck you, Dubinin!"

Emil kicked him until he sobbed.

"You can't have my daughter just because—"

Ivan took over beating him silent.

Once he settled, crying and trembling, I squatted down.

"Gabriella is *my wife*," I corrected.

He growled, thrashing to get up as I stood.

I gestured at the men to stand back.

While I wasn't in the mood to stay here when I could be at home with my family, I was determined to end this once and for all. It was time to get rid of any threats from *this* man, even though there would always be danger lurking near us.

That was the nature of the Mafia life.

Because this wasn't the same old and because this man had threatened the lives of my son and wife, I should've adopted the mindset of taking my time to torture him. But Miguel Lopez wasn't even worth that anymore.

I straightened, gesturing for my firstborn to hand me one of the blades sitting on the table. No other furniture was on offer in this room. Except for this flat surface that housed a variety of torturing tools and weapons, it was just the bloody floor, the sack of broken bones that used to be Gabriella's spiteful, lying father.

I didn't need much. Emil intuited that, wasting no time to put a knife in my hand.

I tested the heft of it.

It'd do.

I didn't care to return to my loved ones overly messy and bloody.

This death wasn't going to be a fancy act of revenge and justice.

But it would be meaningful.

I would forever remember this day that I would eliminate the most direct threat to my love.

"She will never be yours, Dubinin," Miguel snarled.

"You can't just take her. It doesn't work like that. She's my daughter. My blood."

I shook my head, almost sorry for his pathetic ass.

Blood wasn't always thicker. Plenty of recruits we brought into the family were as loyal, if not more, than the relatives I had. Allen was a prime example of such a bond.

"She is my wife," I corrected with savage anger. "She is the mother of my child."

His eyes opened wide as I advanced, showing him the knife in my hand.

"She has given me another heir to enjoy. A grandson you will never meet."

I grabbed his hair, twisting the filthy strands in my grip as I pulled his head off the floor. He grimaced and squirmed, but I didn't release him one bit. Wrenching his head back, I exposed his sweaty neck for the final blow that would end his life. His Adam's apple bobbed as he tried to get free. I lined up the knife to end his wretched life, one that I really shouldn't have taken before. If I'd been hasty to kill him earlier, I never would've met Gabriella. I never would've experienced how much of a beautiful blessing she was to save me.

"I didn't *take* her," I said. "I captured her, just the same as she captured me in the end." It was that vow of love that I shared with my wife that nothing could ever break.

As I dragged the knife over his flesh, piercing it until blood gushed forward, I did the final deed. I killed him with swift deliberation. Just like this, with one movement of my hand, I eliminated the biggest obstacle to the peace I wanted to share with Gabriella for the rest of our days.

Watching the life spill out of him as he gurgled and moaned uselessly, I released his hair. His head dropped at a weird angle, splitting the open gash at his neck even wider.

A crimson pool gathered on the floor where he'd dropped. With every drop that leaked from him, his death was that much more of a done duty.

I rose to my full height, knowing justice had been done.

By my hand, the Lopez name would exist no more.

Gabriella was a Dubinin now, my wife, secure under the protection of my family. She'd submitted to me in love and trusted her role in our family, and I would never, ever take that gift for granted.

I set the bloody blade on the table. Facing my son and my nephew, I nodded once.

"Let's go home."

40

GABRIELLA

Three weeks later...

It didn't matter how I slowed down and tried to take myself back to the basics of all that I knew. It was simply a challenge to move like I used to.

"I don't get it," I complained quietly, more to myself than the spectators in my studio.

Last week, I went through my post-partum checkup. I was cleared to have sex, something Luka and I didn't waste time doing that very night. I was also given the okay to dance and reintroduce more exercise into my life.

Dance was the only form of exercise I ever wanted.

Well, all right. Making love with my husband often felt like a workout too, in the best of ways.

It wasn't as simple as I thought it might be, resuming my skills and dancing again.

I was stiff. Clumsy. Out of sync.

"What's there to not understand?" Luka asked as he held Andre. He carried him with ease, such a confident, quick-to-help father. Sometimes, I wondered if our baby favored *him* with how easily he calmed for him. I knew it wasn't true. So long as the milks jugs were on offer from me, Andre would prefer me.

"You were pregnant. You had a baby. Your body will naturally change."

I winced, trying again to bend and sway my arms in a manner that would enable me to lead into a sequence of steps and spins.

"Yeah. My body changed." I huffed when I couldn't pull off what I considered a simple series in a dance I'd taught myself years ago. Cupping my breasts, I groaned. "Because of these massive things, I don't even feel like this is my body anymore."

He chuckled, pretending to shield Andre's eyes. And that was a smart move. I wasn't all that sure what two-month-olds could see. His vision had to be developing yet, but I swore he had tunnel vision for my boobs.

I smiled.

"Hey, I love those massive things."

I rolled my eyes, frustrated by how hard it was to get back into the groove of it all. "Not as much as he does," I joked.

"It will take time," Luka advised sagely, patiently.

"I know. I know." For some dumb reason, I figured I wouldn't have lost so much. I would be patient, even if my dreams had changed. Going to Juilliard didn't seem as important anymore. Not as much as having another baby with my husband did.

Maybe I'd get on stage later, but for now, embracing this newfound wonder of having a family was more than enough to make my heart swell with joy and love.

"I'm trying to be patient," I admitted, not stopping and going slowly to pay attention to my body. Tendons and ligaments were impacted during a pregnancy, too, so I knew to listen to my muscles and pay attention to aches and pains before they'd cause long-term problems.

"It just reminds me of how I felt before. When I had to beg for lessons and barely get any attention to improve under instructors." That felt like a lifetime ago, when I had to clean that shitty apartment for Miguel to cave and pay for the bare minimum. When I was so scared after Tony almost raped me that I slept at Amy's mom's studio just to have shelter.

I wanted for nothing now. Luka provided me with everything I'd ever need. If I asked, he'd start back up with having instructors. He had made it clear that he would never hesitate to give me anything I wished for.

"Miguel never gave a shit about whether I improved or not. He never cared that I wanted to dance."

Luka didn't reply. Merely watching me stretch and warm up to try to dance, he didn't say a single thing.

"Do you miss him?" he asked at last when I was frustrated about how slowly I was getting in the hang of this.

"Miguel?" I scoffed. "No. How could I miss the man who nearly got me killed? Who wanted to take that precious baby?"

He exhaled a long, hard breath, meeting my gaze. "He's gone."

I nodded. "I know."

"You do?" He raised his brows.

"Yeah, like, the day after you killed him. Blame Emil. He mentioned something about a warehouse and Miguel, and I connected the dots."

"I wasn't sure if and when to tell you."

I shrugged. "I figured. I mean, it's not every day a daughter can wish her father dead." Maybe in this Mafia world, it was. But for me, I clung to some of that former normalcy I had once. My gauge of good versus bad hadn't changed since marrying him and being a part of this family. I still liked to think I was a good person at heart. Wishing Miguel dead wasn't bad of me. It was self-defense.

"Besides, when you took me out to eat for a date, I realized how at ease you were to be in public with me. That convinced me that something had to have changed, and with what I overheard Emil say, I realized he was dead."

He nodded. "I can't always tell you the details of what we do."

I held my hand up, stopping him from elaborating. "Please. Keep it like that. I don't need to know the details."

He smiled. "Not even about that?"

"Okay." I shrugged. "I would've liked to know that Miguel was no longer a threat. But still, it wasn't necessary for you to announce it. No lost love there. And I knew you *would* kill him. I have faith that you'll always protect me. I'm familiar with how you can keep your word."

"I always will."

My father was no longer a threat, no longer an issue, and I was grateful for that.

"Thank you, though." I blew him a kiss.

Maybe I'd go to hell for thanking my husband for killing my father.

But I doubted it.

"You're welcome," he replied, watching me with an increasing flame of fire in his eyes.

Over the last year, I'd adjusted to so many changes. I was a mother. A wife. The head of a household. I was still a dancer, but those other roles mattered more right now.

I no longer worried about being tainted or ruined by associating with this Mafia Family. Instead of assuming the worst and seeing them as nothing but monsters and killers, I knew how fiercely they loved.

Violence was a staple in this life. The more I reacted and waited to freak out, the more I learned that it never touched me directly. It never reached me to the point that my fight-or-flight instinct would flare up.

Because I was safe. I was safer here than I ever would be anywhere else.

When I finished for the night, knowing that baby steps and a gradual approach to dancing would be the way to go, I walked toward him holding a now-sleeping Andre. My heart grew with love each time I saw them together, and I knew that it would never, ever get old.

No spells of being numb and emotionless would ever plague me again.

I had them.

And it was more than enough to fulfill me.

"Ready to get out of here?" Luka asked, carrying our son out of the studio. I sipped my water, eager to shower and get in bed.

"Ready to get out of here and be with you." I smiled slowly, letting him figure out what I meant. I couldn't help but remember when he told me that he'd been waiting for my happiness here, for my smile. I doubted I'd ever stop now.

"Hmm." He put his free hand on my back. "I'll be ready for that too."

I leaned up to kiss him, earning a low growl of desire.

"You shower and get in bed. By then, I'll have him sleeping in his bassinet."

"Shh!" I gave him a stern look. "Don't jinx it."

He chuckled. "You just have to know how to lower him."

I rolled my eyes. I tried. It never mattered. The second I put Andre down, he'd wake up.

I was starting to believe he had some radar for my boobs, knowing where I was.

"It's cute, though, seeing how Emil, Ivan, and Alexsei help with him." I couldn't forget Allen, too. "At this rate, I'll never need a nanny." I opened the door to our room. "Then again, it would be nice to have another woman around here."

He laughed. "You're the only woman in the family now. I guess until we have a daughter."

"Maybe we can practice tonight in making one."

He lightly spanked my ass. "I'll hold you to that."

I knew he would. Backpedaling toward the bathroom, I said, "Seriously. It would be nice to have another woman around here."

"I wouldn't count on Emil bringing someone home." He rolled his eyes.

I agreed. He was too cocky, too arrogant. And too much of a bachelor and playboy.

"What about Ivan?"

He shrugged. "You might be on to something there."

"He's got a girlfriend?" I guessed.

"He almost had a wife. He walked away from her years ago, but I bet seeing how happy we are together has him wishing he could find her again."

I didn't ask about Alexsei. He seemed to hold on to grief yet from losing his wife.

"Regardless," Luka said after I showered, picking up our conversation, "you are the woman of *my* life. The only one." He kissed me deeply, urging me to follow him toward the bed. "And you always will be—all mine."

I smiled, falling on to the mattress with him. Straddling

him and ready to make love, the telltale sound of Andre crying had me hanging my head and groaning.

"I'm telling you, he's got a radar for me."

Luka chuckled, rubbing my back. "I guess you're not *only* mine right now."

I kissed him, smiling as I got up to tend to our hungry son. "I'm yours, Luka. Always." And I was damn proud to say it.

Printed in Dunstable, United Kingdom

72675675R00180